Praise for *Undercurrent of Secrets*

"Rachel skillfully binds dual-timeline love stories together against a fascinating backdrop—the *Belle of Louisville* steamboat. I thoroughly enjoyed uncovering the twists and turns of the mystery surrounding a woman who went missing a century before. Surprising. Heartwarming. A beautiful overlapping of past and present."

–Becky Wade, Christy Award-winning author
of the Misty River Romance series

"Anchored by a historic riverboat, *Undercurrent of Secrets* links past and present in a tale featuring two sweet love stories. Readers will enjoy the lively banter and the relatable themes of finding yourself and following your dreams. Romance, adventure, and mystery abound in this charming split-time story!"

—Denise Hunter, bestselling author of the Bluebell Inn series

"I love a good dual-timeline novel and Rachel McDaniel makes a fantastic foray into the genre with *Undercurrent of Secrets*. I so enjoyed both storylines and found myself relating in many ways to Hattie and Devyn. The romances are lovely and both the history and the mystery kept me turning pages. . .and I especially loved the steamboat setting! McDaniel's latest is sure to charm readers. Highly recommended!"

–Melissa Tagg, Christy Award-winning author
of *Now and Then and Always*

"With her latest novel, *Undercurrent of Secrets*, Rachel Scott McDaniel makes waves in the world of split-time romance with two marvelously intertwined tales set one century apart on the *Belle of Louisville* riverboat. The dreamy heroes and courageous heroines offer plenty of witty banter and moments to swoon over. While McDaniel's talent for designing breath-stealing romance highlights the enchantment of the Belle, her instinct for creating page-turning suspense draws the reader along the shadowy riverbends and into the murky waters below. Be prepared to make room on your favorites shelf with this one!"

–Janine Rosche, bestselling author of the
Whisper Canyon Romance series

Undercurrent

of

SECRETS

Doors to the Past

Rachel Scott McDaniel

BARBOUR
PUBLISHING

Published by Barbour Publishing, Inc., 1810 Barbour Drive, Uhrichsville, Ohio 44683, www.barbourbooks.com

Our mission is to inspire the world with the life-changing message of the Bible.

ecpa Member of the
Evangelical Christian
Publishers Association

Printed in the United States of America

Dedication

*There is a river whose streams make glad the city
of God, the holy habitation of the Most High.*
Psalm 46:4 NRSV

Thank You, God, for Your river of life that washes,
sustains, and carries me home.

Chapter 1

September
Louisville, Kentucky

*S*ome engagements end in happily ever afters, and some just end. . .on social media. Devyn Asbury stared into her master bedroom closet, the sag in her spine a direct result of today's date on the calendar.

Her mood called for leopard print flats. She'd grown up thinking a woman could change the world with the right pair of shoes, but so far all that had changed for Devyn was her spiraling trust issues. That, and her distaste for adventure—to which she had forty-nine million reasons to never fall into its lure again. To go all Lewis-and-Clark into the unchartered cyber wilderness had left her with a bare ring finger and a mountain of misery.

With that oh-so-cheery thought, she slipped on her flats, grabbed her canvas bag off the dresser, and made her way to the door. At least the shakiness that had taken residence in her person all morning had subsided. Sighing, she punched in the alarm code for her penthouse. Under any other circumstances she'd revel in the luxury apartment overlooking the Ohio River in downtown Louisville. But Travis's gifts had come with a hefty price tag. The sooner she shed this address, the quicker she'd free herself of everything that had haunted her these past ten months.

Once out the door, she hustled down the hall, her footfalls loud against the terrazzo flooring. She allowed herself an hour leeway before work, craving those few extra moments to sit by the river. Her Bible was tucked next to a king-sized Hershey's bar in her bag. Breakfast with Jesus and chocolate. The arsenal needed to survive this day.

Her cell buzzed in her pocket. Steph's name flashed, and Devyn came to a skidding halt in front of the elevators.

Steph never called this early.

But then, her superior knew what today was. Or rather was supposed to be. So this was probably a pity call. Dandy. She should no doubt prepare herself for condolence convos from her mom and brother. Mom's would be a short *I'll be praying for you,"* and hopefully out of respect, Mitch would tame his wife Angie's badger-like pursuits of hooking Devyn up with every eligible guy in a thirty-mile radius. Frowning, she answered. "What's up, boss lady?"

"Did you leave your posh palace yet?" Steph's four-cups-of-coffee voice—excitable and with a shaky, elevated pitch—made Devyn blink. "You need to get here. Fast."

"Whoa. Steph. What's going on?" She wedged the phone between her ear and shoulder and stabbed the DOWN button, summoning the lift. "Don't tell me Carla Ludlow called off the wedding and we're stuck with twelve dozen gardenias." Devyn had toiled way too many hours getting things perfect for the ceremony and reception tomorrow. Which reminded her, she needed to call the DJ and make certain he was bringing the fog machine. Not sure why that was a priority for Carla, but if the bride-to-be requested it, then in the name of Vera Wang, she'd get it. Just because Devyn's own dreams had sunk like a diamond ring to the bottom of the Ohio, didn't mean she wouldn't work hard to make others' come true.

"No, it's nothing like that." She rushed the words. "I need to tell you something but not over the phone."

Devyn rolled her eyes. "Then why call?"

"To get your butt moving. I'm going to burst if you don't get here soon. Oh, and I already got you a coffee, so you don't have to make a Starby's run. You know how the line gets at this time of day and if I had to wait any—"

"Breathe, Steph."

"Right." Her boss exhaled.

"I'll be there soon."

"Good." Steph hung up.

Because of the blister-inducing pace, Devyn was winded when she reached the wharf, but paused at her favorite spot on the Riverwalk, taking in the beauty of the moment. The *Belle of Louisville* perched upon the shimmering waters. Sunlight haloed her, as if crowning her white-framed decks with a golden tiara, the glossy paddlewheel on the stern her crimson train. Devyn would never tire of the sight or that stirring within her every time she gazed upon the legendary vessel.

No matter how pushy Steph had been on the phone, Devyn *needed* this moment. If a steamboat could survive over a century's worth of storms with resilient grace, then there was hope for Devyn. Her gaze drifted to the boat anchored beside the *Belle*, which also happened to be a hundred-year-old boat. A lifesaving station. It didn't escape Devyn that her office was aboard a vessel that, for most of its life, had been dedicated to saving lives. Because this job had rescued Devyn in so many ways.

Thank You, God.

After another second of reflection, Devyn took a deep breath of the crisp air and traversed the walkway aboard the green and white lifeboat. She headed straight toward her boss's office, pausing in the doorframe. Her mouth opened to utter a greeting but all words died on her lips as Steph rushed toward her and cupped both her shoulders.

"Before I go into our news, are you okay?" She searched her face, and Devyn wondered if her eyes were still puffy from last night's sobfest. "I should've asked on the phone."

"I'm always good."

"Wow, you're a bad liar. Here." She grabbed a coffee cup from her desk and pushed it into Devyn's hand. "Now try again."

She blew out a breath. "I'm as good as can be expected for a girl who'll devote eight hours to another woman's wedding today rather than attending her own." Saying those words aloud stung, but seemed to satisfy Steph. "Happy now?"

"Yep. I'm telling you, that man's an idiot. I'm glad you're not reducing yourself to becoming Mrs. Idiot."

As if Devyn had a choice in the breakup. She smiled at Steph's narrowed eyes. "Fortune 500 thinks he's a genius."

"What do they know?" Steph flipped her red-and-silver streaked locks over her shoulder with a sniff. With her fluffy, waved hairstyle and penchant for blazers with shoulder pads, it was as if she had stepped straight out of the eighties. "Besides, he stole your idea. So that makes him a jerkface too."

"Space Station was both our ideas." Like a marriage of YouTube and Facebook, Space Station was designed to be the one-stop social media site. Everyone got their own "space" on the global station to upload videos, pictures, or just post about their day. She and Travis had pioneered it.

How could she have known it would become the latest rage? Of course, their videos had helped it along. She cringed and tried to scrub her brain of the toxic thoughts.

"You still should've had a cut."

"Oh believe me. I got my fair share. It just wasn't in dollars." She'd been paid a major lesson in trust and heartache.

"That just makes me so—"

"I kinda hate this subject. Especially today." Devyn braved a sip of the mystery coffee. Ah, pumpkin spice. Her eyes slid shut, savoring the flavor. Things were getting better. It was hard to remain depressed when drinking autumn in a cup. "So what was your crazy call about?"

"This." She pulled a single sheet of paper from a stack of letters on her desk and held it high. "Hope this brightens things up for you. Though I should be miffed because you didn't tell me you entered the *Belle* in *Once Upon a Wedding's* contest." She raised a brow in gentle rebuke, but her eyes gleamed under the fluorescent lights.

"I never heard from them, so I assumed we didn't make the cut."

"Well, we did!" She bounced on her toes. "We're in the contest!"

Devyn's breath stalled in her chest. It couldn't be. She must've heard wrong. "Wh-what?"

"I printed off the email they sent." Her boss handed over the letter.

Heart racing, she took in the congratulatory statements, making certain Steph's claim was legit.

It was.

The leading wedding organization in the country had selected the *Belle* as a finalist. After skimming the body of the message, Devyn lowered the paper, still processing it all.

If she'd submitted the form and photos of the *Belle* five months ago, then why was she just *now* getting a response? "I figured we got rejected."

But the words before her said otherwise.

The Timeless Wedding Venue was the most sought out award in the industry. When the organization had revealed this year's criteria—all settings must be national landmarks—Devyn jumped on the opportunity to apply. Excitement stood in the doorway of her heart, but she was tentative to welcome it in. She'd been numb for so long the feeling almost seemed new.

"The coordinator reached out to me because she never received a response from you. I'm betting her emails are sitting in your spam folder, because I found hers this morning in mine."

Devyn grimaced. "Stupid spam." Technology had one-upped her again.

"The announcement was posted at the end of July." Steph gave her a sympathetic smile. "They listed the finalists on all their social media pages."

Ugh. Social media. Devyn had disabled all her accounts after that horrid night.

"This is huge." Steph glided over to the window and stretched out both arms in an exaggerated Vanna White pose as if showing off the *Belle*. "Our old gal can get prime time exposure if we win."

If we win. As if Devyn needed a further face-plant into reality. "Since they released the list over a month ago, how much time do we have before judges come?" The guidelines had stated that finalists had to host an event which showcased both the landmark's history and why it proved the best location for a wedding.

"That's the thing." Steph's arms wilted to her sides. "The coordinator said they won't allow us any additional days."

Not good. "Talk to me, Steph."

"October twenty-third."

The Hershey bar Devyn had scarfed down on her way here threatened to resurface. "That's less than six weeks away." No way they could do this.

"We can do this." Steph paced the small area in front of her desk. "All we need is a sound plan."

"Don't forget that we have the Benefit Ball to plan for. That's two major events." Two major hits to the budget. Another aspiration ripped from Devyn's hands. At least this time the virtual world wouldn't witness it. A dull ache stretched behind her eyes, making her temples throb.

"How about…" Steph popped her shoulder against a filing cabinet, determination marking her blue eyes. "We combine the events?"

"Um, what?"

She clasped her hands together, the smack of her palms making Devyn flinch. "It's perfect. The Benefit Ball is the second week of November. All we have to do is move it up."

Steph made it sound easy, like switching around pieces on a chessboard. But each shifted chessman altered the dynamics of the game. And Devyn was predicting a *checkmate* in the near future. Another defeat. "It's risky."

"Life is about risks, my love."

Devyn stiffened. She had once been a risk-taker, an adventure seeker, but never again. The past she couldn't alter, but her future? Playing it chill would keep her from landing in another hot mess. "You realize we'll have to adjust all our planning? By sliding up the Benefit Ball we cut our preparation time in half. We need to send out invitations in two weeks instead of four. We also have to tweak our decorations to incorporate a romantic theme to satisfy the *Once Upon a Wedding* people. The whole idea is crazy." Devyn pulled out her phone and opened her calendar app, checking what they had to work with.

"I like crazy." Steph's smile widened. "We have fifty days—"

"Thirty-nine."

"To wow both our beneficiaries and award judges." She zeroed her mascara-laden gaze on Devyn. "I know you have what it takes to pull this off."

Oh to have that same confidence. Steph wanted to take on the universe, and all Devyn wanted was an aspirin.

"Embrace this as an opportunity to show the world what you've got."

Her boss couldn't have chosen a more terrifying turn of phrase. Because Devyn had no desire to show the world anything anymore. She'd shared enough of her vulnerable moments with strangers. But. . .this would be great publicity for the legendary lady. The *Belle* deserved a place in the spotlight, as long as Devyn could hide in the shadows. "Okay. We'll give it our best."

Her sixty-year-old boss shimmied and wiggled her raised arm in some strange version of the Nae Nae—something Devyn would never be able to unsee. "I promise, Devyn. This is going to be fun."

Devyn would settle for survivable.

"I'll let you get to it." Steph ushered her out the door then placed a manicured hand on her wrist, stilling her. "By the way, I heard rumors there can be secret judges who show up any time during the preparations, up until the event. You know, to enforce authenticity of the contest and make sure we're the ones actually doing everything. Thought I should warn you."

Chapter 2

$\mathcal{D}$evyn didn't have time to waste in planning, yet she'd already burned three days since learning about the contest. Granted, Friday and Saturday were booked with weddings aboard the *Belle* that Devyn oversaw, and yesterday was their annual bridal event, consisting of vendors, fashion shows, and every type of fancy dessert imaginable. Now, it was Monday and Devyn's brain was mush. But she'd have to push through. From now on, every second counted. She refused to consider any of her moments free. Not until the ball was over and she had a grand prize plaque on her wall. Well, more like Steph's wall. But Devyn would count the *Belle*'s win as her own.

Though first she needed a theme for the event.

Everything hinged upon it. She couldn't send out the invitations, purchase décor, or secure the entertainment until she had a jaw-dropping theme that would appeal to the judges *and* the *Belle*'s patrons.

Nothing like a little throat-cinching pressure to go with her cold latte.

Since hours of scouring the internet hadn't resulted in anything but a mild headache, Devyn planted herself on the *Belle*'s stern, hoping the timeless lady would whisper some secrets. Or at least maybe an idea or two. Preferably one that would put the steamboat on the cover of *Once Upon a Wedding*'s future issue.

Before Devyn's journey up here, her boss had shoved what appeared to be romance novels into her hands. *"Read them,"* Steph had said. *"Soak your mind in all those swoony love scenes. It'll help with creativity for the ball."*

She perused the cover of the book topping the stack and winced. No, she definitely didn't need a steamy story about a misbehaving duke—as the title referenced—to ignite inspiration. She had all the kindling to spark her genius right here on the *Belle*. She only needed to fan the embers of her imagination.

A few towboats trudged to Devyn's left, and traffic rolled endlessly along River Road with the interstate hovering over it. Yet, the *Belle* was stationary, despite the slight tremor from the water coursing beneath. The boat would be harbored until this Saturday night for the Captain's dinner, but it didn't take much for Devyn to envision one of its thousands of voyages. Her gaze held on the paddlewheel below. Oh the mileage this gal had.

Devyn stood on the most romantic part of the steamboat—the stern overlooking the water. When the paddlewheel was in motion it was like nothing Devyn had ever seen or felt. The planks lifted the river water, creating crystal falls over the crimson boards. The churning, so steady and unbroken, was the pulse of the entire boat, bringing her to life.

Devyn knew firsthand this was the wedding photographers' favorite spot to capture the newly married couples. Even her own parents, who'd been married on the *Belle* back in the eighties, had a snapshot taken right here. But before the nuptials, how many proposals had been vowed at this very spot? How many first kisses?

The ballroom was a floor below, but Devyn was aware of passengers sneaking to this spot to steal a dance. To be under the moonlight, to sway to the rhythmic swish of the paddlewheel. It blossomed something in her, something Devyn had thought all but dead since Travis broke up with her.

Knowing not another soul was around, she allowed her mind to drift. Peeling back the years in her imagination to a different time. An era where social media hadn't existed. Cell phones weren't a thought. When the thrill of the moment was a shriek of the steam whistle. Or a waltz on this roof with a dashing gentleman.

With one arm hugging the books to her chest, she stretched out her other and mimicked the stance of that vintage ballroom dance. Stepping back and forth with an invisible partner, she kept in perfect tempo with the waves lapping the hull. Sliding her eyes shut, she could envision the ambiance of a starlit waltz. Almost hear the hushed vows of love between a young couple.

"May I have the next dance?"

Devyn shrieked at the deep male voice. The books in her arms tumbled to the floor, scattering.

A man with impossibly black hair stood only a few yards away. His hands were stuffed in his faded jeans and his sharp jaw tucked a bit, but the gleam in his eyes totally said his abashed stance was a farce. As if realizing he'd been caught, he unleashed a rogue smile, revealing how highly amused he was at her ridiculous scene.

And here Devyn had thought the coffee stain on her ivory shirt from her stumble in the parking lot earlier had been embarrassing. The beige blob smack dab on her chest seemed nothing compared to her being caught ballroom dancing with an imaginary companion on the back of a hundred-year-old steamboat.

"I don't want to be rude." He popped a hip against the guardrail and folded his arms across his chest, his black shirt pulling taut around his shoulders. "I can wait until the dance is over or until you tire of your partner. He seems pretty boring."

Of all the…

This stranger could startle her out of her red slingbacks, adopt a familiar tone as if they'd been friends for decades, but she wouldn't allow him to insult her taste in men—even if imaginary. "I have no idea who you are, but here's a lesson for you—some women actually favor the silent type." She pinned him with a glare. "They're much more preferable to men who run their mouths, especially ones not welcome in the conversation in the first place."

His grin widened. "I can see for myself the type of men that spark your interest."

She followed his gaze to the steamy romance novel inches from his boots.

The half-dressed duke seemed to smirk at Devyn as if siding with the obnoxious stranger. "Those aren't mine." And why was she defending herself to this man? "Who are you and how'd you get up here?"

He ignored her and moved to pick up another book. "Now this proves you're more refined than that smut novel suggests." He angled the cover towards her.

Her tiny gasp escaped. *Oh Steph, how could you?* A sting of betrayal sliced through her as she glared at the all-too-familiar poetry collection. Would she never escape this? "That's *not* my definition of refinement."

He handed her the book and scratched the back of his neck, revealing part of a tattoo on his bicep. "You don't like Slate?"

"Slate." Devyn scoffed. "That name's as bogus as his poetry. I can't understand all the rage for him. Over three million copies sold." Her muttering took on a sharp edge. "Three million people walking the earth with rot in their brains."

His lips twitched at her severe tone. Was he fighting against a smile? A frown? Maybe he was allergic to opinionated women.

Oh well, it wasn't like she'd see this man again. He was most likely a vendor wanting to burden the *Belle*'s culinary staff. Or a passing visitor who possessed a rebellious streak and jumped the entrance gate.

Either way, he'd inserted himself into her little sphere, piercing her bubble of peace. Her attention landed on Slate's book in her hand, stoking her anger. She held the hardback up to the stranger, shaking it. "This *poet* claims he's a romantic, but his verses are nothing but airy words of nonsense. It's no wonder he remains anonymous. I know I would if I published this kind of garbage." She was taking a risk. All of Louisville adored Slate because he was a local, but seriously, they needed to be more selective about who they prized as a celebrity.

After a few awkward seconds, his silver-hued gaze settled on her. "Are you by any chance, Devyn Asbury?" Something in his tone made it sound like he hoped she wasn't.

She knew that feeling exactly. "Yes, that's me."

"My name's Chase Jones." Gone was his breezy banter, replaced by a professionalism that made her heart stutter. "Your boss, Ms. Dewalt, sent me up here to speak with you."

She lowered the poetry book she was still half-strangling.

With reluctance, his eyes met hers. "I need to tour the *Belle* for special business, and she said you were the person I needed to speak with."

All heat drained from her face. She fought the urge to dash up to the pilothouse and hide under the lazy bench. For the next million years or so. This man was no doubt the mystery judge Steph had warned her about.

She'd just blown her chance at the contest.

Chapter 3

*W*ith his raven hair lifting in the breeze, his golden complexion, and a tiny hook-like scar near his left eye, Chase Jones looked more like a pirate than a connoisseur of weddings.

Maybe he was one of the hired actors for next week's Treasure Island Cruise. But then, why would he have asked for her? And be on *special business*? Devyn held in her groan. She'd just made a colossal fool out of herself. Should she continue in her streak of outrageous behavior by jumping overboard and swimming far far away?

No doubt Steph would follow after Devyn and drag her back by her soggy collar. Might as well face the man and pray she hadn't completely destroyed the *Belle*'s chances at winning.

She fought to keep her chin level. She'd once been a master at disguising her feelings. At portraying someone she was not. But she promised herself never to step into that mode again. Her mind scrambled to remember what he'd just said. "You want to tour the *Belle*, right?"

"If you have time?" His face looked less stricken. Good sign.

"I do." She'd have to brainstorm later. "Would you like to begin in the ballroom? That's where we hold most of our events and weddings." She glanced at the poetry collection in her hand, then to the man who'd fallen victim to her Slate tirade. What had she been thinking? "I'm...um...sorry about my ranting."

His slow smile built, transforming him from pirate to one of those men on the cologne ads at Macy's. "Were you being honest?"

"Yes."

"Then no need to be sorry." The perfect bend of his dark brow only made his lopsided grin more pronounced. "You should've seen that flash of fire in your eyes. It was incredible." He seemed truly fascinated by her ill-timed diatribe. "What is it about Slate's poetry that stirs that kind of reaction?"

"Let's just say I've several reasons to dislike the man and his work." A very strong one, and a few smaller offenses. Though she couldn't slight Steph for slipping this book in. Her boss hadn't known what truly happened.

Aware of Chase Jones's thoughtful gaze on her, she gathered the other books that had fallen and set them on the nearby bench. "Now I'm sure you haven't come to discuss awful poetry. What would you like to see first?"

She took note of his gray eyes. They were intriguing. Not a light gray but a deeper hue. Like graphite. And they watched her with a scrutiny that made her breath stick in her lungs.

"I've seen you before." He leaned back on the guards and observed her, his lazy posture saying he could linger until his mind placed her. "I'm sure of it."

No. No, no, no. If this man was one of the eighty million subscribers to Travis's channel, then he'd no doubt have seen her. Oh, if she could have access to delete all those posts. Mr. Jones was waiting patiently for her response. Jumping into the freezing Ohio was more appealing by the second. "Have you ever toured the *Belle* before? Or attended a wedding here?" She went for the professional approach. "I've been the event coordinator for almost a year now."

"I'm not much for weddings and. . ." He shrugged. "Fluff."

What? Was this man purposely trying to throw her off his scent? Or. . .was he not a judge at all?

He pushed off the railing, straightening to full height. "I'd like to see as much of the boat as I can. Is that possible?"

"Sure." She forced her lips into a perky arc. She needed to figure this person out. And soon. If he was a sneaky-faced judge, she needed to show her A-game, but if not, she had to discover a way to get him off this boat. She had no time to play Tour Guide.

"Let's start at the pilothouse and work our way down. This steamboat was first built in Pittsburgh in 1914."

"And was called the *Idlewild*, right?" He pulled a pad from his back jeans pocket and scribbled something in it.

"Yes." She angled to read what he was jotting down without looking obvious but couldn't catch anything. "It started off as a packet boat loading cargo and ferrying passengers." She motioned him toward the stairwell that reached the starlight roof. He followed her lead.

"What about in the 1920s?"

She paused, fingers twitching on the wooden handrail. "That's the only era where there wasn't much documentation. But mostly because the boat went tramping."

"Tramping?"

"It's a steamboat term for going up and down the river, stopping at various towns and taking passengers for excursions. They probably took on loads of cargo too when they could."

They reached the landing, his attention fixing on the calliope.

"Ah, there it is." He didn't wait for her but took off toward the direction of the musical pipes protruding out of the roof like stubby fingers. His gaze took it in like it was a puzzle needing to be solved. "Where are the keys?" He pulled something from the pages of the notepad—a photo?—and took a few steps back, as if taking in the entire scene.

"The keys have been moved behind the captain's quarters." She pointed to the texas cabin. "It's too loud for our musician to be that close to the pipes. Plus she'd get soaked from all the steam. But you're right. Back in the day, the keyboard would be about where you're standing. Heaven help their eardrums."

He gave her a courtesy look, then returned his focus to the photo. Had he printed off one of the pictures she uploaded for the contest? Wanting to verify it?

"We play the calliope when the passengers board and off-board. But for any other music we hire a live band or a DJ. The sound system here is pretty sweet for a century-old boat."

He lowered the photo and glanced at her, his expression nothing short of curious. "I'm going to be straight with you."

Oh.

"I need your help." He took two steps toward her. "I'm looking for information on someone. She was last seen on the *Belle*."

A missing person? Vanished after being aboard? Devyn's hand leapt to her chest. "I—I think this is a matter for the police."

"No, it's you I need. Someone with knowledge of this boat and maybe access to her history."

"I—I don't understand." Her childhood habit of stammering resurfaced.

"This person I'm looking for was born around the turn of the century. I'm researching her background."

History. Research. Those two words may as well have been her love language. In college, Devyn had majored in computer science for practicality, but her minor—and heart—had been in history.

He handed her the picture, well, half of a picture. Someone had torn it down the center.

Devyn stared at an old photo of a young woman standing in front of the calliope. Despite the sepia cast, Devyn could determine the lady's hair to be dark blond. Maybe a few shades darker than Devyn's own. And the woman had light eyes. She had pretty features, but what intrigued Devyn was her expression. It was almost a challenge. With her chin raised and eyes focused, as if daring whoever looked at this picture to take her seriously.

Devyn liked her. "Who is she?" Then to answer her own question she turned the picture over. "Hattie," she whispered, and a wave of something swirled her gut. Devyn had always been a fan of the classics. Classic movies, books, and fashion. This woman—with her two-toned oxford shoes and drop-waisted dress with pleats on the skirt—had the vintage style Devyn adored. "Is this picture from the twenties?"

He nodded. "I need to know more about her."

In a strange way, so did Devyn. She blinked. No, she couldn't get caught up in all this. Time was not on her side already, and she couldn't go all "cold case" about a missing woman, especially when she didn't even know how to handle such a thing. "So I'm taking it you're not a mystery judge."

That piqued his interest. "Judge?"

"Of the Timeless Wedding Contest. The *Belle* is a finalist this year." Saying those words aloud pushed thrill and panic through her.

"Sorry. I'm not." His full lips pressed together then relaxed, the corners tipping up. "So that must be why your boss gave me the royal treatment. I've been offered chocolate, a latte, and any item from the gift shop on the house."

Devyn couldn't help but laugh. "That's Steph for you. She's a go-getter."

"And you're not?"

"I'm a. . ." What was she? A survivor? A recovering people-pleaser?

"Dreamer."

His lone word snapped her from her deliberation. "Huh?"

"You're a dreamer." Stated so matter-of-factly Devyn could only gawk at him. Which probably wasn't the best thing, because he might mistake her shock for interest, and she could *not* have that.

She settled for a disbelieving snort. "That's quite the assessment for only knowing me a handful of minutes."

"True." He stepped closer, then leaned in as if about to share a secret. "But remember, I witnessed your dance."

"I thought I asked you to forget about that."

"No you didn't."

"Then I am now. Please forget it."

"Can't."

His mischievous grin looked about as dangerous as blow-drying her hair in the bathtub. And she could do without any more shocks to her system. "Thanks for letting me see this." She returned the picture, careful only to handle the edges. "But I can't help. I'm way too busy right now."

"Could we barter?"

She almost choked on a laugh. "You told me you have nothing to do with weddings and their. . .oh, what word did you use?"

"Fluff."

"Yes, fluff." She gave him a decided look. "Weddings and romance and all that is my business. I have to organize an event of the year and only have weeks to do so."

"I said weddings weren't my thing. Not romance. Romance, I can do. Very well."

Oh man. She should've counted on him upping the charm. That's what Travis had always done to get her to give him what he'd wanted. Well, lover boy could take his steamboat-sized ego and conveniently placed dimples somewhere else. "Again. My answer is no. Good luck in your endeavors."

She turned on her heel and glanced over her shoulder. "You better find your way off soon before Gary the guard notices. He takes his job as defender of the *Belle* very seriously."

"I'm an artist."

His blurted confession made her pause. "And how can that help me?"

"I'm sure you need materials, flyers. Invitations, maybe?" He held out his hands, palms up. "I can design them for you."

"Tempting, but no. I don't even have a theme yet."

"I can help you brainstorm. And also help with decorations. I have a good eye when it comes to that."

"But not for fluff."

"Fluff won't win your award. You need something different than the standard. Something that will set you apart."

"You know this, how?"

"Because I've done it. Walked among the routine and come out with something fresh. It was successful."

"Funny, I've never heard of you."

"You just don't know where to look." There was a magnetic dare in his eyes. But there was also something else—truth. He was convincing. Almost too convincing.

As if sensing her resolve weakening, he stood a little taller and delivered the final boom. "And who knows? Maybe unlocking Hattie's past will be something of key importance to the *Belle*'s history. Or it may be your ticket to inspiring the theme for your party."

She sighed. "I need to see some samples of your work before I agree to anything."

"Of course." He dimpled. "How about over dinner?"

Red flags hoisted so fast she felt the burn up her spine. "Purely a business dinner."

"Absolutely."

This man was still a stranger, therefore she needed to be extra careful. There was only one place she'd agree to meet him. "Do you like Skeeball?"

"I give up," he said on a breath of a laugh.

"What?" Her brows lowered. "It was a simple question."

"No, it's not that." He crossed his arms, a smile tugging his lips. "I first meet you, and you're waltzing to imaginary music."

"Not my finest moment."

"Then you launch into a spiel about an anonymous poet."

"You haven't yet seen my full wrath when it comes to him, but you don't know the specifics."

"Care to indulge me?"

"Not particularly."

"Then when I ask you to dinner, I'm thinking you're going to pick some fancy bistro, and here you are talking about arcade games. Point is, nothing you've said during this entire interaction was predictable. Are you always like this?"

She was, once. But for the past several months it had been like she was just existing, just going through the motions. Maybe with this whole not-a-wedding anniversary behind her, she could move on. Feel like Devyn again. Not the Space Station Devyn, but the carefree girl with dreams as deep as the river beneath her.

Instead of giving Chase an answer she wasn't ready for, she held out her hand. "Can I see that photo again?"

"Sure." He handed it over.

She could clearly see the painted word *Idlewild* in the background. A quick Google search would've led him here with ease. "Where's the other half?" She motioned toward the rip.

"I have no idea."

"So you don't know if anyone else was pictured here?"

"No."

Why was it ripped? And who had done it? Hattie? Or maybe someone else. Someone who wanted to remain unknown. Now that Devyn was looking closer, it appeared Hattie was speaking to someone or at least looking at someone. Her eyes were averted from the camera, her body slightly angled. But who? And why the challenge in her eye?

She lifted the photo to the sunlight and noticed something peeking up from Hattie's folded arm. A spark of recognition hit her. "I've seen that."

"What?" The curiosity in his voice was as noticeable as his compass tattoo on his left arm.

"See what she's holding?" She pointed at the picture.

"A book?"

"I recognize it from last year's auction. It's the songbook for the calliope. Maybe this woman wasn't just a passenger, but part of the crew." Or maybe Devyn had just made the biggest mistake in agreeing to help someone she hardly knew, with a mission that could be a major time-stealer.

Devyn wasn't the best at making choices. She had a track record to prove it. Another glance at the picture, and there was that stirring again. That call to adventure. Reviving something in her that had been comatose for far too long. It felt good to feel again. Good and terrifying. *Who are you, Hattie?*

Chapter 4

July 1926
Aboard the Idlewild

*T*he river wore starlight like a jeweled gown, an ancient garment that never grew old. Meanwhile, I couldn't keep my chiffon frock from snagging on the deck railing. With a sigh, I tugged the troublesome dress free from the splintery snare, leaving a sizeable rip to mend later. A trivial annoyance of steamboat life, but one I'd happily endured for all my twenty years. Because this river, like every other waterway, channel, and tributary carved into the dusty face of America, had embraced me when no human arms would. Except for Duffy.

Duffy.

I forced my gaze from the shimmering depths to the whitewashed boards beneath my scuffed oxfords. I couldn't be distracted from my mission.

I needed to find Duffy.

The aged steamboat captain may have been unharmed from his earlier tumble down the staircase, but I'd discovered something that changed the mishap from accidental to intentional. The breeze swept the edges of my hair against my throat as I tightened my grip on the boot Duffy had worn during his plight. I made my way along the deck, the rhythmic churning of the paddlewheel muting my footfalls.

The pale moon's glow hiccupped over a masculine profile stepping out from the cargo hold. I flattened my spine against a support beam, a jagged nailhead biting into my shoulder blade. Until now, there'd been no cause to slink into the shadows. The crewmen of the *Idlewild* had been like a hodgepodge family, but someone had brushed oil onto the bottom of my adopted papa's boot, casting every soul aboard into suspicion.

Breath caged in my chest, I prayed whoever emerged would go opposite my direction. There was no reason for anyone to be browsing the freight at half-past midnight. Unless. . .they were up to no good. My raging heart punished my ribs like the waves pummeling the hull.

Maybe I was being silly. Duffy was forever nagging me about my preposterous imagination. The oily boot could prove nothing more than a foolish prank by a deckhand. And the fellow cloaked in darkness before me could be no more than the engineer's apprentice. That lazy man was always sneaking off to enjoy a cigar. This realization settled my pulse and lowered my shoulders from their spiked position near my earlobes. I rallied my courage to step forward and announce myself, but the shadowy silhouette moved, allowing me a better glimpse.

The sharp angles and plains of his face were as unfamiliar as his large stature, branding him a stranger.

A stowaway!

I'd counted each passenger that had boarded this evening's excursion trip, and subsequently had the exact same number of people disembark. Could I have been mistaken? I'd been distracted because of Duffy's fall, though he'd rallied just fine for the four-hour river gallivant which seemed to please the locals of Paducah.

As for the man before me, how easy it would be to slip away from the flurry of exiting passengers, skitter down to the hold all quiet like a field mouse, and duck behind the wall of crates. For his misdeeds, he'd be awarded a free trip to Evansville. The nerve!

My feverish gaze remained on the trespasser who, judging from his lax posture, seemed unaware of my presence. But for how long? Right now, I held the advantage. Should I charge at him in hopes of shoving him overboard? My mouth twisted. I was just as tall if not taller than a few of the crewmen, but this fellow had the physique of one of those Greek statues from Duffy's worn encyclopedias. And even if I could budge the stowaway, he'd likely drag me into the silvery river with him.

I glanced at the boot in my hand, an idea forming. He leaned on the bull rails as if admiring the water. I lifted the shoe, bent my elbow, and—

"Hope you're not planning to hit me with that." His casual tone disarmed me.

How did he know I was there? The giant of a man turned on his heel, facing me, and my breath seemed to forget which way it traveled.

Must have been a trick of the moonlight. Otherwise I'd deem this man on the suave side of handsome. But a criminal, nonetheless.

He jerked his head toward the Ohio. "Be a shame to pollute the river with an old boot."

"Only if I miss. And I won't." I added a growl to my tone, aiming for intimidation. And failed. The tall feather from my headband had wilted over my forehead thanks to the calliope's steam. I sure loved playing the instrument and entertaining our passengers, but hadn't had time to change to my normal, sensible attire. I huffed with enough force to stir the wispy plume, and I swore a fleeting smirk crossed the intruder's face.

His amusement only stoked my ire. "Your fifty-five-cent fee for the excursion didn't include an overnight stay." My chin notched higher. If I could pilot a thousand-ton vessel, then surely I could steer a two-hundred-pound troublemaker off the boat. "As I see it, you can either take a swim now or I'll be forced to jail you in the brig. You'll be mighty cramped in that four-foot cell."

Ebony clouds slid over the moon, blocking me from assessing his reaction, but I couldn't mistake his low chuckle. "Neither of your options appeal to me. I think I'll stay right here. As a matter of fact, I'm honored to meet you. You see, I'm—" He took a bold step forward.

No. Couldn't let him within grasping distance. I hurled the boot with all my strength. The man angled away, the shoe smacking his spine, giving me time to act. I lunged onto his back and wrapped my hands around his thick neck, squeezing. Maybe I could make him pass out, then tie up his sorry carcass.

The man grunted, but otherwise remained stoic. My foot connected with the back of his knee, though he didn't buckle. He didn't even try to fling me off. Why wasn't he fighting back?

I was glad he wasn't. Because pressed against his frame, I was now acquainted with the solid muscles that the darkness—and his sportscoat—had deceptively hid. All he'd have to do was shake like a wet dog, and I'd go flying into the river.

Maybe if I yelled loud enough Ludwig would hear me from the

engine room and help haul this miscreant to the brig. In all my years on the water, I'd witnessed Duffy imprison only a few rowdy drunkards on the previous steamboats he'd mastered. And here I'd caught a stowaway. My very first captive! It was thrilling! It was—

"Hattie!"

I glanced over at the familiar—if not stern—voice.

Duffy seemed to materialize out of nowhere. He stood slightly hunched from his arthritis, but there was nothing feeble about him. Or the scowl on his weathered face.

"I caught a hitcher."

The stranger grunted again.

"Let him go." Disapproval marked Duffy's tone. "The man you're choking happens to be my new first mate."

Duffy's words struck so hard, I released the mystery man and fell onto my backside in a tangle of tulle and humiliation. The blamed headband slid over my eyes. *First mate?* Since when did Duffy hire crewmen without seeking my advice?

"Miss Louis." The stranger's deep timbre tickled my enflamed ears. "I'm honored to meet you."

He repeated the phrase he'd spoken before I attacked him. Only this time humor glinted off each syllable. I yanked off the headband and peered at the gentleman. The shifty darkness forbade me from distinguishing his eye color, but I spotted a twinkle beneath his lashes. He outstretched his hand, and my gaze snagged on his suit jacket sleeve. Why wasn't he in uniform? If he'd been outfitted like any normal officer, I wouldn't have launched myself at him. With a shake of my head, I refused his assistance and climbed to my feet, nearly tripping forward when my heel got stuck in my frock's hem.

Duffy approached with ginger steps, joining the mystery man's side. "Hattie, let me introduce you to Jack Marshall. As of tonight, he's second in command."

The wheel wash behind the *Idlewild* had always captivated me. The bucket planks spun round and round, troubling the river's serene countenance, leaving a wake of glittering ribbon. A beautiful disturbance.

My mind was troubled but not in the beautiful sort of way. I rolled my shoulders, trying to loosen the crick in my neck from a sleepless night.

"You knew some day this would happen." Duffy spoke above his tin coffee cup. He joined me at the rails, watching the swish of water. "I couldn't keep you in the role as mate. You haven't taken the exam."

My head whipped to face him. "And whose fault is that?" Oh how I'd begged Duffy to let me take the officer's test. To become a licensed mate.

But despite all of Duffy's gruffness, he wavered on the side of convention. A woman being a licensed riverman? Shocking! But I knew every part of the *Idlewild* like my own reflection. Better than. For even my own eye color wasn't dependable, changing shades from gray to green depending on the clothes I wore. Same with my hair, bleaching golden within the summer months. But this boat, she was constant.

A weathered hand cradled my shoulder, and though my annoyance was as present as the sun cresting the treetops, I welcomed Duffy's fatherly touch. He didn't often give affection. Especially lately. So I softened. If only a little.

"I never expected life on the river to be your future, child." His weighted gaze channeled on me. "There's a world out there beyond all this."

I took in the prominent ridge of his brow. Eyes that, not so long ago, could strike terror into any crewman with a single glower. But Duffy had never intimidated me. From childhood, I'd been able to peer beyond his tough exterior. I'd see my only friend who'd sit on the floor and play jacks with me. I'd heard the voice of my first tutor, teaching me port and starboard while other children in one-room schools learned left and right. I became fluent in the language of rivermen. Could splice and tie a line before I could thread a needle. "This is the life I love." I couldn't help the plead in my voice. "Is this about the rumors?"

From the *Idlewild*'s creation in 1914, it had belonged to the West Memphis Packet Group. At first, they'd run cargo with an occasional excursion trip. Though the past few years, the boat had been employed as a ferry in Memphis. But a new highway bridge stripped away that humble job, leaving the *Idlewild*—and all of us—in limbo.

There'd been talk about selling the steamboat. With magnificent vessels like the *Majestic*, the *De Soto*, and the *G. W. Hill* already cramming the Mississippi, the *Idlewild* wouldn't get a passing glance for excursion trips. Duffy had appealed to the owners, asking if they could set course along the Ohio. The uppers allowed it, for who'd turn down a chance to rake in money? But the crew was skeletal. I had to add muscle to the limp places, taking on tasks wherever needed. Not that I minded.

"You know that it's not just a rumor," Duffy at last remarked. "This could be the final season with Memphis."

"Then we'd move on with her." I patted the rails. "No owner in his right mind wouldn't take you on as captain." And me by default.

His heavy exhale spoke volumes. I shouldn't exasperate him with my persistence. Not when we had a full day ahead of us—unloading the freight at Henderson followed by a noon excursion. Then up the river to Evansville for a few days starting with a moonlight trip. Though I didn't want to leave things unsaid. If I didn't say my piece now, I'd have to wait until nightfall.

"Duffy." The word sprang from my lips like one would say Papa with all the sentiment and love my girlish heart could hold. I opened my mouth to begin my spiel, but Duffy spoke first.

"Once we reach Pittsburgh and I deliver the goods there, my obligation's over." Sunlight shone on the brass buttons of his uniform, but his expression was shadowed. "Then we need to start thinking differently."

And there it was. Everything locked into place like the custom fittings in the engine room, roaring to life this new realization.

Duffy was retiring.

No wonder he'd brought on a first mate. He'd be grooming him to take over. While no one felt any qualms about my taking on the responsibilities, there wouldn't be a soul around who would take me seriously as a female captain. Besides, my loyalty remained with Duffy. I owed him that and more.

"You can't quit." The bite of tears made my nose sting. "You have many good years left. Think of all the adventures we'll miss if you hang up your cap now."

"Adventures for you, maybe. But not on a steamboat."

I couldn't believe what I was hearing. Was Duffy's arthritis worse than he let on? My gaze fastened on his left hand still holding his coffee mug. The tremors in his grip didn't seem more violent, rather he seemed less shaky today. "How could you give up something you love so easily?"

He flinched. I'd gone too far and broken the unspoken rule about rivermen. Their devotion to the waters was never questioned. It was in their blood, part of them.

Duffy's mouth pressed into a grim line, and he turned from me. After three heavy steps, he glanced over his shoulder, an unmistakable sadness in every line of his beautiful, old face. "Sometimes life doesn't give you a choice."

Then he slowly trudged up the stairs on his way to the texas roof. Every step he moved higher, my heart sunk lower, scaling the rocky bottom of my soul. We'd reach Pittsburgh in a little over four weeks. It was hard to imagine this could be my last trek on the *Idlewild*. Along the river. An ache stretched in me, a grieving almost.

I had to figure a way to keep him from changing the course of our lives.

Chapter 5

I want all these crates and barrels opened and checked before we off-load them."

My jaw slacked at Jack Marshall's outrageous commands. "You're not serious." From the looks of the crewmen, they hoped the same thing.

"Perfectly." He glared into the cargo hold as if something menacing might emerge.

This was the first time I'd been close to the new officer since my embarrassing assault on him last night. When we landed at Henderson, I remained at a distance. I was still upset from my awful conversation with Duffy and hadn't wanted to worsen my mood by watching this outsider take my usual spot on the wing bridge, assisting our pilot Clem, and commanding the deckhands. Even in my stateroom, I'd heard his authoritative voice, more fit for a naval officer than a steamboat first mate.

I pitied the deckhands. But maybe I should pity our aggressive mate. Did he not understand the workings of rivermen? How they won their revenge one way or another? Something told me this was his first outing as an officer. He seemed as green as the algae on the dock we stood on.

"That task would take all morning." I stood a bit taller, but still only reached his chin. "And I'm sure these men have plans to go up the hill." I jerked my head toward the town of Henderson. Working twelve to sixteen hours a day made the crew possessive over the sliver of free time they were granted. The mate's directive would stoke a fire of grudge he might not be able to extinguish.

"It's a sacrifice we all will make." His gaze finally met mine and my initial assessment was confirmed.

He was handsome.

The kind that would give me a pinch in my gut if I wasn't already prone to dislike him.

His eyes, masked by darkness last evening, caught the early morning light, revealing an icy blue shade. But more than that, it was how he presented himself. His uniform was crisp and creaseless. His cap straight atop his head, the golden hair beneath trimmed and orderly.

The man took pride in his appearance, his role as first mate. I was suddenly aware of how disheveled my appearance must be. It had taken me less than three minutes to throw on my charcoal-colored dress and run a comb through my hair. But I had spent the sunrise moments in the pilothouse with Clem, and the breeze had danced in my hair, whipping it about. No doubt I looked wild.

"The docks at this time of day is no place for a lady."

"Don't worry, I have my trusty penknife. The captain of the *Glory Skies* taught me how to use it." I sent him a razor-sharp look. "If anyone messes with me, I know exactly which tendons to slice that'd make a man uncomfortable for the rest of his life."

His startled gaze swept over me. "You carry a knife on your person?"

"Doesn't every *lady*?" I tossed back the word in the same inflection he'd used. "I thought all young women used a knife for grooming. How else would we pick food from our teeth or clean beneath our fingernails?"

I said this purely to shock the man, but he seemed rather entertained. As if all the words that came out of my mouth were solely for his pleasure. But those laugh lines framing his eyes by no means daunted me. "In fact, I had a seamstress in Owensboro create me a special garter to keep it secure."

"Better be careful not to walk too fast. Those things are known to slip. You could do some serious damage to your leg."

Arg. He was supposed to be appalled at my words. Not join in the scandalous talk. "So as you see, I'm not your typical lady. I've lived on the river all my years and am perfectly capable of fending for myself."

"You can stay, but you need to give me the discharge book." His voice turned back to the business at hand.

I clutched the worn binding to my chest. He was already performing most of my tasks, taking my position, and soon he would take Duffy's. A surge of indignation rushed through me. "No, I'm in charge of the log."

His head reared back at my insubordination. "I thought you were only the perfessor."

Only? "I do more than just play the calliope."

"Such as?" He eyed me. "What exactly is your role then?"

Of all the— "I'm a floater."

His brows rose as if he'd never heard the term in his life. Well, fine. I'd enlighten him.

"I have my hand in everything. Helping Miss Wendall in the kitchen, playing the piano during the day trips, working with the purser on the books." I held up the log. "I've even been a standby coal passer."

He blinked. "Surely not. That's a man's job." His gaze drifted to my arms as if sizing me up. "You shouldn't be straining with wheelbarrows."

"Straining? Oh, please. You talk as if I'm some porcelain creature that could snap in the wind." A hundred pounds in a sturdy wheelbarrow was nothing. What would this man say if I admitted to steering this tonnage vessel? Handling the hardware, controlling this steamboat, demanded a strength I hadn't known I'd possessed. But I'd done it. Many, many times. But seeing as how I didn't have my pilot's license, I wouldn't want this man pestering Clem about it. So it would probably be best to navigate the conversation into safer waters. "I have a system." I tapped the edge of the notebook decidedly against my palm. "A good one." One I poured my heart out to perfect.

"So do I. And it involves checking the articles that go off the boat to match the log to a T."

And now he was attacking how I ran things? My gut bubbled hotter than the firebox that ignited the boilers.

He stuck out his hand for the slim notepad I gripped. We were at an impasse. I was already out of sorts from learning about Duffy's retirement; I felt one more thing would crack my composure.

The deckhands stood on the main deck, watching the show. I lifted my chin, and he did as well, raising his freshly-shaven jaw, his neck boasting several nicks from his razor.

No, not nicks. Scrapes. Shaped in half-moons like my fingernails.

I gasped and dropped the log. "I did that to you." And before I knew it, my hands were on the man's neck for the second time in twelve hours. I ran the pads of my fingers over his throat. There was a medical bag in the galley, but it didn't feel like there was any swelling beneath the scabs. No bruises. "Can you swallow okay? Any feelings of discomfort?"

Surprise filled his eyes, and he stared at me like I was a peculiar creature. Then something else took the place of shock—mirth. He was laughing at me without voicing a chuckle. "The only discomfort I feel is your toes digging into my shoe."

Oh. I hadn't realized how close I was. Come to think of it, I could smell his aftershave mixed with the starch of his collar. "Sorry." I shuffled away and clasped my fingers tightly behind my back. "Just wanted to be sure you were okay," I said by way of excusing my rash behavior. Why couldn't I keep my hands off this man? "I mean, I practically choked you last night."

"Practically?" Humor laced his voice and, despite my ire, I kind of liked it.

No, this man was my enemy. He'd come aboard with the sole motivation of becoming Duffy's replacement. No one could take his place. But maybe, if I acted friendly, I could learn how best to sabotage Jack Marshall's chances. And the first thing in order was appearing remorseful. "I'm also sorry for mistaking you as a stowaway."

He held up a hand. "No need to apologize. You were protecting your boat."

Something in his tone made me study him closer. He wasn't mocking me. Rather it appeared the other way around, as if he held some sort of admiration for me nearly strangling him.

"And besides, it was worth it, for you released your death grip." He bent down and scooped up the precious log I'd abandoned. "Now I can get to work."

My first battle could be tallied as a defeat. I needed to outwit this man and preferably before we docked at Pittsburgh.

Chapter 6

Devyn

MJ's Pizza was Devyn's second home. Not only did she prefer the aroma of carbs to any steakhouse on the planet, but the owner was one of her favorite humans. Most of the time.

"So you invited a man you only met hours ago here? Tonight?" Mitch leaned on the counter beside the register and lifted a brow in that annoying rebuke only older siblings employed. Though he was just older by five minutes and thirty seconds.

"Well, yeah." She shrugged. "If he turns out to be a weirdo, I have you to defend me."

He scoffed. "So *now* you welcome my muscles."

"Umm, the last time you offered to defend my honor you could've landed in jail and had the entire exchange blasted all over Space Station."

"I hate that name."

"You and me both, big fella." After her breakup, Mitch was murderously angry with Travis. Not that Devyn hadn't been grateful for his brotherly wrath, but Travis would have used any retribution as another exploit for his crummy channel. One Asbury publicly humiliated had been enough.

"Besides. Tonight isn't a date."

"Then why are you dressed like that?" He tugged her ponytail, making her Cardinal hat shift on her head.

"A T-shirt and faded jeans is hardly date appropriate." In fact, her attire served two purposes. One being to dissuade any interest from Chase, and the other to avoid public recognition. A baseball hat and comfort clothes were entirely different than the chic always-trendy way she'd dressed last year.

"You don't know dudes, Dev." He shook his head as if he felt sorry for her.

"Whatever." She popped him on the arm. "And for the record, I'm not looking for a dude."

"Because of Travis? I told you he was a loser from the start."

"Yes, yes you did. And I should've listened." But this wasn't about Travis. *For once.* "I'm thinking since you married my best friend, then you totally owe me one."

His brow wrinkled. "What, a new best friend?"

"No, Angie's stuck with me. Since I gave you your dream girl, you need to pony up and supply me my dream guy. I'm thinking Italian, dark, maybe an aversion to anything social media-related. I'm totally cashing in."

He laughed. "I don't know anyone like that. How about a video-game junkie who still lives in his parents' basement?"

"Don't even." She rolled her eyes. "I've suffered enough of that mind decay from your teenage years."

"Good times." He smiled. "So when's your not-a-date friend coming?"

"He's not my friend either. Like I said, I just met him. And he's supposed to be here at six." She glanced at her phone. Ten minutes. She still had time to run away. It would be so simple. She hadn't even given him her number. So he couldn't badger-call her. Though he *did* know where she worked, and—

"You gonna bail?"

"We may be twins, but we're not supposed to share the same brain. Knock it off. It's creepy."

"You're really thinking about ditching this dude?"

"Yeah."

"Don't."

"But I have so many other things I need to do to get ready for the ball." This whole mystery photo could only complicate life more. Granted, she was intrigued, and she could use all the help she could get with the contest. Especially free help. "Besides, just a second ago, you were dissing me for inviting him in the first place."

"Yeah, I know. But you should stay." His voice had an uncommon serious edge to it. "You've been like a recluse since your breakup."

"You know the reason behind it."

"So what if someone recognizes you. You've done nothing wrong. You're the victim."

No matter how many times Mitch said that, Devyn couldn't believe him. Yeah, she was a victim of Travis's manipulation, but she'd willingly put herself there. Willingly allowed him to put their relationship on display. Not to mention all the morals she'd abandoned in order to cling to her former fiancé. She knew better. Man, she knew. But she hadn't the time to go into that with her brother. "I still don't know this guy. He could be a major creep."

"What was your first impression of him?"

"That he looked like a pirate."

He snorted. "Only you."

"He kinda does though. Without the whole hook, wooden leg, and parrot-on-the-shoulder thing going on."

"Does he have a beard?"

"No, but he has a scar."

He lifted his hands as if surrendering, and she laughed. It was good to be around her brother. He always understood her, and in those slim times when he couldn't, he made her smile.

"At any rate, Dev, if this guy turns out to be a jerk you can lodge a skeeball into his skull." He tapped the space between his eyes. "I've never seen anyone with better aim than you."

Being a fastball pitcher for the University of Louisville had always been one of her dreams, however short-lived. Mom's diagnosis had come sudden and fierce. Devyn had quit the team her sophomore year to take care of her. Once Mom went into remission, Travis had reappeared into her life. Then Space Station. Life before Travis seemed so long ago. Almost as if she were a different person.

Mitch's attention drifted to his phone's screen. "No need to be scared, Sis. I'm here. Nothing's going to happen. Never know, you might end up liking him."

Familiar strains of a song poured from the sound system, and Devyn gasped. "Ole Blue Eyes."

Her brother glanced up from his phone, which he must've been using to activate the stereo. "When you texted saying you were coming tonight, I made you a playlist."

"Of the classics?"

"Yes. And nineties Christian songs." He pocketed his cell. "You have the weirdest taste in music. You know that, right?"

Even as he spoke, a DCTalk favorite started. Her eyes misted. The not-gonna-happen-wedding week had been rough on her emotions, and her brother had been the one that had helped the most. He'd texted her funny GIFs, had daisies delivered to her work, and even dropped off the anniversary edition of *Roman Holiday*. The perfect classic movie for the situation, because while Audrey Hepburn and Gregory Peck were always amazing, the ending wasn't sappy. It was real life. And that had been what Devyn needed.

Her six-foot-three, U of L linebacker brother. The best in the whole world. "You have a soft spot larger than Kentucky."

"Tell no one." He tried to look gruff, but the tenderness in his eyes outshone all.

"I'm sure Angie knows already." She nudged his elbow. One thing about Mitch Asbury, he loved the women in his life. He was proof that good guys still existed. Someday, Devyn would find one of those few remaining that would make her soul hum and her heart light. And above all else, love her for who she was.

On that wistful note, she glanced toward the entrance.

Chase Jones had walked in and was staring straight at her.

Chase met Devyn halfway between the cash register counter where Mitch stood guard and the door.

He offered a smile. "I was half-thinking you wouldn't show."

"I considered it. Several times."

His dimples winked at her. "I'm glad you're here."

"You may not say that after I crush you." She gestured toward Game Alley.

"You're serious?"

"I never kid about Skeeball." A smirk teased her lips. "Did you bring the samples I asked for?"

"Right here." He raised a black leather portfolio.

"Good, we'll talk over pizza." She inclined her head, moving toward the pizza buffet.

"Aren't we supposed to pay first?" He cut a glance at the counter where Mitch stood beside a teenage cashier, helping her change the receipt paper.

Her brother chose that moment to glance over and level a look at Chase. Man, he could be intimidating if she didn't know what a teddy bear he really was. "Nope. See that man right there giving you the stink-eye?"

"Can't miss him."

"That's my twin."

He paused. "You're a twin?"

"I am. We hardly resemble each other." Mitch with his tall dark looks and her with her light hair and eyes. They both had an athletic build, though her brother's superseded hers. She had curves and toned muscles, which she'd come to appreciate. But boy, it had taken her long enough.

"Mitch owns this place, so I get all meals free. Yours is on the house tonight too."

"I'm not much for freeloading."

She shrugged. "You can try to pay if it bothers you. Mitch will still wave you off though."

After loading their plates, they got their drinks and chose a booth in the corner. The hanging lamp cast a soft glow.

Chase was the first to break the silence. "Makes sense now."

"What does?"

"Why you chose to come here."

"For the garlic pizza, of course." She tore off a hunk of said pizza and mopped it in ranch dressing.

"That's more like a glorified breadstick," he remarked. "There's no sauce on it."

"Because it's perfect without it." Her lashes slid shut as she took a ranch-soaked bite. She opened her eyes to find him watching her, an amused smile lining his mouth.

"Would you like me to give you two a moment?"

"A man should never come between a woman and her garlic pizza."

"Noted." He winked and took a sip of his drink.

"But yes, it does make sense why I picked this place. I've had a personal bodyguard since birth. Kinda nice." She wiped her fingers on her napkin. "You can't blame me. We hardly know each other."

His bent elbows rested on the table, his tattoo making an appearance along with his impressive bicep. "I know more than you think."

His words froze her blood. He knew. Of course he did. How could she have thought she'd be able to hide her past—her very publicly documented past—from anyone? Maybe Mitch was right. Devyn should quit hiding. Confront it all. But somewhere between now and last October, she'd lost her backbone, and she didn't have the strength to retrace the steps of her memory to retrieve it.

Something glinted in his eyes. "Take a shot at it?"

Fine. Might as well get it over with. "By all means." She took another bite. If she was going under, it would be in a blazing glory of carbohydrates.

"Going by your shoes earlier and your purse tonight, you have a thing for red. I'm guessing it's your favorite color. You haven't outgrown your imagination." His lips curled into a smile. "I'm referring to your waltzing."

"I figured."

"And you have a dislike for poetry."

"Not all poetry," she corrected. "Just Slate's."

A crease settled between his brows. "Seems like there's a story behind that."

"Oh there is." She took another sip of her drink. "Did you bring any work to show me? Or would you rather keep on dissecting me?"

"Not dissecting. Observing." He slid his portfolio toward her, his cologne wafting.

Her intent for a carb overdose was temporarily forgotten. If his samples were half as amazing as he smelled, she could see herself stupidly agreeing to his business terms, signing a contract, and maybe adding a misshaped heart to her name.

She blinked away her juvenile mental lapse. Gucci cologne always had a trancing effect. She opened the sleek black binder, and with a critical gaze, perused his designs of music covers, flyers, invitations, and photographs. He had somewhat of a classic flair. Nothing flamboyant. Or flowery. Clear-cut lines, lots of use of black-and-white. There weren't many pieces though, making her curious as to how long he'd been in business. Either that or he'd chosen his best work to feature.

"Very nice," she finally conceded. "Though I noticed the dates on these are from last year. Have you got anything recent?"

"Afraid not. Something came up that stole a lot of my attention." He folded his pizza in half and ate it like a sandwich.

She waited for him to finish chewing. "What kind of *something*?"

"Sorry, personal."

Hmm. She wasn't about to press. If she knew anything, she knew the value in respecting privacy. But what if the something was a toxic behavior? Like alcohol or drug addiction? "Will this personal business stand in the way of your work for the *Belle*?"

He draped his arm along the top of the bench. "No."

"Do you work freelance, or do you belong to a design agency?"

"Just me."

"Do you have a website?" She scanned the front of the portfolio for any contact information. "Any place I can check reviews of your service?"

He reached over and pointed to a pocket. "There's a business card tucked right there."

"Oh." She slid her hand into the pouch and retrieved it. "I need these designs soon. Like in ten days. Are you able to promise to have the work done and to my satisfaction?"

"I promise to satisfy you any way I can." With one flip of his full lips, the man could deceive any girl that his smile was solely meant for her.

But she wasn't naive anymore. "That needs to stop."

"What?" And now his tone was innocent.

"Your outrageous flirting."

"I can't help it. I have a weakness for beautiful women."

Beautiful? In a worn hat and T-shirt? Now she knew he was being over the top. "This contest is huge for me. Like ridiculously huge. I need you to take it seriously for this to work."

"Why's it mean so much?" The mischief in his eyes waned to something else. He really seemed interested in her answer.

"*Once Upon a Wedding* is big time." Not Space Station big time, but important to the wedding industry. Her industry. "Everyone wants featured in that magazine. It's an honor to be recognized by such an elite organization. Winning this award would bring a lot of traffic to the *Belle*."

"But what does it mean to you?"

So much. To prove she could be successful without Travis. That she could dream again. "Let's just say I had some major things flop over this past year." She held his gaze. "It feels like God's giving me a second chance." To do things the right way. His way. "I don't want to mess it up."

Those dark gray eyes so playful a moment ago were now arrested on her. She almost startled at their intensity. She may have said more than she'd intended, but nothing she hadn't meant. If her mentioning God freaked him out, then so be it.

Whatever lure held him was broken by the tilting of his lips into an enticing smile. "So what do you say? Does my work fit what you're looking for? Do we have a deal?"

Devyn stared at her napkin-wrapped cutlery. Using his services for all the design needs would definitely help the budget. She could use that money elsewhere—securing the entertainment, beefing up the menu, purchasing décor. "We need to cooperate. As in, if I want more *fluff*, you need to be able to adjust your tastes to suit mine. Agreed?"

He hesitated a second, then held her with a look. "Agreed."

"Okay. Good." She swallowed. "Also, if we're going to work together on your project, I need all the info you have on Hattie. What have you got?"

"Not much." He leaned back, a dark curl falling over his forehead. The man really had nice hair. Travis's style was somewhat of a phenomenon, the way it could defy gravity, withstand hurricane winds, all the while holding a glossy shine as if he'd stuffed sunlight into each follicle. It was also untouchable. Not so with Chase's. His hair leaned on the flirty side, purposely overgrown, curling at the tips, daring a woman's fingers to course through it.

She blinked. Her train of thought wasn't only derailed but charging off a cliff into forbidden waters. "Where'd you find that photo?"

"In an old trunk at my great-grandfather's house." He idly toyed with the edges of his napkin. "I was about eight when he died. The last few years of his life, Pap suffered from Alzheimer's."

"I'm sorry."

He accepted her condolences with a nod. "I only found the picture recently, but I knew right away it was her."

"What do you mean?"

"Pap would fall into a dark mood, a place no one could reach him. I was young, but I remember the pain in his voice. He'd get this haunted look in his eyes when he said her name."

"Hattie's?"

"Yeah. He'd say it over and over. Sometimes there was an apology with it. '*I'm sorry, Hattie. It's my fault.*'" His gaze dipped to his fingers. "When I saw her name on the back and the sign *Idlewild* behind her, I thought it was worth exploring."

He spoke as if he was the one who needed closure. As if his great-grandfather's secrets had become his own.

The photo was intriguing. And something about Hattie called to Devyn. Perhaps it was the same reason as Chase's. To discover her story. Her secrets. But sometimes secrets, when exposed, only served heartbreak. "Do you know what connection your Pap had with this woman?"

He peered at her from beneath a fringe of dark lashes. "I think he might have been in love with her."

Chapter 7

Hattie

$\mathcal{T}$he morning breeze that whispered through the cattails lining the riverbank had shifted to an all-out gale by noontime. Passengers brave enough to venture onto the decks for the picnic excursion clamped their hands to their hats lest the felt boaters or turbans be swept into the river. All others seemed satisfied to pass time in the main room. The older crowd gazed out the windows, idly chatting. Those younger loitered around the refreshment table or cut up on the dance floor.

At least my excursion tasks hadn't changed, considering I was the only crewman who could not only play—but tolerate—the calliope on gusty days. Nothing like performing "Swanee River" while being pelted with steam mixed with cylinder oil.

The chipper melody had seemed like a dirge. How many more times would I get to press my fingers to the brass keys? Welcome patrons to their river adventure with merry tunes?

Continuing in my melancholy mood, I'd then endured piano duty in the main room. The snappy jazz music pounded my skull for two full hours, resulting in a fierce headache. Break time couldn't arrive soon enough. I nodded to the bandleader and headed toward the refreshment tables.

Giggles, high-pitched and grating, erupted from a few yards away. I pressed a finger to my temple, squeezing my lids shut against the stab of pain. For the love of healthy eardrums, did they have to screech that way? I cast an exasperated glance toward the young ladies and discovered the source of their enamored glee—Jack Marshall.

During the course of this voyage, he'd done all things with an air of finesse. Nodding with a warm smile to the women and extending a firm handshake to the gentlemen. Yet there'd been something else behind his pleasantries. Something that had carried over from this morning's double—no, triple—check of the cargo hold. As if reading my suspicion, his gaze lifted and locked on mine. The corners of his mouth climbed higher, but I held my face neutral.

Only when a fellow approached him with a hoard of young ladies—the man's daughters and friends, I presumed—did our staring match end, and I realized I could breathe again. Still, I watched the interactions with subtle interest. The older gentleman only hung around long enough to make introductions then abandoned the first mate to the mercy of giggling females around my age.

The July temperatures and multitude of breathing bodies had made the room a few notches above stifling, but these women took their skills with their fans to an entirely different level. Almost like some art form. Fanning their coy faces to stir ringlets of hair, then pressing the silk contraptions to their hearts, drawing attention to their bosoms. The entire charade made my skin itch.

One young lady dressed in a fashionable frock—complete with lace gloves and net-cloche hat—laughed at everything Jack said and every so often gently placed a hand on his arm. She angled forward, stealing streaks of sunlight pouring in from the window to cast a golden hue to her light brown hair.

And this was the world Duffy wanted me to enter? I had no more talent in using a fan than I had in flirting with a complete stranger. Or any male for that matter. Being the only female besides the middle-aged cook aboard the steam vessel, I'd grown up alongside men. I could discuss at length the flow of pipes in the boiler room, but couldn't for the life of me flirt.

I moved to retreat to the other side of the room, though I had to pass First Mate Charming and his host of admirers.

"Miss Louis." Jack Marshall's voice held an edge of authority that made me bristle. "I need to speak with you."

Too soon, the man was at my side. With a hand to my elbow, he led me across the floor to my intended destination.

His searching gaze no doubt read the question in my eyes. "Forgive me." He expelled a sigh. "I didn't know how else to escape." He inclined his head toward the group of women now giving me the devil-eye behind their laced fans.

"I see. Especially since they blocked your goal."

"Goal?"

"You're inspecting the passengers." He was good, I'd give him that. But after hours of witnessing his scrutiny of the freight, I'd noticed the slight crinkling of his eyes as he'd channel his focus. With the passengers, the expression was less intense, but there nonetheless. "What for?"

He grinned. "Are you always this observant, Miss Louis?"

"Are you always this insulting?"

His lips stretched into a frown at my accusation.

"You respond to my honest question with another question. You're purposely trying to divert my attention. And then you throw in a charming smile as if to cloud my mind like the steam out of the smokestacks."

"You think I'm charming?"

"And you're doing it again." I shoved a hand on my hip and ignored the amusement dancing in his eyes. "If you refuse to answer my question, just say so. Plain talking beats word games in my book, sir."

"Please call me Jack." His expression sobered. "I'm sorry. You're right. I'm studying the passengers, but I can't say why. Not just yet."

An odd mix of satisfaction and frustration flooded my gut. "Fine, Jack. But you should turn your efforts on inspecting your stateroom."

His brows lifted, disappearing beneath his cap. "Meaning?"

I pressed my lips together. Should I? This man was my archrival, but could I leave him to the fate of menacing deckhands? "Meaning, I'd give your water pitcher a thorough glance before drinking. Face has been known to put minnows in it. And since you spoiled his chances of going into Henderson and finding a temporary romance, you could very well have a river eel under your bed."

That got him. He pulled off his cap and ran a hand through his blond hair. "Who's Face?"

Laughter rippled in my chest. "Don't tell me they gave you their Christian names?" Oh brother, they must really dislike the man. "Better check beneath your sheets as well."

Poor soul looked like he'd been shoved overboard and was floundering to stay afloat.

I decided to toss him a life ring. "What kind of riverman are you if you don't know the ways? Face is our youngest deckhand."

"Robert?"

I nodded. "Called Face because he thinks he's a looker. Then there's Ludwig. Named after Beethoven because he runs the engine room like a symphony. Has an ear for whenever something doesn't sound right. They all have nicknames except Clem, the pilot." Even Duffy was short for Woodruff.

He blew out a breath. "Looks like I'm going to have to win their comradery." Then his distant gaze focused on me and my breath cinched. "So what's your nickname?"

My fingers fidgeted the helm pendant around my neck. "I. . .uh. . . don't have one." But that didn't make me any less a member of the crew. Though from an outsider's view it must appear just that. The realization burned. Even Duffy was trying to push me out of this life as if I didn't belong. If I didn't fit here, then I wouldn't fit anywhere. I caught a flash of green to my left. "We're approaching Deadman's Island." My gaze lingered out the window. Somehow I identified with the small strip of land. It was stuck between two worlds. On one side lay Indiana, the other Kentucky, yet neither claimed it. It belonged to the river. And so did I. There was no world for me beyond those shores.

"Time to round to," Jack muttered. The scuffle of his retreating footsteps followed.

Caught up in my own musing, it took me a few long seconds to comprehend what he'd said. I dashed to the pilothouse, hoping to catch him before he made a colossal error, but he was already giving Clem the command.

"Cut to port." His order bellowed firm.

The aged pilot shot me an amused glance. Duffy stood beside Clem, arms folded over his chest, content to say nothing. Their silence was unsurprising. Seasoned sailors believed in the traditional way of teaching—by learning from mistakes. But why was Face here? During his free time, the deckhand could be found sweet-talking the prettiest girl aboard. Now here he sat, lounging on the lazy bench, hands stacked behind his head, eyes brimming with deviltry.

My gaze drifted over the three of them, and I huffed. No way the *Idlewild* would maneuver that way. And not a soul was going to warn Jack? Blast the softness of my heart. "Clem," I yelled over the blustery wind. "Don't pull left. You know what to do."

Clem grimaced to the point his bushy mustache hid his mouth. Duffy's eyes gleamed with mirth, and Face's brows furrowed in disappointment.

Meanwhile, Jack blinked at me in what could only be defined as annoyed shock.

I sighed and grabbed him by the wrist, pulling him out of the pilot-house, out of hearing range of the aged rivermen.

The frosty blues of his eyes were colder than a hundred winters. "You just undermined my authority in front of the captain. Clem's even angered by your behavior."

"You better believe he's miffed at me." I matched his scowl with one of my own. "Because I wouldn't let you make a fool of yourself."

A muscle leapt in his cheek. "There's no danger in making a left turn."

"There is if she won't make it."

Another blink.

"You have to treat the *Idlewild* like you would your sweetheart. Not just ordering her about before you get to know her. You need to first understand her strengths and weaknesses. Then she'll give you everything she's got."

He stared at me as if I were some river fairy, unsure whether to believe me or not.

"Since no one else seems keen to help. Here's two things to remember. One, Clem has been piloting steamboats longer than you've been alive. He doesn't need told how to steer her."

"And two?"

"The boat's light on fuel." Which he would know since we were slated for a coal load at Evansville later this afternoon. But he didn't know how it would affect the *Idlewild*. Every boat was different. "As the fuel's burned, her head rises." I gestured toward the bow. "She doesn't have enough in her to face the wind."

Even as I spoke Clem was backing the tail, and I watched understanding dawn on Jack's face.

"So she needs backed into the wind rather than making her turn into it."

"Exactly." The breeze kept whipping my hair against my cheek, and I sighed my annoyance. My fingers gripped the wind-tousled hair, holding it captive at the base of my neck.

The first mate's eyes followed my movement, his gaze traveling the column of my throat and catching on my necklace. The helm pendant.

I raised my chin, defiance roiling through me. If he deemed it silly or outlandish for a woman to wear jewelry fashioned after a boat's steering wheel, then I dared him with my narrowed eyes to utter it.

"Anything else I should know, Admiral?" His crooked smile was all tease, but his eyes said something completely different. He'd given me a nickname, letting me know he saw me as part of the crew, accepted me.

And just what was this peculiar warmth swelling my chest?

So far I'd helped him along far more than I should have. Informing him about the rowdy deckhands and now saving him from making a rookie mistake. I was practically training him to be captain! "Fine saboteur I am," I mumbled.

"Pardon?"

"Nothing." I gave him a stiff nod goodbye and trudged down the staircase. Not forgetting my role as hostess, I chatted with a few passengers in the main cabin, then cleaned up a few lemonade spills other crewmen had overlooked. With the wind subsided, I strolled back to the hurricane deck.

Face stood a few paces away, leaning over the rails and watching the water. He threw me an irritated side-glance. "You ruined all my fun. You should've let the mate figure it out himself."

"And have the *Idlewild* drift sideways down the river?" I shook my head. "It was only fair to warn him."

"He'd find out soon enough." Face's shoulders lifted in a lazy shrug. "He needs to get the feel of her."

"I agree. But not in front of four hundred passengers to witness his embarrassment."

"You're too sweet, Hattie." His lips curved into a fond smile. "Wish you'd be that softhearted with me. Any chance you've decided to run away with me?"

"No."

He chuckled. "Thought I'd ask." He threw me a rascally grin, his dark brown gaze drifting over my head. His mouth flattened into a scowl, and he cursed under his breath. "Be seeing you," he said before sauntering off.

I turned, wanting to understand Face's shift in temper. Jack leaned against the post beside the stairway. How much of the conversation had he heard?

He joined my side, taking Face's spot. "You were right."

I tried not to get distracted by his nearness or how the sunshine highlighted his sculpted jawline. "Only because I'm familiar with the boat."

"I meant about my stateroom."

"Minnows?"

"Salamanders."

I didn't know whether to laugh or cringe. "That would've been an interesting gulp of water."

"One I avoided, thanks to you."

"It was nothing."

The skin framing his eyes bunched, the now-familiar expression in place. He was studying me. My toes curled under his pensive stare. "Why are you inspecting me like a crate of olive oil?"

He stroked the edge of his chin in serious contemplation. "I was considering your voice."

I looked at him sharply. "My voice? What about it?"

"Last night it declared me a stowaway. Today it saved me from two forms of humiliation." His gaze roamed my face, and I felt that irksome flutter. "I'm just wondering if your voice is the sound of an angel guiding me along, or a siren drawing me in to my demise."

"Your guess is as good as mine."

Chapter 8

*M*ist curled over the water. Birdsong awakened the trees just yonder from where I sat in the wooden dinghy. Mornings on the river were majestic. Especially the blazing sky splashed with golds and oranges. It all breathed life into my soul.

"This coffee tastes like cylinder oil."

And then there was Face.

"You're not concentrating." I gave him my no-nonsense tone, and he had the gall to grin wider.

"You flush a pretty shade of pink when you're annoyed. It's a nice sight to see first thing in the mornin'." He set down his coffee mug and finally cast his line into the water. "I thought we weren't gonna fish until we reached Owensboro. What's the rush?"

"I have my reasons."

"And that reason is you wanting to get me alone." He glanced toward the *Idlewild*. "We can row this dinghy further out of view." His eyebrows waggled.

"Perfect." I checked my fishing line. No bites yet. "Then no one would see your embarrassment when I push your sorry hide into the river."

He laughed. "Always the charmer."

"You know that mumbo jumbo doesn't work on me. Read the sentence." I kept my voice low so as not to frighten the fish and pointed at the Bible in his lap. Duffy had taught me how to read using the Good Book, and so I figured it'd work for Face too. And maybe instill some morals along the way.

He winked at me then focused on the page. "The Lord is my shep. . .herd. Shepherd. I shall not want."

"Very good."

He shifted under my praise. These lessons were the only times I'd seen him like this—less than confident. He'd always been quick to flash a prize-winning smile, yet behind those flirty layers was a vulnerable man. Face had been too proud to admit he couldn't read or write, though I'd known. I'd offered to teach him, and he'd accepted on the condition that the lessons were away from the rest of the crew. The only place of privacy was on this hardly-river-worthy boat under the guise of catching fish for the crew's supper.

"How about we practice writing numbers?" I readied myself for an earful of whining; instead he gave a quick nod.

I reached for the chalk and slate I'd packed in my bag. Face nudged my boot with his.

His dark eyes, the same color of the coffee in his mug, fastened on mine. "Hattie, I put the oil on Cap's boots."

"You?" My cutting tone was more accusation than question. My toes itched to give him a swift kick in the shin. "How could you? Picking on an old man. That's a low I didn't even think you capable of. I'm gonna row us back, so you can march yourself to the pilothouse and let Duffy know. Of all the meanest—"

"I told him this mornin'."

"You did?" I lowered the slate, while my right hand kept a firm grasp on my fishing pole. "What'd he say?"

"He forgave me." And from the wonder in Face's tone, he must have expected Duffy to send him packing. "Didn't even require an explanation."

"But I do. Why'd you act that way?"

I could float to the shore and back in the span of time it took Face to fess up. "I got all riled 'cause he docked my pay when I broke that window."

Face had been showing off for some pretty girl in Brookport and had broken one of the panes on the deck. Duffy had let him off easy, considering Face had also been neglecting his duties.

I ground my jaw, my temper sizzling. "What if he'd gotten seriously hurt? I should break this slate in two right over your pretty head for being so foolish."

He gave a repentant look. "I'm done being that way." He held up the Bible as if he was swearing to more than me.

I knew better than to blindly swallow that baloney. "You mean, done with pranks on Duffy? Or in general? Because I'm thinking about a certain first mate with a pitcher full of salamanders."

"That's different." His eyes narrowed. "I don't trust that man. He's not what he seems to be."

My breath stumbled in my lungs. "What makes you think that?"

"C'mon, Hattie. You're cleverer than that. The man shows up outta nowhere. Spends most of his time digging 'round in the hold. Then there's the matter of him having the brains of how to run the boat but no clue about how to handle her crew. How can ya be a mate and not know the ways of a riverman?"

My lips pressed together. "I thought the same thing."

"Bet ya did. You got heaps of smarts behind that lovely face."

My brows rose in gentle reprimand for his flattery, but he only winked. The moment fell quiet and Face's expression turned serious.

"Watch your back around him, Hattie."

"Why, is he prone to pranking, like you?"

He sighed. "I told you I'm done bein' that way. I promise."

"Your promises are about as dependable as the catfish today." I grimaced at the still empty bucket. "Why aren't they biting?" I needed at least five to make a good bribe.

"They'll come 'round. Just gotta be patient."

"Then here." I handed over the slate and grabbed some chalk. "Let's practice our skills."

He gave an appreciative smile, giving me the barest glimpse of how much this meant to him.

For the next couple of hours we worked on the lessons, managed to wrangle seven catfish and several smallmouth bass, and chatted about this evening's moonlight excursion.

"The *Idlewild* was filled to the full last night." Face grabbed the oars and started rowing toward shore. "I thought for certain the dance floor was gonna bottom out."

I agreed. "Wonder if we'll be packed this evening too." This was our last night in Evansville. After the moonlight trip, we'd head for Owensboro. "Bricker did a swell job getting our name out there."

There was at least a full month's worth of advertising already circulating before the *Idlewild* had reached Evansville's wharf. They'd been sold out both nights. The brightness in Face's expression had nothing to do with teeming excursions, but my talk of Bricker. Mr. Bricker had been the charter agent for as long as I could remember. And he'd always excelled in lining up events for the season. "You'd be a good agent, Face."

His eyes sparked with hope. "Think so?"

"'Course I do." He had a natural ability in sales. With his charm, he could sell a face-full of blemishes to a beauty queen. But he had to know how to read and write in order to be an agent. Most of the work was drawing up contracts for future charters and writing advertising bills. Face had a lot of potential; he just needed the skills required to get him there. "That's why we're working so hard, isn't it?"

His gaze lingered on me, and I was reminded why all the gals out there were smitten. "Will you dance with me tonight?"

I laughed. "You know I never dance during moonlights anymore. I learned my lesson."

"That was only one time."

"One time too many." Earlier this summer a passenger seemed to believe my duties extended to taxi dancing. He threw dimes at me and tried to yank me onto the dance floor. One stomped heel to his foot had put an end to that. "You'll have no problem finding a partner, Face."

"If you say yes, I'll even reward you with a kiss." He leaned closer as if to smooch me here and now.

I reached over the side and splashed him with water. "Talk that nonsense again, and I'll soak you even more. You know perfectly well where I stand on that matter."

His eyes flitted heavenward, and his parted lips released a stream of air. "Yeah, yeah, I know."

We shored the dingy, and I grabbed tonight's supper and my teaching bag. All in all, it had been a productive morning. Now to squeeze in the next step of my plan before breakfast.

Face wrapped his pinky finger around his empty coffee mug. "I'll take care of tacking the boat." He leapt out of the dinghy and reached for me.

I waved him off, lifted my skirt with my free hand, and stepped onto shore, not caring that my shoes sank into the mud.

Face kept close. "I'll convince you yet, Hattie." His gaze dipped to my lips. "That kiss you've been saving is as good as mine."

"Ha!" I shoved him, and he playfully responded by stumbling back. "You can't claim a girl's first kiss. It's not yours to take."

His smile was about as relentless as his antics. "Oh, I'm not gonna take it. Just woo you into giving it freely."

A throat cleared loudly behind us.

The unmistakable stature of Jack Marshall leaned against a tree as if he'd been waiting all morning for our return. He took one glance at Face and then a long, sweeping gaze at me, as if making sure I was all right. "What's going on here?"

Face bristled. "I don't see how what I do with Hattie is any of your concern."

Those words caused Jack to rise to full height, his glare spearing Face. The deckhand took Jack's commanding gesture as a challenge and widened his stance.

Oh for Pete's sake. These men were two heaving breaths away from a posturing match.

"Don't get your feathers ruffled, Face."

He ignored me, training his glower on Jack. His hands were clenched into fists. The stony set of his jaw made me skitter between the men.

"Face." I put my hand on his arm, his tense muscles rippling beneath my fingertips. "Remember what you told me earlier. Now's the time to prove to me and yourself that you weren't just jawing."

At my words, his shoulders slacked a little. "For you, Hattie," he muttered and then pushed past Jack toward the *Idlewild*.

His stomping footsteps faded, and I released my breath. All I needed was two grown men sparring along the river's edge. Thanks to Jack, I was now stuck with the task of hauling the dinghy to the *Idlewild*. Pushing a wheelbarrow was one thing, dragging a heavy, cumbersome hunk of wood across bumpy earth was another. I glared at the man who was responsible for my soon-to-be-aching muscles. "Was that necessary?"

"I went searching for you only to be told by the striker that you ran off with Face." A faint pink crept up his neck. "He implied more was going on than fishing."

No wonder Jack was hotter than a triggered crate of firecrackers. He'd thought Face was after my virtue. The engine room apprentice should only stoke the fire in the belly of the *Idlewild*, not the heart of Jack Marshall. "Face didn't lay a finger on me."

Despite my adamant tone, doubt rippled his forehead. "I've seen his behavior around women."

It was all a show. Face charmed the ladyfolk at every port, but he'd never disgraced them. Duffy wouldn't allow it. And in spite of Face's wayward declarations, he had a soft heart. Jack would learn that too, if he'd quit barking at the crew and try befriending them. "Thank you for your concern, sir, but—"

"Jack."

"But, Jack, I've been taking care of myself for nearly twenty-one years. I think I've gotten the hang of it by now." How many times did I have to tell the man?

He stepped closer, gaze searching. "Are you sure he didn't cross a line?" His tone gentled. "You can tell me anything." His open expression enforced the truth behind his words.

I shot a look to where Face retreated. "He doesn't know how to read. And is too ashamed to have lessons in front of everyone. So Duffy allows us to go fishing as long as it doesn't interfere with his duties."

His head tilted. "You're teaching Face?"

"To read and write. He wants to be a charter agent."

The deep groove between his brows eased. "That's kind of you."

I shrugged. "Shouldn't everyone have that opportunity? You know, a chance at their dreams? At the very least be able to read. Words are a gift." I jerked my head toward the bag slung over my right shoulder, my Bible resting in plain sight. "Especially that Word. I couldn't imagine not being able to read God's love notes to me."

His expression slacked in surprise. "You're using the Bible to teach Face?"

"Yes, and I think it's helping him in more ways than one." I nudged a twig with the toe of my boot. "The more time I spend with him, the more he changes for the better."

His gaze hooked mine, locked, and something passed between us. "I can see how that could happen."

I bit my lip, unsure how to tame the surge of what seemed awfully close to attraction.

"Would you like me to take this aboard for you?" He gestured toward the dinghy.

"That would be swell. Thank you. It goes in the corner of the hold. Be sure to angle it against the wall. That way it won't take up too much space."

His lips twitched. "Anything else, Admiral?"

It was the second time he'd called me by that nickname. And that warmth settled around me again. My gaze drifted to the metal bucket I clutched, and everything cooled to icy proportions. I had a job to do. A cook to bribe. I couldn't let these strange flutterings deter me from my original purpose. But then. . . "Why were you searching for me?"

"To return this." He pulled the freight log from his pocket. "I shouldn't have doubted you. You have a good system."

Jack handed me the pad, and his thumb held my index finger for a heart-pounding second. The gentle clasp wasn't romantic in theory, yet every cell in my body responded to his touch.

He offered a friendly smile. "I think we can work well together." With that, he gripped the dinghy and trudged off.

I slid the log into my bag, taking longer than necessary situating the strap on my shoulder, hoping my pulse would return to human levels. What was wrong with me? I didn't have time to explore these bizarre sensations. I had to get to Miss Wendall before the breakfast rush. Determination renewed, I set off, but something snagged my attention.

A slip of paper lay upon dried leaves.

It must have fallen out of Jack's pocket when he retrieved the log. I scooped it up and was about to holler after him, but the markings on the ivory note trapped the words in my chest. I held it to the light, trying to make sense of it. The only thing that became clear was Face had been right—Jack Marshall was not who he appeared to be.

Chapter 9

Devyn

*D*evyn ushered the mother daughter pair, her last tour of the day, into the *Belle*'s ballroom. Yet she could see that the space—decorated for the children's Treasure Island Adventure—wouldn't inspire one to say "I do," but rather rumble a hearty "Arrr!"

A section of the dance floor had been roped where the hired actors would perform a sword-fighting scene. A gangplank suspended off the bandstand. Dozens of wood chests, spilling with fake treasure and jewelry, were scattered throughout. The atmosphere was perfect for the tiny wannabe scalawags coming aboard in a few hours, but not so ideal for a wedding event coordinator trying to convince a moody bride to charter the boat on the best day of her life.

"Just envision." Devyn stepped past a cluster of paper palm trees and swept a hand in front of her. "Twinkle lights strung from the gingerbread trim, reflecting beautifully off the tin ceiling. With the paddlewheel in motion and the sunset as a backdrop, it makes for a memorable romantic evening."

The prospective bride, Larissa Newton, kept her gaze pinned to her phone, her manicured fingers dancing across the screen. "Mmhmm." Her tone proved about as lively as the skeleton hanging from the ceiling fan.

The mother, on the other hand, turned a slow circle and released a wistful sigh. "Yes, that was how it was with mine."

Devyn smiled at the older woman who had a Renée Zellweger look about her. "You were married aboard the *Belle*?"

Mrs. Newton's fingers splayed against her chest, and she nodded. "In '93."

Ah, that explained the mother's enthusiasm and the daughter's lack thereof. The younger woman wanted to have her own fairytale wedding, not a copycat of her parents'. "My folks were married here in the eighties. I'm sure you noticed we've done some updates since then."

Larissa snorted. "Doesn't look like it."

Devyn overlooked the slight. "The *Belle*'s charm is in her timeless beauty. It's our intention to preserve the boat, keeping as much original as possible. When I say things have been updated, I'm speaking more of the surroundings. The Louisville skyline is breathtaking at night." Devyn had given countless tours, and not one of them had been the same. She refused to sink into used car salesman mode and rattle off practiced speeches. Her number one rule was to speak from the heart. Sometimes it worked. . .

Larissa snapped her gum.

And sometimes it failed.

"We'll cater to whatever you wish." Devyn rallied for one more blitz attempt. "Your colors, your flowers, décor, and centerpieces. We also decorate the staircases and areas of the deck. If you're interested, we can go up the steps to the Hurricane Deck."

Mrs. Newton clasped her hands together under her chin, waiting for a response in the affirmative from her daughter.

Larissa finally glanced up from her phone and shook her head. "Sorry. I'm just not sold on having my wedding here. I don't want to take up any more of your time."

Hardly surprising, but her gut sank nonetheless. "If you change your mind, here's my contact info." She slipped a business card from her leather ledger and handed it to the petite bride-to-be. "We'd love to have you."

Larissa mustered a weak smile, and Mrs. Newton fought to keep hers in place.

Devyn watched them exit the double doors to the grand staircase, then pulled out a chair from one of the tables and sank onto it.

With a sigh, she tossed her ledger onto the white tablecloth, nearly knocking over the stuffed parrot centerpiece.

If she couldn't convince a twenty-four-year-old local the value of the *Belle*, how on earth would she persuade the judges? How could she capture the grandeur of this place? That stepping into the ballroom was like stepping back in time—where hundreds, more like thousands, had graced its weathered boards, dancing everything from the Jitterbug, to the Twist, to the Electric Slide. All the dances, all the eras, all the memories, while floating on the shimmering water.

It made her nostalgic just thinking about it. But sentiment wasn't good enough. Maybe she wasn't good enough. Perhaps she should ask Steph to take over this project.

She folded her arms on the table and sunk her chin atop them.

It wasn't wise to make a huge decision with her nerves splintered raw. She should just go home, call for takeout, and spend the evening with Audrey Hepburn and Peter O'Toole.

The unmistakable swish of the entrance doors didn't even stir her. No doubt it was Steph checking in, but Devyn couldn't bring herself to move or glance up.

"Tough day?"

Her gaze whipped to a husky masculine voice. Chase stood several feet away, and her heart smacked against her ribs. How could she have forgotten their meeting?

He approached, his swagger confident, his appearance immaculate in his crisp button-down shirt casually paired with jeans. "What's on your mind?"

"Currently? How to steal a million."

His eyes lit with amusement. "You in a scrape for cash?" He slid out the chair beside her, turned it around, and straddled it. "I thought you smarter than to resort to a life of crime."

"*How to Steal a Million* is a movie with Audrey Hepburn."

"Ah, never seen it."

"You're missing out on cinematography greatness, my friend." She toyed with one of the plastic eye patches arranged by every placemat. "It's kinda my thing. Some girls binge ice cream when life sucker punches them, I binge classic movies."

His dark locks shimmered in the recess lighting. "I'm no Audrey Hepburn, but if it's any consolation, I'm a good listener."

"My college roommate once told me that's an oxymoron." Her mouth twisted. "You know, being a man and saying you're a good listener."

He clasped a hand over his heart, his features taking on a mock-injured look. "I'm trying to be thoughtful and here you are talking smack."

A smile itched her lips. Of course, she'd never believed that. Her brother was the more attentive one in their conversations, but right now Devyn needed her attitude to shift from sullen to light. Her emotional muscles were fatigued from wallowing in a swamp of self-pity. "If I wanted to trash-talk, I'd bring up our Skeeball game."

His deep chuckle rumbled through her. "I had no clue I was dealing with a D1 college pitcher."

"You didn't ask." She'd given him as little as possible about herself during their pizza outing, but after sinking seven 100-point buckets in a row, he'd become suspicious about her "natural" talent. "I should've suggested a wager on our game."

He wagged a finger at her. "Now that would've been cruel. Like some kind of Skeeball shark."

"Maybe I should turn that into a living." It was a joke. A terrible one, but she presently felt the pressure of her current career choice. This kind of stress shouldn't bother her. She'd once been part of a multimillion dollar venture. In comparison, this wedding contest was nothing. Yet to her, it was everything. "I just finished a tour and the bride wasn't interested in holding her wedding here. It's nothing new. And it usually doesn't sink my mood. All part of the business you know? It's just. . ."

"Just what?"

"It made me question myself about the contest. Maybe I'm in over my head."

"It's a pretty head."

"No-flirt rule." She swatted his arm. "You're totally breaking it." Though her tone wasn't as stern as her words due to that irritating disarming effect he possessed.

He lifted a shoulder. "For what it's worth, I think we can pull this off."

We? She only agreed to his help with the invitations. Granted, she'd worked well with a partner. She and Travis created a virtual kingdom, for goodness' sake. Surely there was no harm inviting Chase to brainstorm with her. Besides, she'd learned her lesson. This time around she wouldn't lose her heart. "The first thing on the docket is—"

His cell rang.

He gave a repentant smile and withdrew his phone from his pocket. He peered at the screen and stiffened. "I gotta take this." He rose from his chair. "Excuse me a moment."

"Of course."

He strode out of her hearing radar. Not exactly hard in a 200-foot ballroom. Was it his girlfriend? His wife? And why hadn't she contemplated his relationship status before? Not that she was interested in him, but for the fact alone that he'd been acting unattached, flirting.

"I can't right now." His hushed tone seemed to bounce off the wall. His inflection rose and fell, allowing Devyn to catch the words "agent," "insurance," and "overdue."

Those terms had been pestering residents in Devyn's brain two years ago when dealing with her mom's medical bills. Did Chase have an ill family member? Was he the one who was sick?

Her phone alarm chimed, warning her the purser would be shooing her out soon in preparation for tonight. She grabbed her black ledger, shoved her phone in her pocket, and stood. By this time, Chase had ended his call and was drawing near.

"Sorry." His expression was sheepish. "That was my. . .uh. . .business associate."

Hmm. "I thought you were solo when it came to graphic design?"

"I am." He returned the chair to its place. "This is for something else. That personal matter I was telling you about the other day."

"You're not a drug dealer or anything?"

He chuckled. "No."

"A spy?"

"I wish it was that cool." His phone chimed again, but this time he silenced it. "Like I said, a personal issue. Not a big deal."

Then why the mystery? Then again, she had a slew of secrets she'd rather not share. She reached into her ledger and withdrew her meager list. "Here are a few themes I've been thinking on." She handed him the paper.

She watched him through narrowed eyes, ready to gauge his reactions, but he remained poker-faced. All the proposed themes were love related—*Timeless Romance, Romance Through the Age*s, *Whispers of the Heart*. "What do you think?"

He lowered the page and raised a brow. "What do *you* think?"

"That they're mediocre." A heavy sigh lowered her shoulders. "It's like I can't get my brain to work. Ideas used to come so easily to me before—" Her mouth clamped shut.

"Before what?"

She just had to open that door, didn't she? Might as well stumble on through it. At least she could control what tidbits she gave. "My breakup. I was engaged a year ago. It wasn't a pretty split."

The lines framing his eyes softened. "I'm sorry."

"When you surprised me on the stern. . ." She inclined her chin to the back of the boat. "That was the week I was to be married. I literally found out about the *Belle* being in the contest on my no-go wedding day. And right now, I'm supposed to be in Cozumel."

"Ah, that explains a lot."

"Like my emotional swings on a total stranger? Yeah." She flicked the corner of the list. "And why my ideas on romance are weak."

"They're not weak, but I can tell they're not your best."

And how could he know this? He was right, of course. But they'd only been in each other's company three times. She motioned at the main entrance, and Chase matched her lazy pace toward the exit.

"When I brainstorm, I pick one major focal point and let it roll around in my mind for a bit." He held the door open for her.

She walked past with a nod of thanks. "I don't have time for rolling ideas. I need one soon. Like four-days-ago soon." Her fingers curled around the railing of the grand staircase, and they moved down the steps in silence, the click of her kitten heels echoing off the sconce-lined walls.

They crossed the short distance to the bow doors, and Chase paused. "How many other places are in this contest?"

"Twelve altogether. So we're competing against eleven spectacular. historical venues across the country." Devyn had heard of several of the finalists and had tortured herself by browsing their websites. The venues were stunning.

Chase patted the wood-paneled ticket booth sandwiched between the exits. "Are any of them boats?"

"No, we're the only one."

"Then play off that for your theme. It's what makes you unique."

She'd been aware that the *Belle* was the only moving historical site in the contest, though she hadn't viewed it as a strength. Her gaze met Chase's and hope billowed. "This can work."

"Glad I can pull my weight." His satisfied smile affected her. For all his nonsense and flirting, Chase seemed to truly want to help.

"And here's your reward." She withdrew several sheets of paper she'd tucked behind the event pricing form in her ledger.

"What are those?"

"Scanned pics of the calliope book our girl was holding in that photo. My boss found the hard drive from the auction, and lo and behold." She handed them to Chase. "The book was sold at auction, but I had no idea it's one of a kind. Look at the pictures." She pointed to the one on top. The photos were grainy, but they provided enough detail for Devyn to identify a decorative vine etching on the cover. Maybe she was in the wrong career. Sure, she proved an expert in computer coding, and enjoyed the myriad of challenges that came with prepping weddings, but her heart came alive when around anything vintage. "It's a handwritten songbook. I'm guessing there really weren't songbooks for calliopes and so whoever it was wrote one."

His eyes flickered with surprise. "Think it was Hattie?"

"Possible."

He flipped to the last page and read the information at the top. "Greta Hanson."

"That's the woman who purchased it. Her number is below. This may have nothing of use to us. But then—"

"It very well could." He grinned as he yanked out his phone. "Care if I call now?"

"Let's go outside. It may echo in this spot."

They stepped into the open air and across the grated bridge leading to the wharf. Chase's arm brushed hers as they moved to the closest bench. She couldn't determine if it was the late afternoon sun or his close proximity that had her flushed, but she decided a few much-needed inches of space between them was necessary.

He dialed the number and plastered the phone to his ear. "Hey there. My name's Chase Jones, and I'm calling regarding a purchase from an auction from the *Belle of Louisville*? I believe it was a songbook for the calliope. Any chance I can speak with Greta Hanson?"

Devyn heard a feminine voice but couldn't decipher any words.

"Oh." Chase's expression turned from hopeful to something more serious. "I'm sorry, ma'am. Please forgive me for bothering you."

A couple more garbled sentences and then Chase ended the call.

"Bad news?"

"Greta Hanson passed away this past January. That was her daughter."

"Oh, that's awful."

He nodded. "She's going through her mother's things and knew about the book. Said we can come look at it any time this week."

"Really?"

"Yeah, only problem is she lives three hours away in Ashland." Dark brows lifted over glinted eyes. "You up for a road trip?"

Chapter 10

"Since you're driving, does that mean I have total control over the music and snack distributions?" Devyn swept her hair back in a messy bun, though the breeze from the open window pulled wayward wisps across her cheek. Still not wanting to give Chase her address yet, she'd agreed to meet him at the *Belle*. He'd volunteered to drive, and she had no qualms letting him navigate across Kentucky.

"You're free to listen to whatever you choose." He swigged his coffee then tossed her his signature I'm-hot-without-even-trying smile. "As for the other, it's nine in the morning. Isn't that too early for candy?"

"Pfft. Road trips are all about junk food." Her stomach rumbled in agreement. She opened the Walmart sack filled with all things sugar and calories. "Besides, we have a mission over the next few hours. And chocolate is brain food."

"I'm guessing our mission is finding a theme?"

"You know it." She was determined not to waste her Saturday off. "Before I go farther, are you certain I have complete mastery of the music?"

"What are you going to do to me?" His leery expression made her laugh.

"Nothing too horrible. I ran a search on iTunes for songs that feature water, boats, and romance. We're going to let music inspire us." She connected her phone to the car's Bluetooth and pressed play. The opening bars of *The Love Boat*'s theme song blared through the speakers, and Devyn's shoulders shook with laughter.

Chase squinted as if it was painful to hear. "Probably won't provide us any inspiration."

"Nope. But it's fun to sing." Pretending a Twizzler was a microphone, she belted out the chorus. If he was to be trapped with her today, he would get the full force of her dorkiness.

His chuckle was a deep, low sound, smooth like melted chocolate. And just as tempting. "I don't know if I should be impressed or horrified that you know every word."

She lowered the volume. "I used to watch reruns with my nana when I was little. She had the smallest TV on the planet sitting on the corner of her kitchen counter. Nothing like cutting onions and voyaging on the S.S. *Pacific Princess*."

"Is that why you began working on the *Belle*?" He drummed his thumbs on the steering wheel with the beat. "So you can tap into your inner *Love Boat* enthusiast?"

"Hardly." She bit off a hunk of the Twizzler.

"Maybe we should start there for inspiration. What first attracted you to the Old Girl?"

Her racing heart pumped the brakes as if it had spotted a state trooper. This conversation was speeding into disaster.

"Ah, she grows quiet. This makes me more intrigued."

Devyn swallowed. "It's not as epic as you make it sound. It's actually a tad humbling."

He cut her a sympathetic look. "You don't have to tell me. I'm sorry for asking."

Something about his gentle tone tugged the words from the locked vaults of her heart. "No. It's fine. The whole thing was a result of the breakup I told you about."

"Your fiancé?"

"He ended things in a humiliating way."

Chase's gaze remained fixed on the road, but she could almost hear the questions in his mind.

"We were partners in business. A successful business. When he broke things off, it was like my entire world stopped. My job, my routine, my plans for us, all were gone. I can hardly remember the following weeks. I was in this weird zombie-funk."

"Understandable."

"For days I struggled with sleeping. One classic movie after another. Phone calls to my brother at three a.m. My brain wouldn't rest. I spiraled to the point where I was going to beg the jerk to take me back."

His brow lowered. "Even after he embarrassed you?"

"I was in a funk." She repeated her defense. "I'd given so many pieces of myself to him that I didn't know how to function as just. . .me. He'd take and take but rarely contributed to the relationship. I finally realized how he used me. How toxic those years together had been."

Chase scowled. "I'm glad you didn't return to him. Because the second you try to convince a guy to love you is the exact moment he's not worthy of your heart."

She blinked at him. From all angles Chase Jones appeared every bit the player. Yet his words brimmed with authenticity. "I'm glad I didn't return to him either. Instead, I cranked up worship music and prayed for God's help. I was a sobbing mess asking Him to forgive me for my stupidity in a bad relationship, to save me from drowning in heartache. I must've fallen asleep, because. . ." Should she? Her instincts told her *yes*, but her mind screamed at her to remain silent.

He grabbed a pair of aviators from an overhead compartment and slid them on. "Because what?"

"You're gonna think I'm crazy."

He smirked. "What if I already do?"

Fair enough. Between him finding her dancing alone on the stern, to her off-key rendition of the *Love Boat* theme, and all her emotional behaviors in between, she'd handed him plenty of opportunity to consider her loopy.

She inhaled a calming breath. "I dreamed of water. The sun rested so beautifully it looked like the river was robed in diamonds. I stood at the edge of the shore just staring and then dove in. But instead of floundering, I floated. I felt safe." Carefree and protected. Something she hadn't experienced since before her time with Travis. She should have never let him invade the God-reserved space in her heart.

He shrugged as if she hadn't just shared a chunk of her soul. "Nothing so weird. It was a dream."

"But then. . ." She should just stop. Who was this man anyway? She was basically telling him her inner workings. Could she blame her weird transparency on whacked side effects from a sugar overdose? Or was there a growing kinship between her and Chase?

"Then?"

She sighed. "Then I woke up, went outside, and wandered the downtown Riverwalk." She could still see it in her mind's eye. "The sun was shining on the water exactly like my dream, and the rays outlined the *Belle*. As if God was shining a spotlight on where I was supposed to be." She shifted in her seat, angling toward him. "Do you ever feel that? You know, that you're divinely led?"

"Can't say I have."

"Have you ever listened for it?"

"Can't say I've done that either."

"Maybe you should try. It was the only way I survived my breakup. I saw the *Belle* and had this stirring in my heart. I couldn't explain why, but I knocked on the door to the neighboring boat, the *Belle*'s offices, which I soon discovered was a lifesaving station. And that's what happened. I felt rescued. Steph talked to me and offered me the job as wedding coordinator." Though her boss had thought Devyn overqualified, the kind woman had thrown her a life ring, pulling her from the murky depths of heartbreak.

He slowed at a traffic light. "And you've been there ever since."

"Yes." She smiled. "Right there on my dream river."

His head snapped toward her, his eyes widening with clarity. "That's it."

"That's what?"

"You're brilliant." His voice held warmth and wonder, causing her attraction to triple with those two words. "I knew you'd think of it."

She shook her head, breaking the daze. "What are you talking about?"

"Dream River." His lips tipped at the edges. "Your theme."

Her mouth dropped, but there were no words to fill it. *Dream River.* It was like a veil had been lifted. The entire event would be related to the river—the décor, the music, the cuisine. They could serve walleye, which was commonly found in the Ohio. And for dessert? She had the perfect dish.

Ideas flooded like the rush of the Ohio's current after a deluge. She needed to jot them down. And quick. She rummaged in her purse and found a pen but no paper. Her Starbucks receipt would work decently enough. She glimpsed Chase's notepad peeking out from the console. It seemed the man was never without it. "Can I borrow a piece of paper?" She stretched toward it, but his hand slid over hers.

"Sure." He ran a thumb along her knuckle. "I'll get you a page. Give me a sec."

Ooo-kay. She retracted her hand and hugged it against her stomach. It wasn't as if she intended to peek at anything.

Chase took the notepad, using his thighs to keep the steering wheel steady, not exactly the most secure feeling. He quickly tore a page from the back of the pad and held it out to her.

"Your efforts to keep me from glimpsing what's in your notepad only makes me think interesting things."

"Such as?"

"Like it's filled with women's numbers. Do men still do that whole little black book thing?" Or was that only in the movies? Specifically, Rock Hudson films.

"I appreciate your confidence in my honey-gaining skills, but I don't have that much game."

She snorted. Not much game? She believed that as much as she believed her bag of goodies was calorie-free. "Then maybe it contains something darker. Like the burial sites of all your victims."

"Your imagination is sinister."

"Not always." She wouldn't press him. Even if it only increased the mystery behind the man. He definitely had her intrigued with his secret personal business matter, not to mention the constant texts he'd been receiving during the drive. His phone had buzzed every fifteen minutes. Who was trying to get ahold of him? The person that'd called him when they'd been in the ballroom? It didn't matter. Her mind needed to focus on their new theme. "I can't wait to start working on this." She beamed. "You're good for my creativity, I think."

"That was your stroke of genius, but I'll accept wrongly placed credit if you keep smiling at me like that."

She allowed his ridiculous statement for now. Her mind was occupied with the excitement of making Dream River a reality. Having a flair of romance, yet not too thick, Dream River was a perfect fit for both their patrons and the contest. She relaxed against the seat, excitement threading through her.

The next few hours were spent in casual conversation, getting meals at the gas station, and Devyn almost getting them lost twice. She and

Google Maps didn't get along.

Chase talked about his family. He was the youngest of three, having two older sisters. They grew up in California until his dad had transferred here. He went to the University of Kentucky, her alma mater's rival.

"You realize now that we are forever enemies," she teased. "All because you chose the wrong college."

He raised a brow. "Do I have to bring up the win-loss record between our schools, Miss Asbury?"

"I'm well aware of the unbalanced stats, Mr. Jones."

He gave a bark of laughter. "You mean undisputed."

"You choose your adjectives, and I'll choose mine."

"Agree to disagree?"

"Exactly. Because we're reasonable adults."

He nodded. "Though I'm convinced you have taste buds similar to my four-year-old niece."

"Are you dissing my gas station hot dog? Because it was the best ever." Even if the onions were a bit overpowering. She popped a wintergreen Ice Breaker into her mouth. "You can't tell me that protein bar you inhaled was filling. I totally saw your hand digging into my pretzel bag when I was switching songs."

"I'm glad you came prepared."

"Because road trips are—"

"All about junk food."

She nodded. "Very good. You're catching on."

"I had a charming teacher. I'll adhere to whatever she advises."

She bumped his elbow on the console. "Then you agree U of L is the best college this side of the Mississippi?"

He smirked. "Anything but that."

They finally pulled into a drive that led to a yellow-brick ranch home. They exited simultaneously, meeting in front of the Jeep. A middle-aged woman was stooped over pots of autumn mums lining the walkway. At their approach, she straightened.

"Excuse me." Chase took the lead. "Are you Eleanor Brandish?" He gave her a warm smile, which softened the older woman's features.

"Depends on who's asking?" She shed her gardening gloves and pushed her fluffy bangs from her forehead. "The woman is incredibly busy, but I have it on good authority she can be bribed with caramel macchiatos, hand-dyed yarn, or in your case, a well-placed dimple."

"I'm fresh out of yarn, but if I grin wide enough I can give you two dimples for the price of one."

Such a flirt.

The woman's laughter was as loud as her yellow "Keep Calm and Bingo On" T-shirt. "Don't waste that charm on me. Save it to get yourself out of trouble. Which, by the looks of you, I'd say you'll land in heaps of it."

Chase shrugged, playing along.

"I take it you're Chase Jones?"

"Guilty. And this is my friend Devyn Asbury. She works as a wedding coordinator on the *Belle*."

Devyn smiled. "Thank you for agreeing to meet with us today, Ms. Brandish."

"Of course. And please call me Eleanor. It's been such an ordeal going through Mom's stuff. Finding places for everything. She was a hoarder of all things music." She gave a fond smile. "So I'm glad to have at least one more thing off my hands." She waved at them to follow her onto the front porch and opened the door for them to enter.

"Sorry about your loss." Devyn subtly shuffled her feet on the mat.

She accepted the condolences with a nod. "She lived a long, happy life. Mom was never sick, just went peacefully in her sleep." She led them to a living room with a large picture window, allowing in the early afternoon light. Devyn and Chase elected to sit on the plush love seat, and Eleanor claimed the plaid recliner adjacent to them. "She was a fan of music. Spent decades building a collection of books and prints. Even acquired an original song sheet of 'My Sunny Tennessee' signed by Burt Kelmar."

Devyn gasped, her inner vintage geek rising to ultimate fangirl levels. "You're kidding. That's such an amazing find!"

Eleanor took in Devyn's exuberance with soft laughter. "Next to her great-grandmother's Bible, that music was one of her most prized possessions."

"I'm a huge fan of vintage films and music. Your mother and I would've become fast friends."

Eleanor's expression was warm. "I can see that." She reached toward the coffee table. "Now, I believe *this* is what you came for." She picked up the calliope book, the same from the photograph, and handed it to Chase.

Devyn positioned herself closer to Chase in order to examine it. With such proximity, she noticed faint laugh lines framing his steel-gray eyes, a freckle dotting his left ear lobe, and could see in more detail that curious scar etched near the corner of his brow. She peeled her attention from his remarkable profile and forced it where it belonged—on the book. The weathered beige cover had the same winding vines depicted in the picture.

Chase carefully opened it, and while Devyn had already known the music was handwritten, it still amazed her.

"Look." She pointed. "There's 'Swanee River.'"

A deep groove settled between his brows. "Why would she have to write this one? Why not use mass produced music, since that's a popular song?"

"Because the calliope only had thirty-two keys. She had to change the key to keep in range." Brilliant.

Chase browsed the inside cover, a slow smile forming. "I found our girl's last name."

Devyn leaned closer. "Hattie Louis." The urge to yank her phone out for a quick Google search raged strong, but she refrained. "So it *was* she who wrote this."

"Is this Hattie person a relation?" There was a curious bend to Eleanor's penciled brow.

"No," Chase answered. "Just a mystery woman we've been trying to find information on."

"Gotta watch out for the mysterious ones." She chuckled. "They may not want you learning all their secrets."

"I think I've found one of them. Maybe two." Chase held the book open and peered into the hollow space between the spine and the binding. He set the book on his lap and slid a pencil from his notepad.

Devyn's forehead wrinkled. She hadn't seen him grab his notepad when they exited the car.

"I think something's lodged here. Do you mind?" He flicked a glance at the older woman. "We don't want to intrude on your time."

"Not at all." She reclined against the plush cushions. "I'm not exactly itching to go back outside with the slugs."

Chase smiled, and then, with gentle care, used the eraser end of the pencil and fished out two pieces of paper rolled tightly like scrolls.

Devyn pressed against his side for a closer look, the warmth of his body, the spice of his cologne, reminding her why she put boundaries between them to begin with. Though before she could move away, Chase's free hand settled on her knee.

"Would you like to do the honors?" He held out the papers.

She waved him off. "They look frail. I'm afraid I'd rip them."

"Sure?"

"Very."

With controlled movements, he unrolled the first paper. It was nothing but a jumble of letters. Two lines of capitals.

She squinted at it, as if narrowed vision would help translate the disorder. "Is that a code?"

"Looks like it."

"Maybe the other paper is the translation."

"Good thought." Chase gave the paper to Eleanor for her to see. He then took the second piece and unrolled it like the first.

Devyn bit her lip, taking in the neat, masculine script.

> *Hattie, meet me at the large elm starboard of*
> *the Idlewild at midnight. — J*

Instant goosebumps. "Chase, the person signed it *J*. Could this be from your great-grandfather? Was his last name Jones like yours?"

"Yes." Chase stared at it, his tone quiet.

"Was your great-grandfather in love with the woman who wrote this book?" Eleanor reached for her reading glasses on the coffee table and shoved them on her face. She inspected the code again as if the extra magnification would help interpret it.

"I believe so." Chase's gaze bounced between Eleanor and Devyn. "Though I'm not completely sure."

"Why else would he plan a rendezvous?" Were they going to run away together? Chase had said that Hattie wasn't his great-grandmother. What had happened between them? "Now the question that needs answered is if Hattie went?"

Chapter 11

Hattie

$\mathcal{I}$ entered the galley with the poise of a duchess. Because if I hadn't, Miss Wendall would have ordered me to turn around and try again. The British-born cook bent over a bowl of fruit but glanced up when she heard my footsteps.

"Ah, my dear girl." She acknowledged my presence with a graceful nod suited for a lady wearing a silk day dress rather than an aproned frock. "I've been wondering where you'd gone to."

"I have a special delivery." I raised the bucket, tilting it so Miss Wendall could spy our catch. "You mentioned the other day about wanting some fresh fish. Brought you catfish and bass."

"Delightful." Miss Wendall rounded the small island and joined me. "I can think of a million dishes I could make with this. Now to choose only one."

I'd never seen anyone more capable than Miss Wendall. She could take a tub of kidney beans, a slab of bacon, and a gallon of olive oil and make a feast for a king. Or at least to feed the hungry chops of the *Idlewild* crewmen. "I couldn't rest until I got a bucketful for you."

"Laying it on thick, poppet. Now I know something's stirring in that brain of yours." She clucked her tongue in playful rebuke and took the load from my grip. "Face told me you'd be in soon, so I made tea. Care for a spot?" She set the bucket down, placing it away from the flow of foot traffic.

"Yes please." Though I preferred coffee, I'd learned over the years how to soften the cook's rigid edges. Especially since Duffy had only hired her with me in mind.

You need someone to teach you to be a lady, Hattie-girl. And it never hurts to know how to cook, right?

It hadn't mattered my say-so, Duffy's word had always been law. He'd ask for my advice, consider my input, but in the end, he had the final judgment. No begging or whining would jar him from that position. So I'd been stuck with etiquette and cooking lessons with Miss Wendall.

My prim mentor fixed my tea and handed it to me.

"Thank you." I offered a gracious smile and took a sip, careful to keep my pinky finger extended like she'd taught. I always found it humorous acting like a genteel lady while drinking from a battered tin cup. Instead of sitting on a lush settee, I lowered onto a barrel of flour. Miss Wendall ran the galley like an English parlor. She even made any fella entering bow before speaking. It never stopped being amusing to see the large char-faced firemen dip their chins in demanded respect. But no one defied Miss Wendall. Not if they wanted a warm meal.

"All right, now." She lifted her cup to her lips and took a small swallow. "What's all this fuss for? I already told you I'd make you a chocolate cake for your special day."

My twenty-first birthday. I'd nearly forgotten. Though how could I celebrate when only weeks after that, we'd be docking in Pittsburgh? The tea soured my stomach and I set the cup on the counter. "I've come to chat."

Her mouth tugged down on one side. "You mean gossip?"

I wouldn't attack her intelligence by denying it, but maybe I'd adopt a more tactful approach. "I know you hear everything." The kitchen was the place the crew went in and out all day long. Nothing went on that Miss Wendall wasn't aware of. "I'm thinking of how to help the new first mate adjust to his position, that's all."

"And those fish in that bucket are your means of bribery?"

"Things seem different around here. Only trying to figure it all out."

She took another sip then stood to stir the porridge on the stovetop. "You know how I feel about whispering stories. It's none of my business if I caught First Mate Jack Marshall sniffing the pantry jars."

I gripped the edge of the barrel. "What?"

"Like I said, it's not ladylike to approach a gentleman about his activities. Even if he returned the lids to the wrong place. Or that he placed the vinegar in a different spot. None of my business."

Why would he be interested in the goings-on of the kitchen? Sniffing around, literally. And what about the slip of paper with the bizarre jumble of letters? I moved to help Miss Wendall finish the breakfast preparations. We worked side by side as I peppered her with more questions. She kept her false guise of innocence and answered all of my inquiries about the morning's happenings. Which hadn't amounted to much—Face had been in here asking her what my favorite flower was. The striker from the engine room tried to steal a box of matches before Miss Wendall smacked him on the hand with her wooden spoon.

"Well," I said, grabbing the silverware and placing it on the tray atop the breakfast cart, "I'm glad you aren't a gossip, Miss Wendall, or I'd be tempted to ask if anything else interesting has occurred."

"Heavens be, I'm no gossip. Or else I'd be gabbing about Duffy receiving wires from a man in Pittsburgh. He was in front of me at the office. I needed to check on my sister in Dayton. Not my business, mind you, if I overheard Duffy saying, *We'll be on time, and then you take over.*" She shrugged. "Some status of his delivery or something. I don't really know, because I never eavesdrop."

Pittsburgh. Take over? And who was the man he communicated with? A buyer? I gasped. Duffy's words surfaced like a piece of driftwood to the top of my mind. *Once we reach Pittsburgh and I deliver the goods there, my obligation is over.*

Had he been referring to the *Idlewild?* Delivering the boat to its new owner? Maybe that was why the bosses had let us go on the Ohio. It wasn't to help bring revenue, but to transport the boat. And how did the first mate fit into all of this? The swirl in my stomach climbed to my head, my temples throbbing.

After finishing the breakfast preparations, I excused myself, craving an escape. I grabbed a wrench from the engine room and climbed the steps to the texas roof. Clem had been complaining about the wheel brake needing adjusting. So while the men were below cramming their craws with mushy food, I'd be venting my frustration in the most unladylike fashion. It seemed important to fix something, maintain some semblance of control. Since I couldn't fix my future, I would channel my efforts on the steering system.

With a humph, I plopped onto the gritty floor, stretched my limbs, and shimmied on my back until I reached the desired spot. The river breeze traipsed over my legs, lifting the hem of my skirt. Modesty with this task had always proven impossible, which was why I had to pick opportune times to perform it.

My fingers searched for loose joints, my mind numbing to the rest of the world. It amazed me that this seven-foot wheel controlled the direction of a hundred-and-sixty-foot boat. Reminded me how small decisions held the power to steer my entire life. I'd always been comfortable allowing Duffy to navigate my course over the years, but I sensed that would soon change. A tremor of fear gripped my heart. Floating between two shores had been my one anchor. My only constant. I didn't know my true name, parents, birthplace, or anything else that gave substance to my identity. How could I step beyond all that I'd ever known? Journey past my only stability?

I discovered the wobbly part and tightened it, adding an extra yank for good measure.

Vibrations coursed my spine. Footsteps. Not shuffled steps like Duffy's. Or slow ones like Clem. But heavy, surefooted ones.

And here I was, half my person wedged beneath the pilothouse, my stocking legs exposed up to my thighs for anyone to see.

"Go eat your porridge, Face," I called loud enough for him to hear. "If you say one thing about my legs, I'll crawl out from underneath here and make you wish you hadn't."

"You weren't joking about the penknife garter."

Jack! I jerked, nearly smacking my forehead on a pipe. "What are you doing up here?"

"I was about to ask you the same." Amusement riddled his voice.

Infuriating man. "Turn around. I'm coming out." I couldn't be certain my skirts wouldn't creep farther as I maneuvered out of the crawlspace.

"All clear." His two words and good faith were all I had to go on.

Grimacing, I worked my way out of the narrowed area, yanking my skirt down as soon as my hands could reach, and climbed to my feet. Glimpsing Jack's broad back, my breath leaked from my chest. "Thank you for keeping your word." I smoothed out my skirt, but the fabric remained stubbornly creased. "You can turn around now."

He waited another second before facing me. His fingers curled in a loose fist over his mouth as if to hide a smile. "We do meet under the most amusing circumstances, don't we?"

"You should extend my duties to Boat Comedian, since you find me so ridiculous."

His slanted grin wobbled into a frown. "I don't consider you ridiculous, Hattie. Not in the least."

I returned his scowl, unsure of the meaning of his remark.

"Aren't you hungry?" His gaze dropped to the wrench in my hand. "I would think a full morning of fishing would give you an appetite."

"I lost my appetite. Heard there was this giant rat sniffing around the pantry." My gaze sharpened on him. "I'm thinking of the best way to trap it."

Then I saw it. So clear in his ice blue eyes—a secret. One that made his jawline sharp and his shoulders bend forward, as if his entire, powerful frame strained with the weight of it. His intense focus trained solely on me, his gaze tracing my face.

I held so still the tendons in my neck burned.

Seconds stretched between us, then his mouth nudged into a smile. "I should've known the first night we met that nothing slips by the Admiral." He tugged the sleeve of his uniform, his pensive eyes on mine. "Yes. It was me."

"Why?"

The sun skittered behind the clouds, causing shadows to dance across his features. "I can't tell you."

Fine. If he wanted to play conversation poker, I'd bring all the chips to the table. "Then maybe you can tell me about this?" I reached into my boot and dug out the slip of paper he'd dropped earlier.

His expression was an equal mix of surprise and relief. "I was concerned about where that was. Glad it was you who found it." His hand outstretched, but I slid the paper behind my back.

"I'm not returning this until I know what's going on. This looks like some sort of code." I pinned him with a glare. "Who are you, Jack Marshall?"

He eased close. "Who do you think I am, Hattie?"

My gaze wavered, dropping to his collar "I—I don't know." My voice squeaked, and I hated his ability to rattle me. "But if your name isn't Jack Marshall, then we need to be reintroduced." Regaining my composure, I stuck out my hand. Instead of shaking it, he cradled my fingers and tugged me a step closer.

He released his gentle hold, his chin dipping to my level, his voice as breathless as I felt. "Tonight."

Chapter 12

I clenched fistfuls of my sheet beneath my chin, wishing I could stuff the wadded fabric into my ears. But not even that could muffle Miss Wendall's grating snores. While she lay below in deep slumber, I squirmed on the top bunk at each wheeze that faithfully rent the air every four and a half seconds.

Though my irritation had begun long before Miss Wendall guzzled her sleeping tonic.

And Jack Marshall held all the blame.

Tonight.

That whispered promise which earlier had made my nerves hum with excitement now made my right eye twitch with annoyance. I'd waited through the moonlight excursion, expecting Jack to approach me. To continue our conversation as he'd vowed. But he hadn't.

I was such a fool.

No doubt he'd only invented that sorry excuse for me to leave him be. If Jack Marshall thought for one second I would forget by tomorrow, he'd underestimated me. And to think he'd attacked Face for toying with women's emotions, when he'd done the same—

A gentle tapping pierced my thoughts.

My gaze darted to the door. A hulking silhouette darkened the curtained window. The shadow dipped, and something slid beneath the door. Careful not to wake Miss Wendall, I eased off the side of my bunk, the steel frame protesting with a creaky groan.

Miss Wendall mumbled something and rolled toward the inside wall.

My breath seeped from my lungs in blessed relief, and I scooped up the slip of paper. Angling it to catch the moonlight, I blinked away the blurriness and trained my eyes on the masculine scrawl.

The note was from Jack.

He wanted to meet me ashore. My lips pressed together. The *Idlewild* had been docked at the wharf, so it wasn't any trouble to venture on land. But why? We could easily talk in the hold or in the galley. Most of the crew were either asleep or bunking in town. It was seldom that Duffy allowed anyone to go up the hill for the night, but when he did, the majority of men went.

My fingers curled around the note. Should I? What did I know of this man? Hadn't he all but confessed he wasn't who he'd claimed to be? I could be walking into something dangerous. But then, Jack hadn't lifted a hand against me, even when I was assaulting him. And what if he held information about Pittsburgh?

That alone drove me to snatch my robe from the edge of the bed and throw it over my nightgown. No time for changing into anything suitable. I couldn't risk stumbling around in the dark and waking Miss Wendall. With a steadying breath, I creaked open the door and made my way down the staircases.

All was silent.

I scurried to the bow and reached shore.

Chunky stars paired with the crescent moon, lending a soft glow to my steps. I peered starboard and found the massive elm. A sturdy profile caught my attention.

Jack.

As if sensing my presence, he stepped fully into the moonlight. "You came." His hushed voice silenced the surrounding crickets.

"I'm curious." I drew near, keeping a safe distance. "Is it common for you to summon women to meet you in the middle of the night?"

"You'd be the first." I sensed his smile more than saw it. "It couldn't be helped. I couldn't risk anyone overhearing."

And there it was. The secret. The one I'd witnessed in his eyes on the texas roof, now rumbled in his husky tone. My heart quickened, the intrigue drawing me a step closer.

His gaze dipped to my clothes, then snapped to my face.

I huffed. "You don't have to look at me like that. My nightclothes are about as scandalous as a grandma's. Besides, if you'd been more specific earlier, I would've stayed dressed like you." Jack still wore his mate's uniform, minus his cap, giving me a rare glimpse of his golden hair.

"Didn't I say I'd speak with you tonight?"

"I thought it was a ploy to shirk me off."

"Had I thought you would fall for such a tactic, I would have used one." Just like those first moments we'd met, the night sky complemented him, silvery hues feathering across his strong features. The shifting of shadow and light, so much like my perception of him. I'd like to imagine I glimpsed snippets of his true self, but many facets of Jack Marshall remained in shaded obscurity. "Did you bring the code?"

"It's tucked in a safe place." There was hardly privacy aboard a steamboat, but nobody would tamper with my songbook. The crook in the binding provided the perfect spot.

He beckoned me farther into the darkness. Hesitant, I followed. Twigs cracked beneath my boots, but much more could be broken if I'd made the wrong choice. He led me out of view from the *Idlewild*. I was now veiled in the shadows with a man I barely knew, who happened to be bigger and stronger than me. I should have at least grabbed my penknife before running out. What had I been thinking? I wasn't. So consumed with finding answers about Pittsburgh, about Jack, that I'd left my brain behind as well as my only means of protection.

"I know this isn't an ideal place for conversation." His soft voice contrasted the severe notes of darkness enfolding me.

I scoffed and tightened my robe. "No, it's not, so let's get to it. What's going on? Who are you? Are you really a first mate?"

"Yes. I'm a licensed officer, but that's not my primary profession."

"Go on."

His gaze settled on me. "I'm a prohibition agent. And I have reason to believe someone is using the *Idlewild* to smuggle alcohol."

Thoughts flooded my mind like the time the hull had sprung a leak, my gut sinking along with any intelligent thought. Jack, a federal agent? "You—you think there's alcohol aboard?"

His mouth was a firm line. "It's possible."

"So that's why you've been obsessing over the cargo. Checking and rechecking the hold."

He nodded. "If someone is going to bring anything aboard, the most logical time would be during loading and off-loading."

Very true. Before Jack had forced the reassessing of goods, the crew would offload with no questions asked. How easy it would have been to disguise alcohol in barrels of oil. "That's why you inspected the jugs in the galley."

"Yes." He expelled a ragged sigh. "I've searched everywhere I know to look and have found nothing."

I plucked a blade of grass tickling my leg and rolled it between my index and thumb. "What makes you believe all this about the *Idlewild*?"

"The code. Maybe I should start from the beginning." He crouched beside a sapling. "I served in the Coast Guard during the Great War and made powerful connections with those in. . ." He paused as if weighing his words. "Confidential positions. After the war, I remained an ensign until my contract ended."

It wasn't hard to imagine him as an ensign. Living aboard a steamboat, I'd seen a fair amount of Coast Guard officers. Jack's efficiency and discipline matched every maritime serviceman I'd been in contact with. "Then you became a federal agent?"

"Yes."

"Is Jack your real name?"

"Yes and no."

I tossed aside the blade of grass. "That's not an answer."

"Hattie." It could be the deceit of a moonlit night coupling with my fanciful imagination, but my name rolling off his perfect lips sent chills coursing through me. "I'm already telling you more than you should know."

My brow dug. "Why are you telling me?"

"Because I'm asking for your help."

"My help?" My raspy tone betrayed my surprise.

"You're smart, observant, and assertive. You're a powerful ally, Hattie Louis." His ice-blue gaze sought mine and something built between us, a silent pact.

He thought me helpful. Not a burden, always in the way. But valued. He wanted me to partner with him? For a secret investigation? My blood warmed with excitement. "What would I have to do?"

"Keep your eyes open. Things aren't always as they appear."

"Does Duffy know?"

"He does." Jack ran a hand through his hair. "He's the reason I'm here. I've known the captain since my youth."

My head tilted at this news. "How?"

"My aunt." His lashes lowered, his voice softening. "She was neighbors with Duffy's niece."

"Florence Albright?" That morsel of information served me an entire plateful of how Jack Marshall had been raised—high society. Duffy's niece was one of the well-to-dos in Louisville. Duffy's family was part of the social class that would turn its nose up at an orphan such as me. I lacked good breeding and money. Duffy had the respected family line, but had been shunned for choosing the riverman life. Florence remained the only relative who still spoke with him.

"When I was young, I spent summers with my aunt. I'd wander next door, and Mrs. Albright would tolerate my presence well enough. Duffy would talk to me of steamboats and rivers. He's the reason I became a sailor."

Jack was probably seven to eight years older than me, so this must have occurred before my time with Duffy.

"The Coast Guard intercepted a code about the *Idlewild*. The person who decrypted it knew my connection to Duffy. She recommended me for the job."

She? A woman who interpreted secrets? I couldn't be more fascinated. "What does the code say?"

" 'Diamond aboard *Idlewild*.' " He stood and dusted his hands off on his trousers. "Shakes Donovan is known for calling cases of moonshine 'diamonds.' "

Even I had heard of the infamous bootlegger.

"The man has speakeasies up and down the Ohio and Mississippi. How clever would it be to employ unsuspecting vessels to run his goods?"

Wickedly clever, indeed. "Is that all the code said?" It seemed rather lengthy to only be three words.

"That's the main gist of it." His gaze darted away, making me wonder if there was more he wasn't telling me. "So will you help, Admiral?"

My mouth twisted. "I don't know if I can partner with a man who won't tell me his real name." I could always hassle Duffy to tell me Jack's true identity, but prying secrets from the steamboat captain was about as easy as plucking a star out of the velvet sky.

"Is Hattie Louis your real name?" His counter took the strength from my already-weak case.

"It is to me." Though I had no clue what my birthparents had initially named me. If they'd named me at all. All that had been on my person when Duffy discovered me was a note begging him to take care of me and my birthdate, which hopefully was authentic. It would be unnerving not knowing how old I truly was. "You know about the circumstances with my parents, or lack thereof?"

"I do." His tender response was more than my heart could hold. "I know that Duffy took you in and raised you."

"He's the only papa I've known."

Just like the code, his eyes communicated something I couldn't read. "He's done well."

"Duffy would disagree." I sighed. "He's always saying how much more feminine I should be. That I lack in grace."

Jack gave me a long, meaningful look, then shook his head. "You lack nothing."

Chapter 13

Devyn

"You know I'd do anything for you, Devs." Peirson Brooks's triple-platinum voice flowed through Devyn's cell speaker. "I'm hosting CMAs the following week, but I'm free the Saturday before." Only Peirson would refer to the annual country music awards as one would speak of a routine doctor's appointment.

"You sure?" Devyn curled her feet beneath her legs and relaxed against the plush cushions of the den sofa in her childhood home. "I know you're busy. Please don't feel obligated just because without me you would've flunked college."

That familiar low chuckle made her smile. "Yes, yes I would have."

"Seriously, Peirson, no pressure here. If you can't sing for the ball, then—"

"It's all good. I'll be in Nashville next month, so it isn't any trouble making the two-hour drive to Louisville. Let me do this for you. It'll be payback for all that advertising you gave me. That kickstarted my career."

It had. Despite Travis's complaining, she'd featured Peirson's break-out album free of charge on Space Station. She was glad at least one good thing had come from all that mess. "You don't owe me anything. Friendships don't have strings attached." And neither did relationships. She would never again put herself in a position where she felt she had to earn someone's love.

"It'll be fun. Hey, why don't you sing with me? We can revive our rendition of that Elvis and Nancy Sinatra duet like in English Lit."

She laughed. "That hadn't gone well then and won't now." When she sang "Ain't Nothing Like a Song" with her brother's college roommate, she had no idea the man would move on to be a chart topper. "You nailed it. Me, not so much. I'm just glad no one else saw the video except Professor Andrews."

"No way. I wouldn't exploit you like that. I'm not Leeman."

Nothing like the mention of an ex-fiancé to damper a good conversation. "Which makes me like you all the more." They talked several minutes about the Dream River event, and she ended the call just as her mother entered the den.

With a smile, she handed Devyn a glass of sweet tea and settled beside her, the warmth in her hazel eyes always the same.

Devyn nudged her mom's shoulder. "Guess what? I just lassoed Peirson Brooks into singing for the ball." She couldn't wait to surprise Steph with the news. Her boss was a huge fan of his.

Mom's brows raised in surprise. "How nice of him. It's still strange to think that the twenty-year-old kid who'd steal Mitch's socks is now on my radio."

"He's a decent guy. Glad there are still some around these days." She took a sip of sugary goodness and placed the glass on the coffee table.

"There's plenty out there." Her mom's thin lips bowed into a smile, her bobbed salt-and-pepper hair sliding against her cheek. It had taken two years for her hair to grow back after rounds of chemo.

Devyn whispered her thanks to God. By looking at Mom now, no one would know the fight she'd won against breast cancer. Patty Asbury, the warrior, the survivor.

"Speaking of men, what time's your new boyfriend coming?"

"He's not my boyfriend. Not even close." Oh, please don't let her speak like that when Chase arrived. "Do I look like I'm dressed for a date?" She tugged the rolled hem of her cutoff sweatpants. It had been her day off, so per usual free-time attire, her hair was a messy knot atop her head. But she had slipped on a clean T-shirt. "He should be here any minute."

"Just curious why you picked your parents' boring place for a 'research meeting.'" Her slender fingers air-quoted the last two words. "Especially when you have that amazing penthouse."

"Are you encouraging me to invite single men to my apartment, Mother? I'm shocked." She threw her hand over her mouth with a flair of drama.

"You have a good head on your shoulders. I'm sure you'd never invite anyone over to your place you didn't trust. Which makes me wonder about this man." She raised a knowing brow.

"Chase would behave." She'd been alone with him in a car for six hours plus several times on the *Belle*, and he'd acted honorably. "My reason for coming here is simply because I wanted to be near you. Also, you have better food."

"Don't flatter me." She gave a playful swat to Devyn's shoulder. "You really want me to serve you and your friend Kraft Mac & Cheese and frozen cookie dough?"

"I'd love it actually."

Her mom laughed. "I forgot who I was talking to."

Devyn tamed her smile. "Mom, you know why I can't invite him to my place." She shifted. "He doesn't know about Space Station. Or the specifics about the breakup. I don't want to explain why I live in a luxe penthouse on a wedding coordinator's salary."

Her mom's mouth pulled into a scowl. "You should've gotten more than that penthouse when you two parted ways. You were the whole reason that social media site even started. I should've gotten you a lawyer despite your refusal."

"I couldn't then, Mom. I was struggling to survive the day. And at the time, I didn't want any part of Space Station."

"But all the work you did—"

"Isn't worth the heartache. I got the penthouse. When I sell it, I'll have a nice chunk of change to start my own business. If I get brave enough to do that solo."

She gently squeezed Devyn's arm. "You're braver than you think."

The doorbell rang, saving her from forming a response.

"I'll get it." Devyn rose to her feet.

"Want me to make myself scarce?"

"You're not getting off that easy. You owe me mac 'n cheese." Devyn winked. "Do you care if I crash here tonight? I don't have to be at work until noon tomorrow."

"You never need to ask." Her mom's smile revealed how glad she was for the company. Dad was in Lexington for work and wouldn't be back until late Friday.

Devyn crossed the den and hustled to the foyer. She opened the door and found Chase in jeans and a. . .UK wildcat T-shirt? She wrinkled her nose. "You have to change before entering this house."

With one hand he clutched a sleek folder, and the other he raised, palm flashing. "I wore this for self-protection."

"Ha! How is that self-protection when it makes me want to shove you down the porch steps?"

His mouth twitched as if fighting a grin. "This shirt ensures me you'll keep your hands to yourself."

"You are ridiculous."

He leaned in. *Hello, Gucci cologne.* "You invited me to meet your mom. Every guy knows a visit to the girl's parents' house is a serious elevation in the relationship. We're practically committed to each other now."

She shook her head with a snort. "And for that bit of craziness, I'm totally eating your half of the mac 'n cheese. Get in here, wildcat, before I change my mind."

"Is your friend still on the doorstep?" Mom called from the kitchen. "Quit tormenting the poor soul and let him in."

"I like her." Chase adjusted his baseball hat and stepped inside.

"Mom, brace yourself," she called. "He's wearing a UK tee."

She could hear her mother's snicker. "Does he know how competitive you are?"

"I'm beginning to realize that, ma'am." He answered for Devyn. "I've already sacrificed my portion of mac and cheese to make it this far inside."

Devyn pinched him.

Mom appeared in the archway that led to the kitchen. "Is my daughter being a lousy hostess?"

"The worst."

Another pinch, but this time Chase swerved from her reach, his eyes alight with laughter.

"Just remind her that I can always bring out her baby books and—"

"Nope, nope, nope." Devyn rattled off the introductions and grabbed Chase's wrist, tugging him toward the sunroom. "We'll be out here if you need us, Mom."

She laughed. "Play nice, children."

As soon as they were out of her mother's earshot, Chase turned his wicked smile on her. "I always play nice."

"I'm sure that's debatable." She motioned toward the wicker chairs surrounding the patio table. "So, you texted about having a sample invitation done?" She held out her palm. "Wow me."

Chase opened the folder and set his notebook on the table.

"Ah, the mysterious book that holds all your sketches of the long-wattled umbrellabird."

"Did you just make that up?"

"The bird? No. It's a real species. I went through a Discovery Channel phase in my teens. No more stalling." She snapped her fingers. "Do you want me to make a drumroll sound? I feel like I should."

"Not necessary." He slipped the card from the folder's inside cover and handed it to her.

The first thing she noted was the quality of paper. Ivory with an iridescent sheen, giving the illusion of ripples. Like water. The lettering was navy, and she could hug him for not using Papyrus font. No, the words were sleek and classy. The border too. "It's perfect." She raised her gaze to find him watching her. An intensity in his eyes pulled the air from her chest. "Thank you."

"You're welcome." His voice was raspier than usual, as if her praise had meant something to him.

"Can I take this to Steph?"

"Of course. If she approves, I'll send over the file for you to get them printed."

When he said that, reality struck deeper. They were doing this. Really going to host a ball for the leading wedding magazine in the country with the addition of the *Belle*'s patrons. "I sure hope this all turns out okay."

"I have no doubt it will." He gave her a reassuring nod. "Now it's your turn. What did you discover about Hattie?"

She took a deep breath. "Only that I don't think she exists."

Chapter 14

Devyn carefully set the invitation on the table and regarded Chase with a sad smile. "I can't find her anywhere." With the wicker seat being so large, she pulled her legs up to her chest and curled her arms around them. They'd divvied the next phase of research, Devyn taking on Hattie, while Chase further investigated his great-grandfather. "I've checked every ancestry and newspaper site for a Hattie Louis. Thank heaven for free trials."

He scratched his cheek. "And there was no trace, huh?"

"I found several matches to the name, but nothing for the time and location we were looking for. Plus they all had pictures. None matched her photo."

"That's odd."

"Very. I was hoping for some trail of her existence, a birth or death certificate. Even a census sheet. On one ancestry site there was like a gazillion scans of census forms. All nothing." Her lips twisted. "How should we proceed? Have you done research on your great-grandfather?"

"As much as I could. He married great-grandma Julia in 1933. He wasn't married before that. So if he had a fling with Hattie, it wasn't on record."

"It seems nothing is on record for her. Which leaves us with nothing."

"Not exactly."

"What do you mean?"

His smile flashed. "Remember the other slip of paper? The code?"

"Of course."

"I have a professor friend from UK who believes it went through the Coast Guard. There was a faint set of initials on the corner. E.F."

"Really?"

He pulled out his phone and opened the photos. "Here's a screenshot of this lady." He angled the screen toward her, the motion highlighting the muscle in his forearm.

Devyn peered at a very twenties pic of a young woman sporting a cloche hat, her sturdy frame wrapped in a long overcoat, and her right hand clutching a briefcase. "Who is she?"

"A genius. Her name is Elizebeth Friedman. She was a decoder for the Coast Guard in the twenties and thirties during the prohibition. Pretty much all the codes went across her desk."

"A woman doing a supposedly man's job? And rocking it? I love it." And the lady worked with codes! Of course Devyn's coding had been of a different sort, but there was still the configuration of lettering. Talk about a kindred spirit from a hundred years ago.

"Right? During her time there she was responsible for decrypting over twelve thousand intercepted codes."

"Think she had a hand in this one?" Devyn gestured toward the slip of paper Chase had set on the table.

"Most likely."

Devyn ran a thumb over the paper with a gentle swipe. She raised her gaze to find Chase watching her. "Sorry, it's just so interesting." Even she heard the wonder in her voice. "It's like touching history. Finding something this authentic is kinda breathtaking."

His gaze pulled from the code and aimed fully on her. "I agree. There's beauty in the genuine."

He stared at her with the same enrapturement as she had the code. Something stirred between them. Was he saying she was genuine? Because if that was his implication, he'd gifted her a compliment above all others.

"All right, back to work, my dream girl." He motioned toward the code.

Dream girl? Really? She realized he was probably trying to lighten the mood, but she wasn't a fan of being ridiculed about something so precious to her. She should have never told him about her dream of the river. But then they wouldn't have stumbled upon the theme. Still. . . "Please don't mock me. Not about this."

He flinched. "Who's mocking?"

"You are. Are you ever serious?"

"Actually, yes. A lot of the time." He stuffed his phone back into his pocket and gentled his expression. "I've been accused of being too serious."

"Really? Because you haven't been that way with me."

His fervent gaze zipped heat down her spine. "Maybe all it takes is being around the right person."

She worked to steady her voice. "Or maybe you're trying to sweet talk me so I'll give you your mac 'n cheese back."

"A man can try." He dimpled. "Back to before you distracted me—which you're very good at, by the way—I had a question about the *Idlewild*. Was it ever rumored to have illegally transported alcohol during the twenties or thirties?"

She ignored his remark about being a distraction because right now, with his inviting gray eyes and crooked smile, he was the offending party. "No, not that I know of. Like I told you earlier, there was a lost period of time when there wasn't much documentation with the boat. It did excursion trips, but I never heard about anything like alcohol smuggling. Maybe that's what the message is about. Can we find someone that could crack whatever it says on the code?"

He nodded. "Two steps ahead. I sent a picture of it to my professor friend. He wants to see if he can figure it out."

"What's the next course of action?"

"Keep digging for clues about Hattie Louis."

"What about a steamboat museum? There are several throughout the country. I can call around and see if anyone has anything in their archives about the *Idlewild*."

"That'll work. And if we need to, we can always take another road trip."

She should really ignore the fluttering in her stomach at the anticipation of spending extended periods of time with this man. But really, it was fun to be around him. Even if he was an outrageous flirt. So much so that. . . "I was thinking of watching a movie after this. Would you like to stay for a bit?"

"Love to."

⁂

A gentle hand brushed Devyn's hair from her forehead.

"Devyn." His voice was soft, and she tried to lean into it. "You aren't making this easy."

Her hand skimmed. . .a toned abdomen? Her eyes shot wide, and she sat up straight. She blinked, clearing the haze, and Chase came into focus. He sat beside her on her parents' love seat. Just as he had the entire movie, except at some point she must've dozed and ended up on his shoulder.

"Wow, how awkward."

He smiled. "Not really."

"I can't believe I fell asleep." She yawned, covering her mouth. "I feel like an old lady. Not able to stay up past nine." She knew her hair was a mess and she probably had a crease from his sleeve on her cheek. "When did I conk out?"

"Right when Audrey and the British dude huddled in the broom closet."

Ugh. "I missed the kissing scene." Her favorite part.

"I'm sure I can recreate it for you, if you'd like."

"I think you only say these things to get me irritated."

"I do." His grin broadened. "You get this pucker right here when you're annoyed." He gently pressed his finger between her brows. "I like to see how often I can make it appear."

His phone buzzed. With a quick look of apology, he glanced at the screen and then silenced it.

"You can get that if you want. I don't mind."

"I'll call 'em back in a second." He shoved his phone in his pocket. "I should probably get going." He stood.

"Yeah. . .uh. . .thanks for hanging out with me." Could she sound any lamer?

"I enjoyed it."

"Even though I fell asleep on you? Just so you know, I don't make a habit of cuddling with my guests."

"I hope not. Then I wouldn't feel as special."

She laughed and walked him to the door. "I'll let you know what Steph says tomorrow about the invitation, and keep you updated if I can locate anything from the museums."

"Sounds good." He pulled his keys from his pocket. "Goodnight, Devyn." His gaze lingered on hers and it looked like he wanted to say something else. But instead he gave her a parting smile and left.

She locked the door and made her way to her childhood bedroom. It still had pink walls and butterfly-print curtains. Mom had a sentimental streak the size of the Smoky Mountains. Devyn changed into her pajama top but kept the cutoff sweatpants on because, let's face it, she could live in them till Jesus came.

Devyn awakened late the next morning, and it was glorious. She hadn't slept this soundly in. . .well, she couldn't remember the last time. Her dozing bliss could be attributed to the security of being in her parents' home. But it could just be on account of her pleasant evening with Chase. Even thinking about him made her heart light.

She dressed and met her mother at the table for a hearty brunch. Mom loved to spoil her when she stayed over. It was like retreating to her own bed and breakfast.

Devyn arrived at work with ten minutes to spare, giving her time to gather numbers of the steamboat museums to call later on her break. She'd finished logging them into the notes app in her phone when her cell dinged with a text. It was Chase.

Morning, my dream girl. Just wanted to let you know how cute you were asleep on my shoulder. So adorable I could almost overlook the drool stain on my sleeve.

She laughed. *That's what you get for wearing a UK shirt.*

Then she added the emoji with the silly face.

"What's that smile for?" Steph stood in her doorway.

"I was texting Chase." She glanced up from her phone. "What do you think about the invitations?"

"Same as you. Stunning." She ventured farther into Devyn's office. "I showed the design to Dalia, and she's interested in seeing more of his work. They're looking to update the clothing in the gift shop. Think your man could design T-shirts, hoodies, and such?"

"He's not my man, and I'm sure he could come up with something." Her phone dinged again.

Can I take you out tonight?

Her breath stalled, and she just stared at his words as if they'd magically change into something else.

"You should see the look on your face. What's wrong?"

"He just asked me out." Disbelief registered in her tone.

"And why wouldn't he?" Steph raised her coffee cup to her lips and sipped. "If you'd look in the mirror every once in a while, you'd see for yourself how gorgeous you are. And available."

"I don't think I can date. Not this close to my breakup."

"This close?" Steph dragged the chair by the door to the desk. "It's almost been a year. Travis moved on, and rather quickly."

She winced. He'd moved on before they even broke up.

"And not sure if you know this, but Space Station hasn't been doing so hot lately." She took another sip. "My nephew was complaining about their new format. It's confusing, and it glitches. I guess there's a big to-do about it all over social media."

"New format? I designed it to have updated features, not to be completely revamped." It had been her ideas, her labors with coding, and Travis had changed it all?

Dalia, the marketing manager, peeked her head in the office doorway. "Have you told her yet?"

Steph winced. "I was getting around to it. Circling the airport, you know? And you just crashed the landing."

Devyn's gut twisted. "Told me what?"

Dalia exchanged a glance with Steph. "There's a hashtag going around about you."

"Not again." Why would Travis start another hashtag about her? Hadn't he tormented her enough?

"This one's in your favor." Steph gave a sympathetic smile. "People are so angry about the changes they're demanding your return to Space Station. The hashtag is BringBackDevyn. It's trending."

It wasn't awful, but still, it attracted attention. "Why can't I just be left alone?" Her eyes slid closed. "I can't take off work and hide away." Not when there was so much to do.

"No one knows you work here. Your name isn't even on the website for event coordinator."

That was true. And she wasn't on social media where her location could be tracked. But all people had to do was watch the video where

Travis "gifted" her the penthouse and they'd know where she lived. A sigh pushed from her lungs. She really needed to sell the place. Maybe once the ball was over she'd find a good Realtor. In the meantime, it wasn't like she could run away to her family's cottage in the sticks.

She took a calming breath. "It could be worse. I've weathered this before when it was." Soon Travis would adjust Space Station and her spotlight would dim to nothing.

Dalia flipped her raven-colored locks over her slim shoulder. "Want to go with me to the gym on our lunch hour? Sweat therapy and all that."

The only crunches Devyn did was the kind with her teeth, chomping Cool Ranch Doritos. "Thanks, but I have a hot date with my cell phone." She lifted the paper of numbers listing several steamboat museums.

"Speaking of hot dates." Steph had a special talent for never letting a subject drop. Although Devyn had walked right into this one. "Did you answer Chase yet?"

"Who?" Dalia perked. "That guy who keeps coming to visit you here?"

Devyn downplayed it. "He's not here to see me. He needs information about the *Belle*."

Steph scoffed. "I guarantee you the *Belle* isn't why he asked you on a date tonight."

"I'll answer him soon." When she was once again alone and could think of a polite refusal.

"Nope." Steph smiled. "I know what you're thinking, and *I* think you should go."

"I don't want to go anywhere public right now. Not until this all blows over."

"Then don't leave." Dalia tapped her chin. "Invite him on the sunset cruise tonight. Most of it is in dusk, a nice cover for you."

Steph nodded. "And you could always use your employee advantage and stay on the texas roof."

Which would work. Passengers weren't allowed anywhere near the pilothouse during sailing hours. But did she really want to cross that line with Chase?

"What's one date?" Dalia shrugged. "It's not like you're signing your life away to him."

She was right. What could one night change? Maybe this would be the distraction she needed. Or maybe this would be a colossal flop. Steph and Dalia went about their business, leaving Devyn to her jumbled thoughts. A date with Chase. The staggering hashtag.

Her mind needed to focus on something. Anything. Her tour wouldn't arrive for another fifteen minutes. Not enough time to get immersed in the ball's work, but maybe enough time to flip through Hattie's songbook. Eleanor was kind enough to let them have this one-of-a-kind book. She carefully flipped through the pages until her eyes landed on a light, almost unreadable pencil scrawl. How had they missed this before?

Biting her lip, she reached for her phone and texted Chase.

I found something else in the songbook.

His response dinged almost immediately. *Awesome. Excited to hear about it. Also are you sparing my feelings by pretending I didn't just ask you out? Because I'm pretty sure my pride has already tanked.*

Oops! Though she'd decided to go out with him, she totally forgot to text her answer.

While your pride could use some tanking – my answer for tonight is yes. I know the perfect place. She added a wink emoji and hoped he'd agree to the sunset cruise.

She glanced at the time on her phone screen. Only a couple minutes until her tour. She typed a text letting him know she'd call him later to discuss tonight and then gathered her tour folder.

Her head still swirled from all the dizzying events that'd taken place in just a span of a few minutes. But one thing was for certain, she was going on a date tonight. A thought that both excited and terrified her.

Chapter 15

Hattie

Abraham Lincoln, Charles Dickens, and the woman who'd abandoned me. All had at one time walked the very ground beneath my feet—the Louisville wharf. Though the latter on the list held fault for this pre-dawn visit.

Between the fifth and sixth mooring ring.

Duffy's seven words had been etched in me since the day I'd gathered nerve to ask where he'd discovered me. The smack of my steps clashed with the caw of seagulls swirling overhead. I counted the corroded rings bolted to the coarse concrete and slowed my pace at the fifth.

Heart thudding dully, I lowered to the ground between the rusted, circle boundaries. To the place I'd been deserted.

My thoughts ran murky like the river water beneath my dangling feet. Where would I be had my mother not left me? Were my parents alive? Still in Louisville? Had I passed them on the streets on the several occasions we'd moored here?

It was such a peculiar feeling, being abandoned. I'd often forced myself to approach things logically. My parents may have landed themselves in a situation forbidding them from keeping me. What if they'd thought they'd done what was best? That they granted me a better life than what they could offer? How many times had I rehearsed those reasonings? Until they'd descended into my soul like an anchor, keeping my overactive imagination from drifting. From believing I had been to blame.

Doubt snarled and jabbed its spiky finger into my chest, accusing.

As an infant, I'd been too young to display the myriad of faults that overwhelm me as a twenty-year-old, but maybe they'd suspected me a misfit. What if they'd judged me a troublesome creature that could only belong to the wilds of the river?

My nose stung and I rubbed at the burn, only to have a tear escape down my cheek.

Footsteps sounded behind me, and I quickly mopped the dampness from my face with the edge of my wrap.

"You're up early." Jack's voice floated over my shoulder.

"I'm beginning to suspect you don't sleep." Ever since our talk about the possibility of alcohol being on the *Idlewild*, we'd been overly alert. Jack more so. He was always the last to his cabin and the first roaming the decks. And his agitation seemed to increase the closer we came to Louisville. "I know what you're going to say—that I shouldn't be out here. That the wharf is unsafe for a woman at this hour."

"Actually, I was about to ask if I can join you." He gestured to the spot beside me on the deck.

Oh. I nodded, hoping my eyes weren't shiny from my tears.

He sat near enough that his side warmed mine. I kept my eyes on the water, but I felt his gaze on me.

"We've been to a dozen towns along the river, and this is the first time I've seen you camp out on the wharf. Do you have a certain love for Louisville?"

"Yes and no." I glanced over to see curiosity puckering his brow. "On this exact spot, when I was a baby, Duffy found me. When we travel here, I always make time to visit and think."

The gentleness in his eyes swayed me to continue.

"How different would my life have been if only my parents had kept me? Why *did* they leave me here?" Duffy hardly ever mentioned it. He'd dismiss my questions with a tight grimace as if the topic made him sad. "Who abandons their child on a dirty wharf?"

"Maybe someone desperate," Jack offered. "Maybe your birth mother had to in order to protect you."

"Or maybe she wanted rid of me. Maybe I was a burden."

A wharf worker down the way hollered something unsavory to a passing rowboat. But the man's crass voice was mild compared to the screams in my mind. I'd come here for peace but received the opposite.

I moved to stand, but Jack stilled me with a tender look.

"The sun's coming up." His gaze swept my face. "The sky's destined to be beautiful."

His warm hand wrapped mine, as if offering support. Instead of filling the silence with talk, he spoke with touch.

We stayed like that for several comfortable minutes, admiring the sun whispering over the horizon. God was putting on a show for us with brilliant colors that in theory shouldn't go together, but in the expanse of the sky it was nothing short of a masterpiece. Jack's thumb stroked my knuckles as if it was the most natural thing in the world. Yes, he invited me to be his comrade in investigating, but here, he was my friend.

My nose burned again, but for a different reason. Jack Marshall had no doubt graced the polished floors of the elite, yet he sat on a spit-stained wharf, cradling the fingers of society's reject. A river rat. And his eyes—those bright blues as vivid as the sunrise we'd just shared—were not peering at me in pity or repulsion but in appreciation. And blast it all, if it didn't make my eyes water. I turned away, the emotion overpowering.

We should return soon. A full day stretched before us. I slowly tugged my hand free from his. "Jack?"

He seemed caught up in his own thoughts. "Hmm?" His attention shifted to me, and my breath caught with the gentle force of it.

"Thank you."

His smile was tender. One I tucked in the folds of my heart to revisit.

"Are you helping with the cargo?" His expression slipped into that of a determined prohibition agent.

The freight was to be on-loaded at seven. A little over two hours from now. Then we'd head toward Tell City. I pushed back an errant lock of hair, causing Jack's focus to stray, following my movement. "I'll be there. After I burn a few eggs and toast." The poor *Idlewild* crew had to suffer with my cooking since Miss Wendall was in town gathering more supplies to stock the galley.

We made our way to the boat. I spent the next harried moments preparing breakfast, beating my personal record of only dropping one egg on the floor and burning just the tip of my index finger on the frying pan. I may have lost shards of shells in the scrambled eggs, but no one complained about their food. Not even Ludwig, who had an opinion on everything.

After the plates were cleared and washed, I scurried to the wharf where the deckhands, the purser, and Jack were waiting for Duffy's signal to on-load. With the logbook back in my possession, I continued my role accepting payments from merchants for their shipment. Within the half hour, I'd received cash for crates of grain, barrels of Karo syrup, and bags of mail.

I paused at the next piece of freight. "Who does this belong to?" I motioned to the large crate mostly obscured by a wall of boxes containing soap chips. "Should I run to the dock office and see if the merchant left payment for us?" Some storekeepers and vendors hadn't the time to wait around, so they'd pay in advance.

Jack glanced from the barrel of vinegar he was checking in. "Money was left for it at the wharf office."

"Ah, I was wondering where you wandered off to during breakfast."

Duffy gave the signal to start loading. Jack and I inspected the crates then waved the deckhands to haul the freight into the *Idlewild*'s belly. We worked in orderly chaos. My next crate was the one that had been left unattended, the one which Jack had already collected payment for.

I crouched, mindful of my skirts, and pushed on the edge, attempting to scoot it closer to the other freight. It wouldn't budge. "Did the missive say what's in here?" I popped the lid with my crowbar and studied the contents—boxes of matchsticks. My hand dug deep until my fingertips brushed the bottom. Odd. "Hey, Jack?" I waved him over, and he held up a finger as he finished business with an older gentleman.

"What's the problem, gorgeous?" Face stepped beside me.

I wasn't in any humor to respond to his teasing. "It's filled with matchsticks."

He perused the crate, his eyes holding amusement. "So it is."

"Don't sass me, Face." I glared.

"Step aside. I can lift it for you and haul it aboard."

"That's not the point. That box is—"

"What's the trouble?" Jack approached with his usual confident demeanor.

"She was talking to me, Mate." Face didn't even bother to conceal his annoyance.

"But she asked for me," Jack countered, his expression neutral.

Men could certainly be ridiculous. "Both of you, quit yapping and try to lift that box." I pointed sharply at the wooden beast. "It's only matches. I should at least be able to move it. But I can't." My chin jutted, daring them to question my strength.

The men wisely remained silent. Jack hunched over and inspected the box while Face made an effort to pull it toward him. It scraped only an inch.

Face whistled. "Are those matchsticks dipped in lead?"

Jack and I exchanged a meaningful look. This crate could be what we'd been searching for. Was there a false bottom crammed with illegal alcohol? I lowered my voice. "We need to search this freight thoroughly."

Jack nodded. "Face, please fetch the captain." He waited until the deckhand turned before speaking again. "If this is what—"

A dark blur loomed at the fringes of my vision. I flinched. A massive man, clad in a black workman's uniform, careened toward Jack and lobbed a punch. Jack swerved but caught a knuckle on the lip. He recovered and launched himself at the assailant. Face turned at the commotion and joined in the ruckus, spearing an elbow to the attacker's back. A fierce growl erupted from the man's lips, his fiery red hair falling over his feral dark eyes.

He lunged toward Jack, but this time Jack was prepared. He dipped and launched a punch to the man's gut, causing the brute to double over. Face moved in, grabbing the man's arms and wrenching them behind his back.

"Who are you?" Jack's tone was low and powerful.

Rather than recognizing defeat, the goon writhed in Face's grip and kicked his right leg, his heel not quite reaching Jack.

"Let's try this again." Jack spoke through clenched teeth. "Who are you?"

The man let loose a string of curses. Jack raised his tone, but his words were muffled by the man's vehement threats. Face struggled to keep him subdued. A strong tobacco odor clogged the air, adding more confusion as I gawked at the scene. The rest of the crew in the *Idlewild*'s cargo hold should suspect something amiss by now. Why weren't they—

"You're a fair view if I ever seen one."

I jumped at the deep snarl and swirled around. Another man stood several feet behind me. Where on earth had he come from? With the river to our left, and the wall of soap chips freight to our right, his appearance was impossible. He was my height and maybe even my weight, but he held the advantage in his right hand—a pistol. He yanked me closer and pressed the barrel to my neck, the bite of metal like ice against my flushed skin.

"Call off your friends."

"Jack." My voice rattled a weak whisper.

Thank God Jack glanced my way. His left hand bunched the man's collar, his right fist cocked, readying to deliver a penetrating blow, but his entire frame tensed at the sight of the thug with the revolver.

Face caught sight of me and the gun, his face blanching. The first attacker broke free from the deckhand's white-knuckled clutch.

"Keep your hands to yourselves and your traps shut." The armed man's venomous spittle sprayed my arm. "Then little missy won't get hurt."

His words ignited my blood. He spoke as if I was a helpless female at his mercy. My fingers tightened around. . .the crowbar. I tucked it into the pleat of my skirt and angled as far as his grip allowed, keeping him from spying my weapon.

The thug skimmed the gun's tip from my neck to waist, his finger curled around the trigger the entire time.

Face stiffened.

Jack's eyes narrowed. "Don't touch her."

The man's fingers dug into my side, pulling me with him in the opposite direction of the boat. "How about you takin' a stroll with me. My partner 'ere can tie up your pals, in case they decide on bein' heroes and comin' after you."

So this man was going to use me as a way to escape? "You won't be able to just walk away."

He paused, easing back so I could view his full glower and sucked air through his yellowed teeth. "I can and will."

"Not if I break your kneecaps." With all my force, I swung that hunk of metal, nailing his legs with a sickening crack.

He howled in pain and doubled over, clenching his right knee. His spindly fingers released me, but not the pistol.

Shouts and whistles erupted from the boat above, heavy footsteps charging down the stage. The other crewmen were coming to our rescue. The first brute landed a solid punch to Face's gut and dashed forward, linking an arm around the injured man. They took off.

I lunged forward to chase after them, my trusty crowbar in hand, but Jack caught my free wrist.

He gently spun me around to face him. "Don't go after them. They're still armed."

Oh. Right.

Frustration tightened the corners of his eyes. Yet his wrath at the attack didn't stop his gaze from roaming over me slowly, methodically, as if making certain there weren't any broken spots. All the while, his bloodied lip dripped like a faucet.

I set the crowbar down and searched my pockets for a handkerchief. "Here. Take this."

His expression turned downright grumpy. "Why?"

"To stop the bleeding." I huffed and stretched on my toes, pressing the handkerchief to his busted lip.

He stiffened, whether from his stinging mouth or from my touch, I couldn't tell.

The excitement of the past few moments sank into my bones, turning my joints wobbly. I flattened my hand against Jack's chest, using his sturdy build for support while keeping the handkerchief in place. His heart hammered against my palm, making my own race. "Hold it with light pressure until I can clean it."

Several other crewmen approached, and I stepped back from Jack. My mind needed cleared, and being that close to the first mate only hazed things. Who were those thugs? Why had they attacked us?

Duffy drew near, concern deepening the grooves in his forehead. His age-spotted hands cupped my shoulders and he stared into my face. "You okay, my girl?"

My heart clenched at the anguish in his voice. "Yes."

"Is it true? Did that ruffian threaten you with a gun?"

I nodded.

His aged blue eyes lit with wrath. It had been a while since I'd witnessed such a reaction. All my tears on the wharf earlier now seemed foolish. This man may not be my birth father, but he was my papa in every sense of the word.

"Then Hattie clobbered him with a crowbar." Face had made it to his feet, admiration stretching his grin. "Here we thought we was protecting her and 'twas the other way around."

Duffy didn't share Face's humor. Instead, his scowl tightened. "This shouldn't have happened," he muttered. "It's all my fault."

I set my hand on his quivering one. "You're not to blame. You couldn't have known this."

"Well, lookie here." Face crouched beside the massive crate holding the matchsticks. "Seems we were fixin' to load a stowaway."

"What?" I rushed to the crate, Jack following. In the surprise, his hand holding the handkerchief had dropped from tending his wound. I nailed him a glare and he pressed it back to his lip.

A hidden door hinged open at the bottom of the wooden box.

I gasped and dropped to my knees, peering inside. My nose wrinkled at the familiar odor. Tobacco. The stench identical to the man who'd held me at gunpoint. He'd been hiding in this crate. Why?

"At least your lip stopped bleeding." I dipped a washcloth into the lukewarm water in the washbasin in Duffy's cabin. "I still need to clean the area." Then possibly swab it with peroxide. But admitting that wouldn't improve Jack's mood.

Fury rolled off him in waves. His hands clenched at his sides. His body was as rigid as the chair he occupied. Was he fuming because the goons had escaped? Or because the crate held no alcohol and the investigation seemed at a standstill?

I wrung the cloth and stepped in front of him, taking in his disheveled hair, his blood-and-grime-stained uniform, and the split flesh of his mouth. Oh, his mouth. And oh, how alone we were.

Focus, Hattie. As the *Idlewild's* unofficial nurse, I had a job to do. Although this was nothing like putting salve on a blister when the striker accidentally burned himself on a scalding pipe. Or splinting a thumb when the deckhand jammed his finger in the capstan. And this was nothing at all like the time I snapped a dislocated shoulder back in place when the watchman took a tumble. This was only a busted lip. Easy. And yet my nerves tangled like a thousand mooring lines at the thought of touching Jack's face.

With a steadying breath, I bent close to him. But before my fingers could reach the swollen flesh, his warm hand came to mine. Our gazes bonded, and I realized I was wrong. His eyes weren't filled with rage, but haunted, the blue hues like stormy waters.

"I'm sorry, Hattie."

I blinked. "For what?"

He released my hand. "You could've been hurt. Shot." His throat worked. "I should have protected you. I would never forgive myself if something happened to you."

My chest squeezed at the note of raw strain in his voice. The emotion he'd been battling was directed at himself. Not because of the case or even about the thugs. But stemming from his concern over me. "You didn't know a man was hiding in that crate. Or that he was going to attack me." I lowered into the chair beside him so our eyes were level. "You were taking care of the only threat you knew about—that brute. I'm glad I got the scrawny one."

"But he was the one armed." Jack's brows furrowed. "I wonder what he was doing hiding in there. It seems he was more than just a routine stowaway."

"Would the wharf office have any information that could help? Maybe they saw the person who paid shipping for the crate?" Though how easy would it be to invent a fake business card and leave a wad of cash?

His thoughtful gaze dipped to his folded hands. "It's possible. I'll look into it."

"As for the stowaway part, do you think the man wanted aboard to retrieve hidden alcohol?" Wherever it was. Jack and I had searched this boat from top to bottom. If someone had hidden liquor aboard, they'd stored it in an excellent spot.

"That'd be my guess." He appeared deep in contemplation, then shifted his focus on me. The skin framing his eyes—bunched in pain only a few seconds ago—were now crimped in amusement.

"What?" I hadn't bothered to check my appearance as we entered Duffy's cabin. Was there grime on my face too?

"I was just thinking about you. How you swung that crowbar like you belonged at Yankee Stadium." All merriment fled, the admiration in his blue gaze making my breath flutter. "You're a brave woman, Hattie Louis."

His words latched on to my heart with a sturdy grip. But I couldn't allow him to picture me this way. "That's not true. Not when I'm afraid to go beyond the river's shore."

His head tilted. "What's so scary about it?"

"This is the only place that accepted me after the world cast me aside." I motioned toward the cabin door. "Out there, I'm the unwanted orphan. Here on the *Idlewild*, I have purpose. I belong." My tone reflected my sadness. "Outside this boat, I could never blend in."

"What if God designed you to stand out?"

"Why? I don't have anything to offer. I don't even know my true name. Duffy named me Hattie and gave me the surname Louis because of the wharf." I couldn't bear to look at Jack. I'd set out to disillusion him, but now I feared I'd done much worse—I'd made him pity me.

His knuckle trailed a tender path from my elbow to wrist, causing me to brave a glance at him.

"I've never met a woman like you, Admiral."

The room, the space between us, felt as though it were shrinking. "You make it sound like a good thing."

"Because it is. It is very much."

May as well have said "bon voyage" to my heart, because it had sailed free from my ownership and dropped anchor in Jack's hands.

Chapter 16

Devyn

"What do you think so far?" Devyn sipped her iced tea, pulling her gaze from the glistening waters to rest on Chase. They'd chosen two chairs on the deck and watched the Louisville skyline. One would think Devyn would tire of this view, but she hadn't. Lights from the cityscape painted the river with brilliant strokes of color, like moving art.

"It's impressive," he said. "Hard to believe this boat's been coursing waterways for over a century. She ages well." He raised his Coke as if in cheers to the timeless gal.

"There's something admirable in that, isn't there? Throughout the decades, this boat's weathered countless storms, surviving hits and damages." Devyn idly stirred the ice in her drink with her straw. "It's like life has thrown everything at her, yet she still paddles along. Her whistle a victory cry."

As if in response to her words, the whistle sang loud. Devyn laughed. The pilot only pressed the steam treadle to signal to the tugboat passing the opposite direction, but the timing had been perfect. She glanced over to remark on it and found Chase watching her. This hadn't been the first time she'd felt his gaze. Tonight she'd worn her hair down, having styled it with loose curls. Since the weather dallied on the warmer side, she'd donned her favorite sundress, showing more of her athletic frame than her sweatpants and baggy T-shirts. Chase's appreciation had been evident in his lingering looks.

She tugged down the hem of her dress as she stood. "Are you ready to head back inside to the ballroom?"

"To dance?" He rose to his feet. "Gladly."

"I was thinking more on the lines of food."

He chuckled and followed her inside the air-conditioned space. They moved through the concession line and claimed a table close to the windows. Her barbeque chicken would be several minutes yet, so the workers offered to bring both dishes when ready. Devyn grabbed the opportunity to excuse herself to the restroom.

By the time she returned, their dinner had arrived, but that wasn't what snagged her full attention. Chase had his mystery notebook open and was hurriedly writing.

He glanced up, and their gazes collided. His fingers snapped the notebook closed and a flush climbed his neck. Why the embarrassment?

Then it hit her.

The food on the table. Him jotting things down. This had been her family's situation two years ago. Mom had kept a journal of all she'd eaten to help determine which food had agreed with her while on her meds and which hadn't. Devyn had also used that same notebook, upon advice from the doctor, to keep records of appointments and insurance claims.

Everything fell in line with Chase's behavior, confirming what she'd already suspected. The phone calls he'd taken in private. Those times she'd overheard him say "insurance," "agent," and other health-related words. And oh, hadn't he mentioned that he'd been accused of being too serious? That could no doubt be blamed on a sickness too. Now tonight, he recorded what he'd eat, then was subsequently embarrassed. She wished she could tell him he had nothing to be ashamed of. That in a way she understood his struggle. She pulled her chair out and sat, her heart softening even more toward Chase Jones.

His lips twitched. "I'm not sure what I did to earn that look in your eyes, but I hope you tell me so I can do it again."

She smiled. "Are you always this observant?"

"I try to be. Especially when a gorgeous woman is involved." He popped a fry into his mouth with a wink.

They ate with light conversation mingled between bites. After Devyn polished off her milkshake, she regarded Chase with a satisfied look. "Now that I'm adequately sugared, I can relay to you my progress with Hattie." She could bore him with updates on the ball. Although she was secretly pleased with the progress that had been made—the invitations printed and sent out, the flowers ordered. But tonight, she'd decided not to dwell on work.

Chase leaned in. "Did you find a record on her?"

"Not yet. But I called the steamboat museums and one of them returned my message, saying they've an archive room stuffed with old discharging logs."

"Discharging logs?"

"They're books usually kept by the purser, listing cargo and inventory on the packet boats. The museum's system is organized by years, so I asked about the *Idlewild* during the 1920s. We may learn the names of the captain and crew. Not sure what that will tell us, but it may lead to something else that could give us more information on her."

Chase idly toyed with his straw paper. "I think we should quit our search."

Devyn blinked. "Wait. What?" She thought he'd flash his mischievous grin, teasing her once again, but he remained straight-faced. "What brought this on?"

He tossed the wrapper onto his empty plate and looked up, hesitancy deepening the granite flecks in his eyes. "We haven't been able to locate her. What if she never wanted to be found? What if she remained anonymous for a reason?"

Devyn thought on his words. Of course by now Hattie Louis had passed on, but Devyn understood what Chase was getting at—respecting Hattie's privacy. Or. . .he was nervous about what they would uncover. Maybe a deep secret that would involve his family. But wasn't that why he began the hunt in the first place? To discover why the name Hattie had brought anguish to his great-grandfather? "What if the result brings closure to your family mystery?"

"It could." He nodded, thoughtfully. "Just want to be sure the outcome is worth digging up another person's secrets."

"What if her remaining in the shadows wasn't her fault? What if she wants her story brought to light?"

"That's a possibility too." His lips tilted in that familiar smile she was beginning to adore. "Let's keep searching then."

She opened her mouth to reply, but a teenage girl trailed by a young man about the same age approached their table. Their adolescent eyes on Devyn.

The girl wore a bashful expression and stroked the length of her long, dark ponytail. "Are you her? I mean, are you Devyn?"

No. No, no, no. She wasn't ready for this. Not now. "I am."

"See?" The other teen, the girl's boyfriend, Devyn assumed, nudged her shoulder. "I knew it was her."

"I wasn't sure until we got close." The girl released a nervous giggle. "You look different in person than on Space Station. But I think you're prettier without all that." She motioned in front of her face and Devyn got her meaning. All that makeup. Fakeness. "But you should totally come back. Everyone is calling for you. Even T-Man is—"

The boyfriend's brown eyes widened. "Aubrey, don't bring him up."

She waved him off. "Maybe he's sorry for what he did. Though gotta say, that was wicked cruel."

Deep breaths. In. Out. They're only kids. But oh, that curious look Chase sent her turned her milkshake to concrete in her stomach. She pressed a hand to her abdomen to quell the nausea.

"Can I take a selfie with you?" Aubrey slid her phone from her pocket like a gunslinger, but Devyn would rather face a revolver than the threat of her face being plastered all over Space Station.

"I—I don't think. . ." But no other words would budge. It was like her tongue had fainted.

"Sorry, guys." Chase stood. "But this is our song." He gave Devyn a convincingly besotted look. "I promised to dance with her."

The kids shared a confused glance, especially since the song the DJ was playing was "The Chicken Dance." Chase seemed to realize a little too late but held his features as if the silly birdie music was truly *their* song.

The teens kindly took the hint and stepped aside. Chase held out his hand, beckoning her, and while her fingers trembled with the residue of the shaky moment, her lips pulled into a grateful smile.

He escorted her to the dance floor, dodging a spirited elbow belonging to an old lady flapping her pretend wings. Someone clucked loud, and Chase winced. "This has to be the most unromantic gesture I've ever done."

She disagreed. He'd thrown her a lifeline. He'd realized her distress and, without hesitation, had come to her aid in the sweetest way. In her eyes, it was remarkably romantic.

Chase took in the surrounding scene with an exaggerated shrug. "I promised you a dance, and I'm a man of my word." He waited until the next round of movements started and joined in.

Surprised laughter burst from her lips.

Those teens had exposed her. Devyn should be yanking Chase's hand and dragging him to the pilothouse. But at the moment, she didn't feel like running away, hiding. She shoved her anxiety overboard and shook her tail feathers with the best of them.

They flapped and wiggled through the entire song, and by the end, Devyn's side hurt from laughing. Chase rewarded her with a beaming grin. Neither of them made a move to leave the dance floor but waited for the next song, which could have been anything since the DJ was taking requests.

The strums of Tony Bennet's "The Way You Look Tonight" crooned through the speakers, and Chase raised his brows in question. Devyn needed no further invitation. She moved to wrap her arms around his neck, but instead Chase reached for her hand and curled an arm around her waist, imitating the waltzing stance she'd done that day on the stern.

She inclined her face to peer into his. "Are you trying to upstage my imaginary beau?"

"Of course I am." His hooded gaze paired handsomely with his lopsided smile. "Is it working?"

"Maybe." She rested her cheek on his shoulder, breathing in his cologne. But the niggle in her chest made the blissful moment short-lived. "I suppose I owe you an explanation."

His fingers caressed her lower back. "No, you don't owe me anything."

His warm words thawed her frozen fear. She lifted her head. The soft grays in his eyes were like her favorite wool blanket—comfortable and cozy. "I told you I was engaged, and my fiancé ended the relationship in a horrifying way."

He nodded and adjusted his grip to hold her closer.

"My fiancé was Travis Leeman."

His brows shot north, but he then schooled his surprise. "The guy that created Space Station?"

"Not all of it. Space Station was originally my idea. But you would never know, because he never gave me credit. I coded it. But he funded the entire thing and promoted it. And he was the mastermind behind our videos." Devyn shuddered. "Remember when we first met, you said I looked familiar?"

His gaze was intense, as if he saw something in her, deeper than those superficial videos. "The girl on those posts is different than the one I'm dancing with."

"I'm glad you think so." She allowed a small smile. "Travis wanted me to act and look sexy. He picked my outfits." Almost all skin-tight and revealing. "Preferred me to wear my makeup thick and spider legs on my eyes."

His mouth quirked a smile. "Spider legs?"

"Fake lashes." Not that she was against false lashes in general, but the idea that Travis wouldn't let her go out in public without them made her despise them. Now she only wore a bit of eye makeup and lip gloss. "He even made me talk an octave lower."

Chase's eyes flashed. "You're kidding."

"Nope. Sultry and hot. That's what he required, and that's what I gave him." Day after day. Video after video. "I thought at first it was no big deal. We were trying to launch our baby, wanting it to be a success. But then Travis started getting more controlling. All those videos were supposed to appear like *us* in real life, but he scripted it all."

His voice dropped with his gaze. "I've only seen one of your videos."

"The breakup one?"

He nodded and lifted his chin, something unreadable in his eyes. "I'm sorry he did that to you."

"Nothing like dumping your girl in front of millions of viewers." Devyn should have realized something was majorly wrong that day. He'd never recorded anything unscripted. She'd thought maybe he was finally being spontaneous, transparent. But no. She was just another gimmick to get even more clicks, more subscribers. "Now you see why I can't stand Slate."

His Adam's apple bobbed. "The jerk used a Slate poem to end things with you."

She stilled. "Not just to end it, but to slam me. He told the world *I* was the one who changed *him*. As if I took advantage of him, when it was the other way around." The words of that poem had haunted her.

I'm letting you go because our souls never reflected each other. Every moment spent with you cost me more and more of myself until I didn't recognize my own image. So it's better for you to be the stranger than to never know my own heart again.

But at that devastating moment, Devyn had been too shocked to defend herself. She'd just stood there like an idiot, tears streaming down her face. It had taken all that was in her to scurry out the door, as the cameraman chased her to her car.

"The video went crazy viral. Travis invented a terrible hashtag—DitchingDevyn."

Chase's jaw tightened. His eyes flickered with harnessed anger, and Devyn felt oddly comforted. "He had no right." Though his features were rigid, he held her a little tighter, sending a wave of comfort stretching through her. "He was never worthy of you."

The song ended. Chase led her by the hand back to the table. Only this time he claimed the chair directly beside hers, rather than opposite, as if placing himself as a protector between her and the rest of the world.

"I should've seen it coming." Her gaze fell to their locked hands. Her fingers fit so perfectly within his. "Travis charmed his way to get everything in life, me included. But then he turned his focus on the camera. He noticed viewers liked grand gestures. Everything was a publicity stunt to gain more subscribers—like giving me a Tesla, buying me a penthouse apartment. All for show. Of course, the biggest stunt was breaking up with me. It's the most watched video." She raised her lashes and hazarded a glance at Chase. "I guess people love drama."

"Not all people." His fingers gently squeezed hers.

"After that I shut down all my social media accounts and basically logged out of life for a time."

"Until you had your river dream."

Her gaze clung to his. "Yes."

With his other hand, he pushed a tendril of hair behind her ear and his fingertips traced the curve of her jaw. "I'm glad you were still able to dream after the nightmare you had."

Devyn's breath rippled in her chest at his touch. "I had to discover what real love was. What I had with Travis wasn't it. He never did tell me he loved me. He'd say he wanted me. Needed me, even. But that's not the same."

"It's selfishness." Chase's face turned thoughtful. "But people are often confused where love is concerned. Many don't know what it is."

"Funny thing is, I've been taught what love is all my life, but never realized it until this happened to me."

His brow creased and she smiled.

"Love is bold."

The inquisitive bend to his brow encouraged her to continue. "It doesn't cower, but expresses itself. Think of Jesus. What He did on the cross was bold. He gave His life without any guarantee that anyone would love Him back. It was daring and beautiful." What was that verse in Romans? Something about while people were still sinners, Christ had died for them.

Her date squirmed. And no wonder. She'd just preached a sermon, but she wouldn't apologize. She'd told him before about her faith, and if they were going to continue with—whatever this was between them—he needed to know that she and Jesus were a package deal.

She'd made the mistake of abandoning her relationship with God in pursuit of Travis. She would never make that error in judgment again.

Chapter 17

$\mathcal{D}$evyn and Chase walked hand-in-hand under the cityscape lights toward her apartment, the scene seeming straight out of a nineties romcom.

"Thank you for my song." Devyn broke the comfortable stretch of silence.

The glimmer in Chase's eyes, framed by dark, thick lashes, really wasn't fair for a girl who had a weak immunity to charm. "Which one?"

She laughed, catching his meaning. The chicken dance had been hysterical and special in its own right, but she'd referred to what happened after their intimate conversation about her breakup. "I've never had someone dedicate a song to me." There was a designated number for passengers to text a request. The baldheaded disk jockey had announced, "*A certain someone here dedicates this next one to his Dream Girl.*" Chase had sent her a mischievous smile and on cue, the song "River of Dreams" thrummed throughout the ballroom.

Chase shrugged as if it were no big deal, but the warmth in his expression said otherwise.

He'd taken her in his arms, but this time, he'd gone all 1940s style by twirling her, spinning her out then curling her back to him. Of course, she'd spoiled his smoothness by stumbling into him, then stepping on his foot. But her clumsiness hadn't broken the sweetness of the moment. Or the fun of it. They'd smiled at each other through the dance, and in true exaggerated fashion, he dipped her at the end.

Her fingers tingled at the thought of his toned muscles and harnessed strength.

They paused at the crosswalk, and Devyn pushed the WALK button. "I haven't laughed that much in a long time."

"I liked hearing it."

"You did?" Why his confession caught her off guard, she didn't know. Maybe it was the sincerity in his voice when she was so used to his playful tone. Or it could be the heady feeling from just being in his presence. Or the simple fact that her laugh was nothing spectacular—not the sexy throaty sound Travis had demanded from her, or even gracefully melodic like some other women. Just a plain, unremarkable laugh.

"Yes." He leaned closer, his breath stirring wisps of hair at her temple. "There's a lot of things I like about you."

Her heart went full WWE mode against the cage of her ribs. "I can say the same," was all she could breathe out. She angled toward him, matching his stance.

It could be illusions of nightfall, but the grays of his eyes burned darker. The smolder lingering beneath his charcoal lashes was enough to draw her on her toes, closer. The light changed, signaling them to walk, breaking their moment. Chase squeezed her hand, and they crossed the street. Disappointment feathered across her shoulders and settled in with surprising weight. Had she really wanted Chase to kiss her?

It wasn't quite ten o'clock, the city still abuzz. With the Cardinal's game just ending, traffic clogged the streets and people made their way to the parking garages.

Devyn adjusted her purse on her shoulder and made sure it was zipped as a precaution. "I just live over—" She stumbled to a halt.

Cameramen. Reporters.

Dozens of them hovered outside her building, like circling vultures ready to swoop on their prey. Her bones locked, unmoving. "No. Please, no."

Chase's hand settled on the small of her back. "Has this happened before?"

She blinked, hoping this was some strange hallucination from her sugar overdose. "They've never come to my place. Not even after Travis broke up with me. They only hounded him." Which had been fine by her. Travis adored the spotlight.

Chase's chest broadened as if he were bracing to take the weight of the situation solely upon his squared shoulders. "Do you think those teens posted on Space Station?"

"Possibly." Some people loved snatching a few minutes of fame. "I can't go in there." She retreated a step. Then another.

"You don't have to." The calming lilt of his voice drew her gaze from the media hornets to his reassuring eyes. "But you have no reason to fear them. You've done nothing wrong."

He was right. Just like Mitch always said. She had no reason to flee. If she ran now, who was to say they wouldn't keep badgering her?

But could she face them?

She inhaled deep, and something stirred within her. It was words. Words she'd recited as a kid swept to the forefront of her mind. *Perfect love drives out fear.* And that love was embedded in her soul. "Love is bold." She murmured the phrase she'd said to Chase only a few hours ago. With God, she could face hard things.

"I won't leave your side." Chase strengthened his grip, still gentle but sure.

"Let's do this." Her wobbly ankles protested, but she forced her legs into motion. Each step forward a declaration against the fear that had controlled her for the past year.

No more hiding.

A short man with a terrible goatee saw her first. "Devyn Asbury, is it true you're returning to Space Station?"

She knew better than to acknowledge their probing questions. No matter what she said, her words would get twisted. Flashes from cameras shuttered, reducing her vision. She was sure Chase was blinded as well. Yet their determined paces didn't hitch.

"Who's this man you're with?" Another voice—feminine this time—hollered from the side. "Does this mean the rumors about you and Travis getting back together are false?"

The crazy impulse to kiss Chase and send a clear message sluiced through her, but she wouldn't dare take advantage of Chase that way. She'd been on that end. Any intimacy between them—if there was to be—was not for the cameras. She'd learned that lesson too. Their relationship would not be for public consumption.

More questions sailed her direction, which she ignored. She and Chase reached the steps. As if realizing they were getting nowhere with Devyn, the scavengers changed strategies and fired verbal darts at Chase. A muscle leapt in his tight jaw as he yanked the front door open.

Hans, the security guard, ushered them inside with a growl and glower directed at the disappointed horde.

"I'm sorry, Hans." Devyn sounded as winded as she felt. "I had no idea."

He gave a stern nod, his watchful gaze never leaving the entrance.

Devyn stole a glance at Chase, who seemed completely unfazed by the whole incident. She, on the other hand... It would probably take several vintage films to return her blood pressure to non-threatening levels. She shifted her attention to the fiftysomething security guard. "I hope this is the first and last time of craziness."

Hans grunted. "I don't think any of those leeches got inside, but I was away for a bit helping another resident. Do you want me to see you to your place?"

"I'll do it," Chase offered. "That way you won't have to leave your post." He gestured to the throng. Several of them had left, but there was still a good ten to fifteen people loitering on the steps.

Hans looked to Devyn for the *okay*. She gave him a smile, shaky at best.

She and Chase entered the elevators, and Devyn sighed against the wall. "That was unexpected."

Chase remained close as if one of the cameramen would rappel from the ceiling. But Devyn didn't mind. His nearness was comforting. She stabbed the PH button.

"You weren't joking about living in the penthouse," Chase remarked.

"Nope. That's why we met at Mom's house instead of my place. I knew you'd have questions."

"And here I thought it was because you couldn't trust yourself around me."

"Well, that too," she teased back, grateful the moment had lightened. Her heart still hammered in her chest, but at least she wasn't so rattled that she couldn't joke around with Chase.

The elevator dinged open and her door came in view.

"Sorry for the lousy ending to our date." Of all the crazy incidents that could have happened. "I'm thankful you pressed me to face them. It was ..."

"Liberating?"

She smiled. "Yeah." Oh, she could kiss him. But with her emotions all wacky, she wasn't certain that would be the best choice. She leaned against her doorframe.

Chase's gaze zeroed on her. "Is this the part where I tell you I had a good time? And ask you out again?"

Her heart lurched. "Only if you want to."

He took a step closer and palmed the wall behind her. "I do. Very much."

What was that about not kissing him? Because she'd completely forgot the reason, especially with him so kissably close. His head lowered, and she tipped her face toward his.

The doorknob clicked behind her. What in the world? She jolted and clung to Chase's arm.

The hinges whispered. The door yawned open. A shock of blond hair rattled her vision before the rest came into focus.

Travis.

Chapter 18

Hattie

My eyelids cracked open. Whispers of dawn tiptoed across the cabin floor. Another day, but this one held significance. For I was now twenty-one years old.

Where most women would be celebrating the day of their birth in a parlor crammed with family and presents, I'd be coursing the river. Two excursions were scheduled back to back, leaving no time for dawdling.

I threw my legs over the bunk and jumped down like I'd done when I was ten. My toes twinged at the impact, clearly not in support of my youthful gesture. I reached into the narrow closet, skimming past Miss Wendall's faded dresses and grabbing the last hanger on the wardrobe bar. My thumb brushed the chiffon fabric of my lilac frock with burgundy trim. The uncertainty I'd sparred with last evening returned with fresh boxing gloves and eager swings at my confidence. Perhaps I should wear one of my drab dresses. Though it was tradition for me to don my best frock on my birthday, I wasn't certain Duffy would remember the importance of today. After the attack on the Louisville wharf ten days ago, he'd been more aloof than I'd ever seen him. He'd kept to his cabin, allowing Jack to bear most of the leadership duties.

With Duffy's neglect came Jack's attentiveness. He'd hardly left my side during freight checks, as if he feared another gun-toting villain would materialize any moment. During crew meals, he'd claim the seat beside mine, engaging me in conversation as if I were the only one in the room.

With a contented sigh, I snatched my prettiest frock from the hanger and made myself ready for the day. My normally rebellious hair decided to cooperate, allowing me to sweep the sides back and secure it with a matching ribbon. I caught sight of the shears in Miss Wendall's sewing basket that sat atop the wooden two-drawer dresser we shared. By society's standards the length of my hair—a little past my shoulders—labeled me out of style, but the last time I'd attempted to bob my honey-blond locks, it looked like I'd given the task to a toddler. Better to have a longer hairstyle than an uneven one.

With a shake of my head, I made my way toward Duffy's stateroom. We always shared a special breakfast on my birthday, just me and him without the fuss of the crew. The recollection of Duffy's recent behavior slowed my steps. Maybe Miss Wendall had seen to the preparations. Or maybe I was going to encounter my first disappointment of the day.

My knuckles rapped a tentative knock.

"Only birthday girls are allowed to enter."

The air whooshed from my lungs at Duffy's standard reply. His withdrawn mood hadn't carried over to today. *Thank You, God.* My fingers curled over the knob, and with a relieved smile, I opened the door. "Good morning, Duffy."

The aroma of blueberry hotcakes sent my stomach growling.

Duffy must have heard the rumblings, for he laughed. "Miss Wendall was up early making your favorite breakfast."

"I must thank her later." I pecked a kiss on his cheek and sat across from him, claiming the chair Jack had sat in the day I'd washed his wound. The day he'd told me I was unlike any other woman he'd known. My heart swelled at the memory.

Steam climbed from the coffeepot's spout, and I poured us both a cup. Duffy accepted with a more steady hand than usual. His eyes seemed brighter too. Maybe the extra time he'd spent in his room had improved his health.

We ate in contented silence, the occasional holler from a deckhand below interrupting the quiet. After we had our fill, Duffy stood and rummaged around his closet, emerging with an armful of boxes. Instead of elegant paper and ribbons, the presents had been wrapped in old newspapers tied with twine. To me, the packages couldn't be more beautiful.

"My girl only turns twenty-one once." There was a somber hitch in his tone, but before I could question him on it, he nodded at the table, still cluttered with the remains of our breakfast.

I stacked the dishes onto the tray, making a clearing for the gifts. Duffy set them down and reclaimed his seat, waiting for me to begin unwrapping. It could be the shifting of light through the door's window, but Duffy seemed hunched in his chair. Where were the traces of life and strength so visible earlier?

Sadness crashed into me with the force of turbulent waters. I blinked, hoping to keep the emotion from flooding into my eyes. Forcing a smile, I opened the first box. My fingers stilled on the lid's edges. "Duffy." My tone was breathless as I gawked at the silver-plated vanity set—a brush, a handheld mirror, and a powder box. Never mind I'd never dusted my face with cosmetics in my life, the items had to have cost a small fortune. "I've never owned anything this expensive." The gold necklace and helm pendent hanging from my neck had been my sole extravagance since I'd turned eighteen, when Duffy had gifted it.

He dismissed my words with a shrug. "If I had my inheritance, I could've bought you a townhouse on Fifth Avenue, New York, but this felt good to purchase." A tremor of satisfaction rippled in his craggy voice, making me love him more.

Oh the things he'd given up for love of the rivers. It had cost him a world of luxury, but his choices had allowed him to navigate his own course rather than have it set by his family.

"I admire you, Duffy. I couldn't have had a better example. Nor a better father than you."

His eyes shined with emotion, yet his mouth pressed into a straight line as if my words made him sad. Maybe he was disappointed that it had taken this long for me to acknowledge it.

"I know I've never openly said it, but I've always considered you my papa."

His vein-bulged hand settled on mine. Callouses from years of being a riverman scraped rough against my skin. "Let's not get all sniffly. You have two more gifts to open."

I gave him a warm smile and opened the second. Jeweled hair combs. Rubies arranged as flower petals glistened in the light pouring in from outside. I trembled at the thought of touching something so beautiful. "Stunning." But where on earth would I wear them?

I didn't need anything this lavish. But maybe Duffy had remembered what his sister received on her twenty-first birthday and wanted me to experience it. My heart softened. I wouldn't protest these expensive gifts, for Duffy's sake. "Thank you. I'm overwhelmed."

"Last one." He nudged the final present my way. The box was twice the size of the others. I made quick work of the paper and lifted the lid.

"A new dress!" I unleashed a grin, but I took in the frock, and it too was fancy. Ivory silk fabric trimmed with delicate lace around the capped sleeves and neckline. I couldn't wear a near-white gown about the boat. It would turn a darker shade of ash at every hiss of steam from the stacks.

All these elaborate gifts didn't make sense. Duffy had always been practical. Perhaps his mind had been affected as well as his body. That would explain the recent moodiness. I looked over and realized he was waiting for my response. "I don't know what to say."

"I realize it's different than other years. I made mistakes by giving you tools and books. It's about time you got something just because it's pretty."

"Everything is beautiful. Thank you."

"Maybe. . ." He shifted in his seat. "This is a good start to a hope chest."

A hope chest? I'd never heard him speak along those lines. And his eyes were shiny, as if I was going to be married and gone tomorrow. Or maybe he thought *he* was the one who was soon to be gone. Did he think he was dying? It was more than I could bear. "Duffy, is there something you're not telling me? I feel like—"

Voices resounded from below. The men were singing "Happy Birthday."

"That's for you, my dear." Duffy smirked as if he'd planned the entire thing. Maybe he had.

My thoughts swirled from all the shifts in emotions during the past half hour, but I managed to move out the stateroom door. All the crew from Clem to Ludwig lined the deck and held their caps over their hearts. My gaze landed on Face, who winked at me. Jack's expression was something else altogether, as if he were the only one serenading me. My heart flipped at the pleasant sound of his tenor voice. The song ended, and they whooped and hollered.

"Thank you, gentlemen!" I blew an exaggerated kiss and Face pretended to catch it.

He cupped his mouth. "I told you that kiss belonged to me."

"You have to share it." I rolled my eyes and turned my back just as Jack was climbing the staircase toward me.

His sweeping gaze set free a thousand locust wings in my stomach. I hadn't worn this dress around him before, and his eyes, as clear and blue as the sky above me, were warm with interest.

He paused at the top of the steps, only a few yards from me. "It's not fair for you to look so fetching. Not when I have to report to the wing bridge and don't have adequate time to spend with you."

I believe Jack Marshall had just flirted with me. A flush of pleasure raced down my neck, spreading down my arms.

He stepped closer. "You didn't tell me you were turning twenty-one today."

I inclined my chin and adopted Miss Wendall's British accent. " 'Tis not becoming for a lady to reveal her age."

His chuckle was well worth my awful impersonation. "That doesn't give me much time to get you a present." His crooked smile flattened, his eyes taking on that determined edge I'd grown to admire. "But I promise I will."

❧

My workday began with prepping food in the galley for the cruises, then scaling the flights of steps to play the calliope to welcome the passengers as they purchased tickets. I pressed the final key to "Swanee River" and rushed to the landing bridge to help Jack count every person boarding.

Each excursion felt like a mini-adventure, and though I'd been on hundreds of cruises, the churn of the paddlewheel and the shriek of the steam whistle never became ordinary.

It was midday before I realized I'd left my gifts in Duffy's cabin. He hadn't remarked about it, but I didn't want to appear ungrateful.

The *Idlewild* had a couple more hours of cruising and enamoring the Carrolton crowd. Duffy had resumed his duties and now seemed in good spirits. When I'd last seen him, he was explaining the workings of the piston arm to a group of children.

With quick steps, I made my way to the texas roof and to the captain's stateroom. I studied the gifts again. So refined. So unlike me. The idea of handling these expensive tokens forced me to the washbasin to scrub my fingers.

Duffy's coats were haphazardly hanging in his closet, and my heart tore. Simple tasks like tidying his cabin were getting harder for him.

With quick movements, I straightened his grooming area, then rehung his extra uniform and suit jacket. I bumped a hanger, and his trousers puddled onto the floor. Sighing, I scooped them up, but a piece of paper slipped from the pocket.

A letter.

The word *Pittsburgh* seized my attention. I snatched the paper from the floor and read it.

> *I know the risk you're taking but it won't be without reward.*
> *I trust I don't need to remind you to keep quiet. I realize it's hard*
> *with the federal agent snooping around. Stick to the plan and he'll*
> *be none the wiser. Too much depends on you and your delivery.*
> *Off-load before Pittsburgh. I'll be in touch with the name of the*
> *contact who will be meeting you.*
>
> G. Jones

Who was this Jones person? I read the note again, a fierce shiver chasing a chill down to my fingertips. Contact? Delivery? Risk? Everything pointed to one conclusion, but my brain wouldn't accept it. My heart wouldn't allow it.

Duffy couldn't be the one Jack was looking for. It defied everything I knew about him. The honorable steamboat captain had always been a stickler for the rules. He would never risk his captain's license for a few barrels of liquor.

Would he?

He *had* been more distant since Jack had come aboard. This Jones gentleman was aware that Jack was a fed and here on a mission, while also admonishing Duffy to "stick to the plan."

My breath stabbed my chest. The evidence was too blaring for it to be anything else.

Duffy was a rumrunner.

Chapter 19

Devyn

*D*evyn hadn't heard from her ex in almost a year, and now he stood in her doorway, all casual-like, as if he hadn't fed her heart into the social media shredder. His gaze roamed her body, and that familiar note of approval—that masculine regard she'd once craved—reflected in his brown eyes.

"What are you doing here?" Her voice was absurdly calm. Yet there must have been some trace of emotion in her eyes, for Travis blinked and his lazy smirk crumbled into a frown.

"We need to talk." He noticed Chase standing behind her. "Alone."

She barred her arms in a tight fold across her chest, barricading her pounding heart. "You have nothing to say to me that hasn't already gone viral. Now leave your key and go, or I'll have security drag you out."

"C'mon, Dev. A couple minutes." He held out his hands in a plea. "That's all I want."

All I want. How many times had he said those three words to her? Everything had always been about what Travis Leeman wanted. And with zero consideration for others. Her jaw clenched until her back teeth ached.

"Please?"

Tension snaked through her. She knew him well enough that if he didn't say his piece now, he'd badger her until he could. "Five minutes. That's it."

Travis gave a satisfied nod and strolled back into her penthouse as if he lived there.

Ugh. What a way to ruin a first date.

Chase cupped her shoulder and leaned close. "I don't want to leave you. After what you told me about him tonight, I really want to crush his jugular. But I'll go if you want." Struggle burned the silver flecks in his eyes deeper, no doubt his protective nature at odds with his considerate side. He removed his touch and stepped away, as if giving her space to make a decision.

She reached toward him, and he caught her hand in his. "Give me five minutes, then come in. That'll ensure Travis leaves."

With one last steady look into Chase's face, she took in a lungful of air and entered her penthouse, leaving him standing on the other side of the door. Travis lounged on her sofa, directly in the center, making it so if she sat on either side, she'd be touching him. Might as well stand. Looming over her ex-fiancé provided her a weird sense of advantage

Their lifestyle had been demanding, and while she was no longer tied to it, she could see its effect on him. Like the faint lines rippling his forehead. The man still dressed like he'd just emerged from a GQ photo shoot, but he didn't fill out his clothes as he had before. He was thinner.

"Okay, Travis, out with it."

He leaned his elbows on his knees, clasping his hands together in the space between. "I tried to get ahold of you, but all your accounts are disabled."

"Can you blame me?"

"And you changed your number."

"And now I need to change my locks and alarm code," she said in a dry tone. "Though I never considered you would add breaking and entering to your skillset."

Travis's gaze floated around the room. "I'm actually surprised you kept this place."

"Yeah, well, considering Space Station was pretty much my idea *and* my work, I figured I should get something out of it."

"You're right." The sheepish expression looked foreign on his face. "It was jerkish of me."

"Which part?" She popped a hand on her hip. "Cutting me out of everything I worked for or jilting me in front of millions? Or is it billions now?"

"I deleted the video."

Her brows spiked, then flattened just as quickly. "I'm shocked you'd remove your most viewed post."

"It wasn't. The proposal is the most popular."

"Oh that's right. I even had to share *that* moment with all your followers." The words she'd swept into the dark corners of her heart axed through the barred gates, demanding to come to the light. "How could you? All that time, you knew how uncomfortable I was sharing our life with the camera. You cheapened what we had together, cheapened me. But still, you broadcasted our entire relationship."

"Not all of it." His suggestive tone punctured her flimsy composure.

She'd lost more than her heart to Travis. Thank God for His forgiveness, but oh, what she wouldn't give for a do-over, for a chance to correct her mistakes.

"What I'm trying to say, Dev, is I shouldn't have ended it that way. I'm sorry."

Her jaw slacked, lips parting. Travis never apologized. Not once in all her years of knowing him. It had always been excuses. Always something or someone else to blame. "You said what you wanted, now please leave. And take your entourage with you."

"Entourage?" His innocent tone and the slight widening of his eyes almost seemed convincing.

But she wasn't fooled. "All the cameramen and reporters outside this building. We got bombarded on the way in, thanks to you." She should have realized something more was at play. The media continually followed Travis. He thrived on their attention. Just like all his other ploys. Which made her wonder. . . "This isn't another one of your schemes, is it? Where's Stu?" That devoted cameraman trailed Travis like a shadow. "Because if he's secretly filming this right now, so help me—"

"Stu's not here." Travis stood and stepped toward her. "No one's filming anything. C'mon, Dev, give me some credit."

"I don't have to give you anything. Again." She held up a ringless hand. "We are nothing to each other. And I'm pretty sure your five minutes was up five minutes ago."

She turned on her heel toward the door to usher him out, but his fingers wrapped her wrist.

The door opened and Chase entered. His gaze dropped to her ex's grip on her arm, and his expression went from placid to thunderous. He strode toward Devyn, his hand flexing at his side reminding her of his throat-punching remark in the hallway. Surely Chase would keep his cool, even if his eyes were hot like molten steel.

Travis dropped her wrist and stepped back.

She gave Chase a quick nod, letting him know she was okay, then leveled her glare on her ex. "You need to—"

"Come back," Travis blurted.

"What?" She hugged her arms to her middle, her fingers rubbing the spot of his touch. He'd left no mark, but the residue of his manipulating manner pricked like fire ants on her skin.

"Come back to Space Station. People are spamming the feedback logs, begging you to return."

She shifted her weight from foot to foot. The longer she stood, the more her shoes pinched, but her cramping toes were nothing compared to the tightness wringing her chest. "Travis, you can afford the very best. Hire some genius to do the coding. You don't need me."

Chase's scowl remained aimed at Travis. Devyn couldn't see Travis turning violent, but then she'd never imagined him ditching her the way he had either.

"Come back." His low murmur had once stirred her longing. Now it gave her low-key nausea. "I miss you."

"And I miss the kid who had a maxipad stuck to his back. But he's gone. Fame destroyed him."

Chase shot her a confused look. But Travis knew exactly what she meant.

Her ex shoved his hands deep into the pockets of his designer jeans. "I made the biggest mistake when I broke up with you."

She scoffed. "Because Space Station suffered?"

"No, not because of Space Station."

He could claim that all he wanted, but she knew better. Everything was about that dumb site. That was why he was here. The public wanted her back, and Travis was nothing if not swayed by the public. He'd finally gotten the attention he desired from the world, and now he was losing it.

"Okay, so the site has slid in ratings compared to other media platforms, but we're gearing for a comeback. I've contracted heavy hitters to promote it. Some A-list celebrities. And I'm close to securing Slate to reveal his identity on my station."

Fingernails biting into her palms, she inclined her chin. "Looks like you have everything in order then, so you certainly don't need me."

"Dev, don't be like this." He reached to touch her face, but she shrank away.

Chase's jaw hardened and he widened his stance. Devyn placed a hand on his bicep, his muscle tense beneath her fingertips. She gave an I-can-take-care-of-it look, then faced Travis. "I've moved on. I have another job. One I love."

His brows furrowed. "A wedding coordinator for that decrepit boat? Planning paltry dinners?" He gestured toward the dining room where she had all her charts and spreadsheets for the ball on the table. How long had he been in her apartment?

"The *boat* is called the *Belle*, and it's not decrepit." Her tone was low and sharp. "The answer is no, Travis."

"You can't be satisfied with something like that, babe." And now he used an endearment? The man must really be desperate. "You have too much talent to settle for something like that. Come back to me." His voice cracked with emotion, but so much more had been broken between them.

Come back? Her heart wouldn't survive Travis's careless handling, his constant deceit. She recalled the final months of their relationship. The lies murmured in her ear had dripped one by one into her soul, flooding, until all she'd thought of life was a falsehood. No. She didn't need him to be happy. And adventure wasn't pretending in front of a camera but living under God's divine smile. She faced Travis, a thousand retorts stampeding her lips, but Chase beat her to it.

"I believe you heard her answer." He took a bold step between them, his chest broad, his glower intimidating.

"Who are you again?" Travis snapped. "So what if you had a few dates with her. I know Devyn better than anyone."

Ha! He'd never taken the time to know her, just the Devyn he'd created.

"She's capable of making her own decisions." Chase ignored his snide comment. "And she made it clear they don't involve you."

Travis tensed, his golden complexion flushing red. "You have no idea who you're—"

"Enough." Her voice rose above his, silencing him. "Goodbye, Travis. There's nothing more to discuss."

With a downward slash of his hand, Travis strode toward the door. His long strides came to a stop, and he glanced over his shoulder. "Think about it, Dev." His gaze trained on her and softened, his tone strengthening with hope. "We were good together."

She flipped her hair over her shoulder. "Leave your key."

Chapter 20

*D*evyn fanned her fingers on her collarbone, her pulse thudding at the hollow dip in her throat. "What. Just. Happened?"

"Your ex tried to win you back." Chase nodded toward the door Travis had retreated through only a moment ago. "In more ways than one."

"What person breaks into his ex's apartment?" At least he'd returned the key. She eyed it with suspicion. Would he have made a duplicate? "I'm going to write a memo to change the alarm code and staple it to my forehead." She regarded Chase with an apologetic smile. "Sorry about all this."

"Nothing to forgive. Glad I could be here for you." Sincerity laced his voice.

Chase's protective demeanor had earned him a forever spot on her all-time admiration list, ranking slightly below her brother and just above the person who'd invented microwave popcorn. "I'm glad you were here too." She kicked off her shoes, her toes flexing in response to their freedom.

Now that Travis was gone, Chase seemed to take his time glancing about her place. "This is really nice."

Devyn plopped her purse on the coffee table. "Thanks. Hopefully a potential buyer would feel the same."

Chase's brows lifted. "Looking to sell?"

"I never asked for this. I'm grateful for a roof over my head, but it doesn't have to be such a swanky one." Her gaze floated from the sleek flooring to the vaulted ceiling to the posh furniture in between.

There was a bemused twist to his lips. "Most women would love a place like this."

"I don't mean to sound ungrateful. It's just my style is much less extravagant." Devyn's taste was rustic and down-to-earth. One day she'd like to design her own living space, minus the luxurious details. "This space is too Travis-y. He furnished it without my input. He's all about control. That's how he operates. Like tonight. He arranged for the press to be here. I'm sure of it."

"Why would he do that?"

"So they would report that he'd gone to my place. So it would appear to the Space Station fan base that he's trying to get me back." A heavy sigh lowered her shoulders. "Just another way to pacify them. He's freaky weird about pleasing the public." She motioned for him to follow her through the living room to the kitchen. "You being with me wasn't something he factored in. You know, I had the crazy thought to kiss you in front of all those reporters."

"Why didn't you?" He stood opposite her, the kitchen island between them. Good thing, because his husky tone was borderline dangerous to her self-control. "It would've disproved any rumor of you two getting back together."

She opened a drawer beneath the counter, grabbed a bag of M&Ms, and tore it open. "This is called eating my feelings."

He gave a compassionate smile.

She offered him some candy, but he declined with a shake of the head. Tonight called for at least two palmfuls of chocolate remedy. "As for the not kissing you part, I didn't because that would be using you." She poured a generous amount into her hand and tossed all of it into her mouth.

He palmed the quartz countertop and leaned forward, his muscles taut, his tattoo on full display. "I would've whole-heartedly complied."

She almost choked before swallowing the mouthful. "Nope. I wouldn't waste our first kiss like that."

"Ah." His slow smile built. "So we're planning on having a first kiss, huh?"

"Um. . .well. I don't know. But if we do, I'm not having the world watch. Oh man. My emotions are all over the place right now." She stuffed more candy into her mouth, her palm growing sticky and multi-colored.

"Understandable." He rounded the counter, moving closer. "Are you okay?"

"I am, actually." The first few weeks after the breakup, Devyn had imagined scenarios of how'd she feel running into Travis. Never had she thought of him being in her apartment.

"Was this the first time you've seen him since. . ."

"He ditched me? Yes." She crumpled the bag and tossed it in the trash. "This was the first."

He gave her elbow a friendly nudge. "You handled yourself like a champ."

"Well, one doesn't prepare for situations like this." She turned for the sink and rinsed the candy residue from her hands, wishing she could wash away her memories of her time with Travis just as easily.

"What's the deal with the maxipad?"

She cringed. "About that. . . Travis and I went to the same high school. Though he was a few grades ahead of me. He came from a wealthy family but was kinda nerdy. His face was covered in acne. He was thin as a toothpick. A terrible dresser. The guy was a bully target." She flipped off the faucet and grabbed a hand towel. "Some football players stuck a pad to his back. He had no clue. Everyone was pointing and laughing as he walked down the hall. When I saw, I pulled him into a vacant classroom and yanked it off." She tossed the towel onto the counter and faced Chase in time to see the flash of his dimples.

"Of course you would. You're bighearted like that."

With an answering smile, she opened the fridge and retrieved two Dasanis. "Want a water? Or I could make you a coffee? Espresso?"

"Water's perfect."

She handed him the bottle.

"Thanks." He twisted off the top and took a swig.

"After that, Travis and I became friends. Occasionally hung out. Then he graduated, and I didn't see him until my sophomore year at U of L. I hardly recognized him. He'd filled out, lost the acne, and gained a whole bunch of charm. I found out we were both majoring in computer programming." She took a drink, the crisp water slaking her thirst. "It made sense to pick up where we left off in high school. We started as friends then things went further. Then of course we launched Space Station together."

"Which was a success." Chase downed the rest of his water and crumpled the bottle.

"Was it though?" She relieved him of the trash and tossed it in the recycling bin. "Space Station changed him. It's like all the attention and popularity he never had but wanted hit him at once. We didn't take an income the first year. The money from advertisers we poured back into the site, but once it took off—like really took off— I totally lost the man I fell in love with. He became obsessed with work, with public opinion. I faded into the background."

His soft steel eyes locked hers. "Which makes Travis the biggest loser."

"The site is now worth a fortune." She set her bottle on the island. "And from what he has lined up, he'll be back on top again. Especially if he can nab Slate. I mean, everyone's been after this guy for years. Prime time TV, late night shows, magazines."

"What if he doesn't want to reveal his identity?"

Chase had asked a similar question about Hattie earlier on the *Belle*. "This is way different than our research on your picture. Hattie may have had strong reasons for keeping secrets, but Slate? He's all about money. Have you seen him releasing any new books lately? Yeah, the first was a hit, but where is he now?" She leaned against the counter. "The mystery behind his identity might be the only thing he's got going for him. All the more for him to cash in now, right?" It only made sense. "Ten bucks says he'll do it. The guy sounds like a total sellout. He's another walking publicity stunt, just like Travis."

Chase stuffed his hands into his pockets. "How can he be a publicity stunt when he's choosing to remain anonymous?"

"I think it's all strategic. You know, build up the intrigue regarding his identity. He's a total show stealer. *Kentucky Local* all over again."

"Huh?"

"Oh that's my second offense against the famed poet. The *Belle* was supposed to be featured in *Kentucky Local* magazine. But when Slate's book sold two million copies, they gave the spot to him. If that's not enough, the interviewer asked him about the Space Station mogul using his poem to break up with his fiancée. Do you know what Slate said?"

His brows pinched.

"He told the interviewer, 'Well the guy must not have loved her if all it took was one of my poems.'"

Chase winced.

"My thoughts exactly. So I bet ten bucks he'll sell out." She stuck out her hand.

Chase straightened and shook it. "Deal." He held on to her fingers, his thumb caressing her knuckles. "And I make a counteroffer that we stop talking about ex-fiancés and mystery poets."

"Deal." She squeezed his hand and released it. "And you're right. It's unfair to you for us to be talking only about me. Tell me something about you. Anything."

"Sure." He rubbed the back of his neck, his discomfort evident in his detached gaze. "What would you like to know?"

Oh. Wrong move on her part. Last thing she wanted was to make the man uncomfortable, especially since he'd been so sweet to her tonight. With exaggerated taps to her chin, she purposed to correct her error, to keep the conversation light. "Tell me about. . ." She eased closer and folded up the hem of his sleeve, revealing his tattoo, ignoring the surge of pleasure at his nearness. "This ink on your arm."

On closer inspection, she discovered she was mistaken. His tattoo wasn't entirely a compass, only the left side of it. The other half was the face of a pocket watch. With her fingertip, she traced a slow outline of the inky sphere, enamored by the intricate details—the jagged index lines of the compass, the roman numerals ranging from one to six. Her finger stilled on the orienting arrow pointing North. "May our sights always be aimed toward heaven," she murmured.

Chase swallowed. Hard. Did her touch affect him? Or her words?

She pulled her hand away. "Why'd you pick this design?"

"Because it looked cool in the parlor catalog." The corner of his mouth hitched. He was teasing her, returning the moment to its familiar playful state.

She tilted her head in a mock challenge. "I'm two seconds from pinching you again. My mom's not here to protect you this time."

He chuckled and raised his palms in surrender. "Okay, you win." Then his grin dwindled, and a seriousness overtook him. "I got it as a reminder."

"Of what?"

He regarded his tattoo, his mouth flattened to a curious line. "That time is valuable. 'Teach us to number our days, that we may gain a heart of wisdom.'"

Her tiny gasp made his eyes light with amusement. He'd recited a verse from the book of Psalms. "You're a Christian." Her tone came out accusing—not her intention, but— "You told me you weren't a believer."

His light laughter was addicting. "No, I didn't."

She gave him an easy shove. "Yes, you did. I remember it clearly. It was during our road trip when I was talking about my dream."

His grin was all-out mischief. "No, you asked if I was ever divinely led. And I was honest. I've never had a dream like you that led me to God. It was all my failings that brought me to that place."

Her chest lightened. Chase was a believer. What had been a source of strife between her and Travis was something she shared with this man before her.

"May our sights always be aimed toward heaven." Chase repeated her words in that husky way of his. "My time and life course belong to God." He shrugged. "That's why I chose this design."

"I love it." She beamed at him. This evening was ending on a way better note than how it had looked only a half hour ago. "Now follow me. I want to show *you* something." She grabbed his hand and led him through the living room and onto the balcony. "This is my favorite part of the penthouse."

He took in the view with appreciation. "I can see why. It's beautiful. You can see the riverfront."

Devyn inhaled a nice hunk of crisp night air and gazed out. "I never tire of this view."

"I agree." But he wasn't peering out at the water, he was looking at her. "It's breathtaking."

Heat zip-lined her spine. "You think so?"

"Very much. It's hard to peel my gaze away." He slid his arms around her waist, drawing her into an embrace. "Which is probably why I should go."

Well, she wasn't expecting that. She tipped her face toward him, brows lifted in question.

He tightened his grip for one delicious second, then stepped back. "You had a crazy end to your night. I won't take advantage of those emotions."

"Chase Jones." She raised on her toes and kissed his cheek. "I really like you."

"Took you long enough." He quirked a smile. "And likewise, Devyn Asbury."

His phone buzzed, and she eased away so he could fish his cell from his pocket. He glanced at the screen and smiled. "It's a text from my professor friend. He cracked the code."

She sucked in a breath. "What does it say?"

" 'Diamond aboard *Idlewild*,'" he read aloud. " 'Off-load before Pittsburgh whatever means necessary.'"

Chapter 21

Hattie

The sun tucked behind the jagged tree line, hushing daylight's vigor.

Jack's sturdy arms rowed us along the quiet river, paddling away from the *Idlewild*. There was no moonlight excursion due to the town of Carrolton's anniversary celebration tonight. Most crewmen headed up the hill to join the festivities, watch fireworks, and no doubt scour the tobacco market which the town was so famous for.

Instead of joining the men, Jack had asked if I'd take a short journey with him in the dinghy. He'd changed from his uniform into beige trousers paired with a matching vest over a cream-colored shirt. The sleeves had been rolled past his forearms allowing easier movement for working the oars. I hadn't glimpsed him in civilian clothes since the first night we'd met. It was as if he'd removed anything that separated us in station. Tonight, he wasn't the first mate of a steamboat, my superior. He was just Jack.

The metal bucket I'd previously used to slop fish into settled between our feet, holding our picnic dinner.

I tugged the hem of my dress and, careful not to reveal my knees, recrossed my ankles for the fifth time at least. My restless gaze bounced over the still waters. I should be thrilled about this alone time with Jack. Instead, I was troubled.

Because of the letter.

Because Duffy was breaking the law.

And I couldn't tell a soul.

How could I betray the man who'd found me, raised me as his own? He'd devoted years to teaching me the ways of the river, the ways of Jesus.

It made no sense. Duffy wouldn't forsake his morals and partner with a known criminal like Shakes Donovan for a cut of soiled money. Would he? A steamboat captain's salary could be considered enviable. Duffy had always squirreled it away. Or had he? My fingers squeezed the splintery edges of the bench. What if he'd spent it? Lost it somehow? And now, with him retiring he had nothing for us to live on?

But then why purchase those expensive birthday presents?

"Turning twenty-one has made you pensive." Jack's kind voice snapped me from my daze. "I've never seen you so quiet."

How was I to respond? That Duffy was a whiskey smuggler? Jack was a prohibition agent, for goodness' sake! If I leaked word about the letter, Jack would row this dinghy back to the boat and haul Duffy away. Both Jack and Duffy—the two men I admired most—would be plucked from my life in one evening. Fine birthday gift that would be. "I suppose I'm tired."

Not untrue. My mind had been drifting all day with scenarios of Duffy's involvement. And it had taken a toll on both mood and energy.

Jack's smile was comforting, and my fingertips itched to touch it, trace the steady curve, and absorb his strength. "Then I'm glad I stole you for the evening. You could use some time away from the boat."

Jack was such a good man. But so was Duffy. I just couldn't understand it. "Have you ever thought a person was one way—someone you thought you knew really well—only to discover they weren't what you always believed them to be?"

His arms stilled mid-row, elbows locking straight. "Yes."

I leaned forward, mindful not to rock the boat. "What did you do?"

"I confronted them." His somber tone reflected in his eyes. "But it didn't work out as I hoped."

"Oh." I'd thought to question Duffy about the letter, but perhaps that wasn't wise. Though what if this was all a misunderstanding? I could have interpreted the letter wrong. I drummed my fingers along the side of my seat, stopping when a shard of wood pricked my pinky. No, the words had been very clear. Why else would this Jones guy warn Duffy to remain quiet about the *delivery*? And why even mention Jack in the letter if the freight had nothing to do with alcohol? With a grimace, I picked the splinter out of my flesh and flicked the sliver into the water. "How did it all go wrong?"

"She married someone else."

My hands dropped into my lap. "What?"

He resumed rowing, his gaze fastened on the line of ripples extending from the oar. "I was engaged to Gertrude Albright."

"Duffy's great-niece?" Oh dear mercy, why hadn't I heard this before? Two summers ago, Gertrude had married a congressman's son. I'd only met him once on a visit with Duffy. The fella's handsome features and padded bank account made him a dandy of a catch, but not as good a man as Jack Marshall.

"We grew up around each other. In the same circles." His fleeting frown appeared for only a second before tugging into a ghost of a smile. "But then my family lost everything in a bad business decision during the Great War."

My hand pressed to my heart. What a terrible time to lose all. "I had no idea. I'm sorry."

Jack released a humorless laugh. "I had no clue either, until I arrived back from my enlistment. The house was sold. Dad was working at a warehouse and Mother at a textile factory."

My brows lowered. "They never wrote, letting you know?"

"No. I was on the coast at the time. They didn't want to alarm me." He pressed his lips together then relaxed them to expel a shaft of air. "They knew I'd abandon my post to come help. They didn't want me torn between serving my country and loyalty to my family."

I pressed a hand against the ache in my heart. What a sad homecoming for Jack. For him to finally return to his family only to be met with devastation and ruin. "How that must've shocked you to find everything different."

"It wasn't easy." Something shifted in his eyes. "But the peculiar thing was, the loss brought my parents closer to each other and to God. They called it their wake-up moment. I've never seen them happier than when they'd lost everything and found each other and a faith in something greater than themselves."

"In a way that's beautiful." Their circumstance reminded me of a scripture Duffy had often quoted—what good was it to gain the whole world and forfeit one's soul?

"Not everyone viewed it like you. When Gertrude realized my family's drop in society, she dropped me as well."

Not surprising. Duffy's family had all but banished him because of his *reprehensible* choice in profession. And I couldn't say my heart held much love for Gertrude Albright. She'd tolerated our visits because she had to, but she hadn't bothered to hide her disgust with me. She was beautiful, elegant, and wealthy.

Everything I wasn't.

A piece of my heart withered. Now I knew the kind of woman that captured Jack's attention. I couldn't compete or attain that status. "I'm sorry she did that to you."

Jack shrugged. "We wouldn't have worked out. I didn't realize how shallow she was. Love is more than the rung you cling to on the social ladder. She didn't want to take the risk with me. Her life was privileged and coveted."

Though Jack would have treated her like a queen. Foolish girl. "But isn't that what love's about? Taking risks? Committing to a person no matter what the future holds?" My head tilted as I thought. "Kind of like when we choose to serve God. We don't know the entire course, what lies behind life's many river bends, but He does. We can trust Him to hold our hands and lead us through difficult waters." And I'd be good to remember that in a few weeks when we arrived in Pittsburgh. God had always taken care of me and He always would.

Jack peered at me with the most intense expression.

I tried not to squirm. How silly of me to rattle off such things when I had no experience. "Though what do I know of love?"

His gaze traced my face. "A great deal more than most."

I warmed under his approval. I needed to change the subject before I melted into the splintered cracks of the dinghy. "Where exactly are we going? By the way you're rowing we should hit Cincinnati by nightfall." Though I wouldn't complain about the interesting show of muscle rippling he was putting on.

He chuckled. "See the mouth of that stream over yonder?"

I peered in the direction of his jutted chin. The Kentucky River was up ahead, but that wasn't what he referred to. There was a small opening past a cluster of oak trees. "Is that a distributary?"

"Yes." He nodded. "Therein lies your present, Admiral."

Chapter 22

Devyn

"Welcome to the middle of nowhere." Devyn tossed a grin at Chase as he drove his Jeep up the familiar lane leading to her family's vacation cabin. "Isn't it glorious?" It had been several months since she'd visited the area, but there was something soothing about this wooded wonderland.

Chase cut the engine and tugged his keys from the ignition. "It is." He returned her smile. "And also far from civilization." He grabbed his cell and checked the screen. "No bars."

Oh. She'd forgotten about that. What if a doctor or some other health professional needed to get ahold of him? "There's zippo service out here. Is that going to be a problem? We can go back, and I can come here another time."

He set a calming hand on her jiggling knee, stilling it. "It's perfect." His smile grew the longer he looked into her eyes. "Now I don't have to share you with your ex-fiancé."

Ugh. Travis had somehow managed to get her number and had been texting over the past two weeks. "He'll get a clue when he realizes I finally blocked his number."

Chase gave her knee a gentle squeeze then removed his hand. "I think he realizes what he lost."

She let out a disbelieving laugh. "No way. With him it's all about appearances."

"You have a beautiful appearance." His thumb ran along his keys disinterestedly, but there was nothing casual about his tone. Chase was fluent in the language of flirting, but there were times, like this, when the pitch of his voice deepened in such a way, causing Devyn to think there was more to his playful remarks.

And of course, her heart responded with a predictable thud. She tugged her Ray Bans from their position atop her head and slid them over her eyes. "Come on, I have so much to show you."

They exited the Jeep, and she led Chase up the porch steps to the Asbury Getaway Lodge, as her brother called it. Humidity stuck the door to the jamb. With a little shove, the wooden entry gave way, and Devyn was greeted with a wave of must and memories.

She invited Chase inside and left the door ajar, allowing in fresh air and sunshine. Her smile buoyed at the familiar space. Roughhewn beams ran along the high ceiling and the stone hearth featured on the opposite wall was bookended by large picture windows. Devyn could almost see Nana in the rocking chair working on a crossword puzzle and humming a Gaither Vocal Band song.

Chase glanced around the room, and Devyn's heart pinched. She hoped his reaction to her beloved log cabin wouldn't match that of the last guest she'd brought here.

He shoved his hands into his pockets. "So what's our mystery mission?"

"Ah, it worked. I've intrigued you." The entire car ride, Devyn had kept silent as to their purpose for coming here. Although, Chase didn't need much convincing to join her, his words still whirring through her— *As long as I'm with you, it doesn't matter where we go.*

She met his gaze and hoped her eyes didn't reflect the sappy condition of her heart at present. "We need to head into the basement. Apparently, there's a Victrola down there Mom wants me to bring back for her. Then you and I are on official ball business." She tamed her smile. "First I need to turn on the electric." She went to the utility room, opened the panel box, and flipped the circuit breakers.

The house hummed alive.

Devyn emerged to find Chase browsing the picture wall.

"Is that you?" He leaned in, and she knew exactly which picture he was examining.

"Yes. Some girls want to grow up and be movie stars and models, I wanted to be Annie Oakley." She laughed at the image of her nine-year-old self clutching a shotgun with an exuberant grin.

"You look adorably dangerous with that rifle." He chuckled.

"My grandpa taught me how to shoot." She straightened the picture and smiled. "It was a valuable skill, especially later on when learning how to pitch. I already knew how to adjust my vision to perfect my aim." She spent the next couple of minutes showing Chase pictures of her and Mitch, her parents, and grandparents. "My brother and his wife are expecting a baby next February. So this space will get some fresher photos." Would Devyn get the chance to add to this generational wall? She ignored the stab of uncertainty and watched Chase's meandering gaze.

He caught her staring, and his grin turned wolfish. She braced herself for a Chase-sized teasing, but instead, he returned his focus to the wall. "Are there any of your great-grands?"

"Only one." She pointed at the photo on the top left. "They're older here. Sorry it's grainy, I think it's from my parents' wedding." She joined him in viewing the blurry image of two grinning old people. "I wish I could've met them." Though in an odd way, Devyn felt connected to them through this place. Her great-grandfather had built the cabin for his young bride. Their only son, her grandpa, had preserved the home and passed it on to Devyn's father. Love and laughter had been breathed into each nook and crevice, and Devyn inhaled wistfully before leading Chase through the kitchen.

They descended the paint-chipped steps into the dusty basement. "Mom said to look in the far right corner." Devyn wrinkled her nose at the cluttered space. "If we can get there." The cellar was crammed with piles of boxes, walls of plastic tubs, and pine shelving stuffed with rows of glass jars, mostly empty.

Devyn maneuvered past an old dining table with chairs stacked on top. Her careful steps halted at the sight of something fuzzy. She squealed and skittered back, colliding into Chase's chest.

His hands encircled her waist, stabling her. "What is it?"

She turned into him, clinging to his neck, burying her face into his shirt. Her voice pitched high. "A mouse." Rodents and any creature with eight legs turned her into the biggest wimp. A low sound rumbled against her forehead. "Are you laughing?"

With his hands still on her waist, he eased back to look fuller into her face. "I thought you stumbled on a dead body or something. But it turns out Annie Oakley is only afraid of a dusty rag."

Devyn released her death grip on his neck and glanced behind her. Sure enough, it was a shriveled, black cloth.

She gave him a mock glare and poked his chest. "Tell no one."

He released her with a grin. "Your secret's safe with me." But then the smile faded from his eyes, and another emotion claimed residence.

Rather than question him on it, she grabbed his wrist and led him through a narrow path between the rows of boxes. Devyn's nose itched from all the dust. The light was dimmer in this area of the room, but she spotted something bulky covered with a garbage bag and duct tape. "That has to be it." She pointed.

He followed her as she picked her way to the Victrola. Using her index fingernail, she dug a hole in the bag and tugged, exposing a curved, gold-toned speaker. They worked together uncovering the rest.

Chase stood beside her, admiring the antique.

"It's from the thirties, I think." She brushed the hair away from her forehead with the back of her hand. "Mom wants it for a decorative piece." Her finger carved a dust trail along the main box. The needle seemed in good condition. Her attention snagged on the tray, and she gripped Chase's arm, too stunned to speak.

"Another mouse?" he teased.

"It's a Perry Como record." With gentle handling, she lifted the shellac disc from the tray and used the edge of her tank top to brush away the filth.

Chase arched a brow at her crud-stained shirt.

"Anything for Perry." She gave an exaggerated wink. "He's like the twentieth-century version of Michael Bublé."

"Ah. A crooner, is he? Should we see if it works?" Chase gestured toward the crank. "Try to hear Perry's golden pipes?"

She bit her lip, subduing a smile. "Sure."

But he didn't move, his gaze steady on her. "You have. . .a little something." He eased near, and with the pad of his thumb, brushed her temple. "There."

She thought he'd step away, but he didn't. Neither did she.

Chase's gentle caress. The smolder in his eyes. The visible rise and fall of his chest, all made her head swim and her chin lift ever so slightly, inviting him to erase the distance between them. To kiss her.

Her want must have been reflected on her face, for Chase slid his hands into her hair, his fingers taking their time traveling down her back, sending a shiver through her which he no doubt felt. His gaze flicked to her mouth, then to her eyes. "I meant what I said in the car." His voice was like that first sip of coffee on a sleepy Monday morning, bringing every part of her to life. "You're beautiful, Devyn." He nuzzled her temple. "In so many ways."

His head dipped, but then he paused, his jaw locking. Some sort of struggle carved deep grooves between his brows. What was wrong with him? Or maybe it was her. Maybe he didn't want to cross that line. Then why had he been looking at her with such hunger?

His Adam's apple bobbed and his gaze, now distant, dragged over her shoulder. "Should we see if it works?"

Huh? Oh, the Victrola. She bit back her disappointment and pasted on a wobbly smile. "Of course." She stepped aside, letting him have full access to the ancient gramophone. Maybe he didn't want their first kiss to be in a crusty, mothball-reeking basement. Whatever it was, he was now back to his casual self with a sure hand poised on the tarnished lever.

He nodded. With a "Here goes," he rotated the crank.

The tray didn't turn.

"Maybe I can get it fixed." She reached into her back pocket to grab her phone to check the time, and her elbow brushed a pile of records on the shelf behind her. The top cover caused her to suck in a sharp breath. "Dean Martin." Her fingers tugged the entire stack off the pine plank, and she thumbed through them. "The Andrew Sisters, Ella Fitzgerald." There were some older looking ones with names she didn't recognize. "Who needs Space Station, I can get filthy rich selling these on the internet."

Though who was she kidding? Like she'd ever part with such treasures. Some families would pass down jewelry to future generations; it appeared her great-grandparents' heirlooms consisted of vintage records. Devyn had never been one for bling, but Bing? Oh, she'd go for that swoony voice over a pretty trinket any day of the week.

What other sorts of awesomeness had been left as spider bedding down here? Her gaze drifted over the tall shelves. Coffee cans filled with screws and washers. There were stacks of *McCalls* sewing pattern catalogs from the early nineties. She paused in front of an Avon cardboard box filled with miscellaneous things. As if someone had emptied out a junk drawer and shoved the box down here, leaving it to collect dust.

Her focus glued on a yellowed envelope wedged between a tomato-shaped pin cushion and a plastic cup filled with pencils. She reached for what she hoped to be a little token from Nana.

Chase stepped behind her. "Find something?"

"Every time Mitch and I spent a weekend here, Nana would kick off the visit with a scavenger hunt." Devyn tugged the envelope from its longtime home and raised it for Chase to see. "She always tucked clues in envelopes like this and we'd go nuts running around the cabin in search of 'em."

"Your Nana sounds fun."

"She was the best." Beautiful flashbacks rolled through her mind, memory after memory, like one of those old-school slide projectors, making her fingers tingle to open the brittle envelope resting in her hand. She angled toward the light and peeked inside. Her brow lowered. Not a clue written in Nana's flowery script. "It's a picture."

Gently, she eased it from the paper sheath, wincing when one of the edges tore. But. . .the picture had already been ripped. Right down the middle. "Chase?" She studied the image and turned it over, reading the name.

"Yeah?"

"I think I found the other half to Hattie's photo."

But it wasn't Chase's great-grandfather.

It was hers.

Chapter 23

Hattie

Stones grated the dinghy's bottom. I gripped the sides so I wouldn't spill into the shallow water as Jack rowed us ashore. The boat scraped to a halt on a craggy beach as narrow as it was long, the setting sun glinting off the sand.

Jack climbed out, grabbed the bucket holding our dinner, and reached for me. I placed my fingers in his warm ones and carefully stepped onto the closest rock protruding from the rippling stream. My sturdy T-strap shoes and faultless balance would prevent me from slipping, but Jack, being the gentleman he was, placed a protective hand on my side. Together we trekked our way from stone to stone onto dry land.

Instead of withdrawing his touch, he threaded his fingers through mine. If my ribs hadn't been so determined on keeping my heart caged, the jittery thing would have soared higher than the surrounding treetops.

My gaze roved the tangle of ferns, searching for a path. There wasn't one. Yet Jack was surefooted, snaking us around giant maples and through tall grass as if he'd been here a million times. But how? This place held no trace of human interference. No houses. No roads. Nothing but rugged beauty that nourished my weakened spirit. After all the lows about Duffy, this place supplied solace. "Thank you for bringing me here." My tone hushed in the splendor of it all. "I couldn't ask for a better gift."

"You haven't seen your gift yet." His lips edged into a smile that flushed warmth to my toes. "But you can hear it."

I slowed my pace and listened. The birds and crickets engaged in a shouting match, and my ears couldn't register anything beyond it. No, wait. I closed my eyes. "Water," I murmured, the faint burble as recognizable as the voice of a lifelong friend. My lashes fluttered open, and I glanced over my shoulder. The stream we'd beached the dinghy near was no longer in sight.

"Up ahead." Grin widening, he resumed walking, and I matched his eager pace.

Within minutes, our steps slowed on the fringe of a bank leading to a meandering brook. I peered at the flow of water, how it whispered over rocks and sparkled with the final breaths of daylight.

"In honor of your twenty-first birthday, I present to you. . ." Jack's voice roughened with emotion. "Hattie's Creek."

My eyes widened. "You're naming a creek after me?" A shiver of wonder coursed through me. This had to be one of the sweetest gestures someone could bestow. And yet, it couldn't be right. Didn't this property belong to someone? It wasn't like Jack to bend rules. To claim what belonged to another.

Jack squeezed my hand. "Ready to explore?"

The lure of adventure beckoned, but I silenced its call. "I would hate to get caught by the owner." However unlikely. It didn't appear as if another body had stepped foot here in a long while. But that didn't make it okay to traipse across a person's land.

"I'm the owner." The blues of his eyes brightened with certainty, leaving no question of truthfulness. "This land belongs to me."

"I thought your family was from Louisville?"

His thumb absently stroked my knuckle, his gaze never straying from the brook. "This property belonged to my grandfather. We used to come fishing here when I was young. He really loved this land." Jack's voice took on a reminiscent tone. "He wanted to build a log cabin on the clearing not too far from where we're standing, but Grandmother demanded they live in Louisville. Before he died, he gifted it all to me."

"What an amazing gift."

He nodded. "When my family lost everything, I tried to sell it. No one was interested."

I blinked so hard I was surprised my lashes didn't knit together. "I can't imagine anyone not falling in love with this land."

"It's the location. The area's too far from Carrolton. Or any other town for that matter." He set the bucket on the soft earth. "I couldn't find a soul who could see the value in it."

"You've found one now." I inhaled the loamy air. "The problem with most people is they look without really seeing."

His arrested gaze fastened on me with sudden intensity. "How does it look through your eyes, Hattie?"

The edge of daylight slanted through the trees, glossing the leaves, rendering them almost translucent. The winding creek, constant as my heartbeat, rippled between two sloped shores as if God swept a fingertip along the earth, carving the waters to His liking. Truly, I could see His heavenly prints everywhere. "It's a wild beauty." My voice was quiet, and Jack leaned in as if my words were of utmost importance to him. "Something that should never be tamed, but cherished, just as the Creator designed."

He swallowed. "That's exactly how I feel."

Naming his creek after me was thoughtful, but could I accept? This was his land. It was doubtful I'd ever visit this place again. I had no idea what my future held beyond Pittsburgh. That thought alone, sobered my judgment. "As much as I'm grateful, I can't allow you to name a piece of your property after me."

"I'm not just naming, I'm giving it to you. The creek is yours, Hattie." His hand cupped my jaw, a tenderness overtaking his expression. "I could've easily gone to town and bought you flowers or candy. But I wanted to give you something that means something to me. A present with value."

No one ever looked at me like this. Or touched me with such soul-rousing affection. I didn't want to move. To speak. But the question burned within me, scalding. If I didn't release it, I'd be charred with the fear of never knowing. "Why?"

He paused as if he chose his words with the same care he held my face. "Because you mean something to me. Your heart is valuable. . .to me." Though he pulled his hand away, I remained caressed by what he'd spoken.

My breaths turned shallow. I had no idea how I could be of value to anyone. I, a scrawny orphan with nothing to my name. I had no training of anything useful. All I had was a head full of steamboat knowledge. Before I lost nerve, I placed my hand on his jaw, mirroring his exact touch only a second ago, his late-day stubble scratching my palm. Our eyes held with a fierceness I couldn't explain but could feel to my marrow. "Thank you, Jack."

He gave a tight nod, his entire body tense as if harnessing a surge of emotion. I stood there for several heartbeats, then slowly peeled away from him. But Jack caught my hand and pressed a kiss to the inside of my wrist.

My skin tingled from the gentle pressure of his mouth, from the heat of his breath.

He released me with a smile that lit his eyes. "Ready to explore your creek?"

I could barely contain the swell of feelings. "Yes."

He turned to retrieve the picnic bucket, and I ducked behind a massive oak. With quick fingers, I unbuckled my shoes and slipped out of them. Now for my stockings.

"Hattie?"

"Right here," I called as I hopped on my left foot, pulling the soft cotton over my right toes. There. I released my skirt and emerged.

Jack's gaze traveled to my bare feet.

A blush stretched to my earlobes. So far in this man's presence I'd been caught ambushing him with a worn boot, discovered sprawled on the dirty floor beneath the pilothouse, and now seen exposing my freckled toes. Jack must have thought I hadn't an ounce of feminine grace in me. "You can't gift me a creek and not expect me to experience it." Strengthening my grip on my shoes, I stepped into the water, moving inward until it reached my shins, the minnows scurrying at my intrusion.

Jack chuckled. "Then I must follow suit." His acceptance of my antics oddly touched me. He leaned against the tree trunk and shed his boots. Within seconds, his trousers were rolled to his knees, his muscular calves in plain view.

Dear mercy. I was getting several gifts this evening. "Perfect. Now c'mon." I grabbed his hand and we traipsed through my creek. We talked and laughed, and nothing on earth could have been finer.

"There's something else I want to show you." Jack moved a few paces ahead, then turned to face me. "It gets deeper from here on out. Venture to the shore, unless you're in the mood to swim."

Tempting, but I was already being scandalous enough. The ground was spongy beneath my soles as I treaded carefully toward the bank. As soon as my feet reached a grassy patch of shore, my eyes latched on to a familiar sight. "Paw paw trees!" I squealed at the row of fruit trees that grew native along the Ohio River. Clusters of bright green, varied-size paw paws dotted the branches. Could this place be any more perfect?

"There's a larger patch farther up." His tone dropped with hints of mystery. "Along with something else."

I hastened my pace, mud pulling at the arches of my feet, but even that couldn't slow me. Jack's pleasing laughter carried over my shoulder. I descended the small hill along the brook's edge and came to an abrupt stop. I was pretty sure a twig was wedged between my toes, but I couldn't yank my gaze from the sight before me. "My creek has a waterfall."

"Of course it does." Jack came up behind me, his hand settling on the small of my back, bringing my attention to his smiling face. "I wouldn't dare give you a waterfall-less creek."

The whole scene seemed like a page from a fairy tale. Fairy tales had never been part of my world. But here, with Jack, it seemed anything was possible. Fireflies blinked every so often. A canopy of paw paw trees hedged both shores. The water—so murky a few steps backs—turned glassy as it poured off the cliff of rocks.

I faced Jack, who watched me with pleased interest. My breathless tone revealed my heart. "I love it."

"I'm glad."

It was then I noticed a pocket of space just behind the waterfall.

Jack followed my gaze. "Ah, you found our picnic spot."

Dinner behind the falls? "Really?"

"We might get a tad damp, but—"

"As if I care about that." I snatched his hand in mine, tugging so hard I felt a knuckle pop under my grip. I threw a sheepish smile over my shoulder, and it prompted his deep chuckle.

There was a sliver of space between the water and the wall of earth. I slid into it, the mist from the falls spraying me. Jack handed me the bucket and angled to squeeze through. It was larger back there than I'd imagined. Someone could use this for a shelter. Maybe even light a fire. Though with twilight, the space was also darker than out in the open. More intimate.

Jack lifted the tarp from the top of the bucket and spread it over the damp ground.

I moved to unload the bucket, but Jack set a hand on mine. "No, allow me to serve you."

With a smile, I sat on the tarp, placed my shoes beside me, and tugged the hem of my frock over my knees.

Jack went to work, grabbing a Beech-Nut Ginger Ale. I smiled. Had to have been Miss Wendall's doing. Only she knew my weakness for ginger ale. He used his soldier knife to remove the bottle top and then handed the bottle to me. Next, he served a paper-wrapped sandwich and a tin of potato chips.

"Hattie." He hesitated. "I know it's not a fancy cuisine fit for a proper birthday party but—"

"It's lovely." I was gently emphatic. "All so very lovely."

"And so are you." Jack raised his bottle in a toast. "Here's to you and your twenty-one voyages around the sun."

We clinked our bottles and sipped. I couldn't keep from grinning. No doubt I looked like the silliest creature on the planet, but Jack didn't seem to mind. In fact, he hardly tore his gaze from mine.

Our picnic dinner was consumed, and even my constant swatting at mosquitos couldn't lower my mood. The steady rush of water cascading only a yard from where I sat, the dotting lights of fireflies, the satisfied swell of my filled stomach, all worked together, prompting my contented sigh.

"Happy Birthday, Hattie." The way he said my name, as if relishing each syllable, wrapping the word with all the care in his heart, affected my own in the most beautiful way.

"Thank you." I twisted my napkin in my lap. "It's all been. . .tonight's just. . ." How could I smash giant feelings into little sentences? "Words are failing me."

Jack eased closer, bringing with him the scent of spice, masculinity, and everything that made me thrum with longing. "I never thought I would see it."

The deep rumble of his voice drew me closer to him. "See what?"

"You short on words."

I gasped at his wickedness. "Maybe I can let this speak for me." I leaned and reached my hand under the waterfall and splashed him. The icy water dotted his face, and a chuckle burst from my lips.

He blinked and wiped the moisture away using his sleeve. "When I was younger, I used to dip my head under the falls. It was exhilarating." The corners of his eyes narrowed with merriment. "Perhaps you should try it." He reached for my waist, and I squealed.

"Don't you dare, Jack." Not that I cared a straw about getting wet, but I refused the shame of being dunked. I laughed and squirmed out of his touch. I scurried away, but he caught me by the waist. "Of course I could always dunk you first." I shoved hard against his chest, but he didn't budge, my movement only bringing me closer to him.

Too close.

All amusement slipped into something else entirely. Something new.

His hands explored the curve of my waist as mine flattened against his expansive chest. I tipped my head toward his face, and my breath squeezed at the aching tenderness in his countenance.

His chin lowered an inch. Then another. The question swam in his ice-blue eyes. He wouldn't dare make another move until I gave him permission. Because that was Jack. He'd never take what wasn't offered.

Gaze tethered to his, I nodded.

His mouth captured mine, and my lashes drifted shut. I had no idea how else to respond, what to do, but the teasing pressure of Jack's touch awakened everything in me. His lips coaxed mine, his mouth a gentle leader. His hands slid up my back, tangling into my hair.

He eased back and peered into my eyes. I'm not sure what he saw there, but it was enough to encourage him to press his lips against my temple, then trail delicious kisses along my jaw, each one causing my heart to pound harder. His mouth met mine again, and this time I was prepared, answering with inexperienced fervor. Jack moaned and crushed me into him. I nestled in his embrace, but then I yanked back in surprising reality.

"What's the matter?" His brow creased in alarm.

My fingers flitted to my swollen lips. "I just kissed you."

He relaxed and smiled. "You did."

"But I don't even know your real name. Which means I kissed a stranger."

He brushed the hair from my forehead, his gaze following the movement as if every part of me fascinated him. "I'm actually named after my grandfather, Marshall being my first name. It was intended for me to go by my middle—Jonathan. But soon everyone started calling me Jack. And my last name's Asbury."

"Well then." I wound my arms around his thick neck. "Now that we're acquainted, Marshall Jonathan Jack Asbury, kiss me again."

He did.

Chapter 24

Devyn

*D*evyn's knuckles whitened as she held the half-torn picture with a shaky grip. Her great-grandfather? The photo was yellowed from age, but there was no mistaking his white officer's uniform or the embroidered letters on his cap reading *Mate*. It didn't seem possible. An officer of a steamboat? Her steamboat! Why hadn't she known this?

Chase retrieved Hattie's photo from his notebook and lifted it to meet the one in her hand.

A perfect match.

Goose bumps rose on her arms. She would have never identified him if it hadn't been for his name scribbled on the back. "Marshall," she whispered. She glanced to see Chase's brow lift. She flipped the photo around, letting him read the faded scrawl. "That was my great-grandfather's name." Which didn't make any sense because. . . "Oh." Her hand fell limp to her side. "How could I forget?"

"Forget what?" Chase handed her Hattie's picture, and she placed them side by side on the shelf.

She looked at the reunited pair. "His name was Marshall, but I think he went by his middle name. Jonathan. Or was it Jack? I can't remember. Either way, it matches the mystery initial on the note we found in the songbook."

Understanding marked Chase's eyes. "So it's possible it was *your* great-grandfather who planned the rendezvous." He leaned in, his sleeve brushing her elbow, and examined the photo. "Makes sense."

"Hardly. I never heard of him being an officer on the *Idlewild*. I thought he was a farmer."

Chase gave her a small smile. "I mean it makes sense that he was the one who wrote the note. Wanting to see her."

Her nose wrinkled. "Why do you say that?"

"Look closer."

Hattie hugged the songbook to her chest with her right hand and with the other—Devyn gasped. "They're holding hands." In Hattie's half, her left wrist and hand had been torn out. But in Marshall's half, his fingers clasped hers. "Check out the way he's gazing at her. It's like—"

"He loves her."

"No, no. He couldn't." But there it was, evidenced in sepia tones. While Hattie faced the camera, Devyn's great-grandpa was angled toward Hattie, his eyes shining with affection. "He was married to my great-grandmother Mira for sixty years."

Chase seemed impressed. "That's a long time to be with one person."

"Right? It's creeping me out to think he was in love with someone else. You don't think. . .he had an affair with Hattie?" Fire gathered in her chest. "Maybe that's why the picture was torn. So no one would know they were ever together."

His face softened. "Maybe Hattie was a secret love *before* Mira."

Devyn's gaze snapped to his. "Secret. That's it."

"That's what?"

"Can you drive a quad?"

His lips curved into an amused smirk. "You win the award for the most random remark of the day."

Devyn smiled despite her crazy emotions. "What you just said reminded me of something. More like some place. And it happens to be in the same area I planned to take us to get what we need for the ball. We can walk, but the quads will get us there quicker." She reached to lift the Victrola, but Chase was there.

He dimpled. "I got it." With complete control, he gripped the sides of the gramophone and followed Devyn back up the stairs. He loaded the Victrola into his Jeep, and together they went to the large steel-framed barn.

With their quads freshly gassed and their heads properly helmeted, Devyn led the way. She'd forgotten a hair tie, and her makeshift knot lasted only a few turns into the drive. Chase dutifully followed on the well-worn trail, and they reached their destination in no time.

They killed their motors and tugged off their helmets.

"It's pretty out here." Chase's gaze wandered the wooded space. "Do I hear water?"

"Behind you." She pointed to the narrow path that had born the marks of her sneakers for years. "I'm going to show you my favorite part of the property." After grabbing a few burlap sacks from the dump cart and tossing a utility knife into one of them, she motioned for Chase to walk with her. Of course, she'd only taken a few steps before he insisted on carrying everything.

Her fingers ran across the tips of the tall ferns. "I wanted a special dessert to serve at the ball. Something that grows along the Ohio River to go along with the theme." They reached the creek, and she gestured to the patch of trees surrounding them.

"Paw paws." He inspected the low hanging fruit. "You know, I've never tasted one."

"What?" Devyn's brow spiked. "Pfft. And you call yourself a Kentucky boy." She examined several on the branch. They were all in varying states of ripeness, but the last week of September was the prime time for picking. "Here's a good one." She snapped it free.

Chase looked doubtful. "How can you tell?"

"It's kinda like bananas. The blacker it is, the riper the fruit. The solid light green ones aren't ready to eat yet. But this beauty?" She raised the pear-sized, black-speckled paw paw. "Is perfect right now. Ready for an education, Mr. Jones?"

"Only if you're the teacher."

She pulled the utility knife from the bag Chase held and sliced open the paw paw. She showed him the inside of the fruit.

His face puckered in disgust. "It looks like snot."

She laughed. "Let's say it's a custardy texture." She used the tip of the knife to remove a handful of seeds. "Ready to taste?"

"Are you getting me back for teasing you about the non-mouse rag?"

"Here, I'll go first so you know I'm not poisoning you." She swept up a dollop of paw paw flesh onto her finger and ate it before it slid off, the flavor a gentle blend of banana and mango. "Now, your turn."

He took the smallest sample possible and hesitantly tasted. All doubt left his face. "Not bad." He scooped some more onto his finger. "I'm impressed."

"Now imagine this as a pudding with a little more sugar and some fancy garnish. That's what we're serving our esteemed patrons and judges." She sampled another scoop of fruit before closing the knife and returning it to the bag.

"So how many paw paws do we need?"

"At least a hundred. More if we can."

Chase let out a low whistle and turned a slow circle. "I'm game. But are there enough?"

"There's a decent cluster here, but let's start at the larger patch up the creek." And up the creek held one of the most beautiful spots in all the world. At least to her. Her gaze connected with Chase's. He'd given up a beautiful Saturday to trudge into dirty basements, trample muddy paths, and perhaps blister his hands with the amount of picking ahead of them. All with an easy grin on his handsome face.

She wove her fingers into his.

His dimples appeared like a stamp of approval, and he tugged her closer until their sides brushed.

"It's just up that small hill." She nodded ahead. "Careful, the shoreline gets rockier here."

They crested the incline, and Chase paused. "A waterfall."

"It's nothing epic." And it really wasn't, compared to the Ohio Falls or even the others around the state. But it was special to her.

Today her little waterfall was showing off. The creek water cascaded over the rocks, the mist catching the light and producing a rainbow of sorts.

Chase's expression turned thoughtful, and Devyn tried not to read too much into it. She'd learned her lesson after bringing Travis to this exact spot.

" 'Secret Creek,' " Chase read, his gaze pinned to the wooden sign that'd been cemented into this soil longer than she could remember.

"My great-grandfather named this creek. He built this sign." She brushed a hand over the two familiar words etched into a sturdy plank of wood. "This is what had me freaking out over what you said in the basement. *Secret*. You see, there are stories and traditions surrounding this place."

"What kind of stories?"

"According to Grandpa, this creek once had another name. But my great-grandfather refused to tell anyone what it was."

"Interesting."

"That's not all. Grandpa said that his mother, my great-grandmother Mira, would tease his father about this creek being named after one of his loves. It was all in jest, but what if. . ." She hesitated. "What if it was Hattie? What if he brought her here?"

"We definitely know he had a thing for her. It's clear enough in his expression."

"But then, how was your great-grandfather involved in this? Why did he have the other half of the picture?" Devyn's fingers fanned against her open mouth. "Do you think there was a love triangle?"

Chase smiled at her theatrics. "Could be. Great-Grandpap was certainly distressed about something concerning Hattie." He leaned against the sturdy signpost. "Maybe she was a player and ditched them both. It was the twenties, after all. The era of the flapper and rebellion."

But Hattie didn't look like that kind of woman. Her dress seemed plain, her face void of cosmetics. She had a wholesomeness about her. But if neither Chase's nor her great-grandfather had married her, what happened to her?

"So you told me the story." Chase folded his arms, the afternoon sun playing in his hair, giving his dark locks a blueish cast. "What of these traditions?"

"You sure you want to know?" She leaned closer to him, as if her words held a world of mystery. "The tradition is that every time a person visits here, he or she must confess a secret."

Chase's eyes widened as if he'd swallowed a paw paw fruit whole. Was he afraid she'd make him play along? Of course he held a secret. But she wouldn't make him uneasy about it. Or make him confess about his illness. Maybe she should she tell him she had already figured it out. Or kinda figured it out. Perhaps that would make things easier for him. "Since you're not a family member, you're not obligated to anything." Which had never been a rule, but with traditions there was always leeway, right?

He stood to full height. "Actually, there's something I need to tell you." He swallowed. "It's not easy for me."

She flashed her palms. "You don't have to. Really."

"But with the secret comes the fear that you'll look at me differently. With all the phone calls, the texts. I'm sure you've been wondering." He blew out a breath and raked his hand through his hair, tousling it.

Her mother had that same fear when she reentered society after chemo. She hadn't wanted people to treat her like she was fragile, easily breakable. Mom hadn't liked the way even her closest friends had viewed her. "It's okay, Chase. We can leave things in the past. If it helps, I kinda already know." She placed a hand on his arm, and he instantly tensed. "At least I have an inkling."

Chase remained frozen, his eyes filling with what Devyn could only label stark terror. "You do?" He stepped back, and her hand fell to her side. "How? When?" Another step. "Did you look at my notebook?"

"No." She shook her head. "I didn't need to. All the signs were there."

He blinked with a shake of his head. "I can explain. I wanted to tell you. I was afraid of what you might think. It's a part of my life I'm not used to sharing."

She'd never seen him this shaken. Her heart tore at his labored breathing. "We don't have to discuss it. I know it's hard for you."

"It's awkward for me to open up about it."

"Then I won't press you to."

His head reared back. "Just like that?"

Devyn smiled with a nod. "Just like that."

He moved toward her and kissed her forehead. "I don't deserve you." He nuzzled her hair.

"How about I take your turn?" Her pulse pounded at his nearness. "I'll tell two secrets to cover us both."

Chase eased back and opened his mouth to argue, but Devyn shook her head. "I'm an Asbury. I have to keep the tradition." She smiled. "Okay, first." She took a breath and looked around. "I confess I enjoy this view more than the one on the balcony at my penthouse." She was certain Chase would call her crazy. Who would trade the lights and colors of the city for this spot?

But instead he nodded. "I can understand that."

Her jaw slacked. "Really?"

His chuckle was low, deep, and stirred a longing in her to hear it as much as possible. "You seem shocked."

"I am."

"This place has natural beauty. The city lights are nice, but they're still artificial. That's not the case here."

"No, this is all God's artwork." Her gaze lingered on the creek, glistening with the sunlight's kiss.

He draped the burlap bags over a low hanging branch and turned in a slow circle, admiring the surroundings. "I can see why this is your favorite spot on the property."

"This isn't my favorite spot. It's over here. Come see." She moved to take his hand, then stilled. "Oh, you may get a little wet." He may not even value it like she did. Her arm fell to her side. "Never mind, it's a stupid idea. I don't want your boots to get ruined."

Chase swept both her hands in his and eased closer. "There's nothing stupid about this. Take me to your favorite spot." His touch was as soft as his eyes. Those granite hues now a warm gray like her favorite fall sweater. If only she could wrap herself up in them.

"We're going behind the waterfall." She took a few steps on the squishy ground and stepped onto the larger rocks to avoid the muddy bank. "Just right here. See this little space? I used to fit through so easily when I was younger." She cast him a quick glance. "Ready?"

"Ready."

She tugged him close and they squeezed through the narrow opening between the rock and waterfall. Once again, her heart filled with awe.

He studied the space, his gaze lit with interest. "I've never stood behind a waterfall."

"I love this place. Always have. When Mitch and I were younger, we begged Grandpa to let us camp all night here. Of course he never let us. Now, all grown up, I think it's so. . ." She'd better not finish that. This spot was precious to her. She knew better than to expect others to value it like her.

"You think it's what?" he prompted.

"It's special here. We're tucked into the heart of the earth. The waterfall closes us in from the rest of the world. It's just me…and you." She did everything she could to avoid saying it was romantic. But to her, it was.

"So how many men have you lured back here, Miss Asbury?"

"Only you."

His eyes revealed his shock.

She ran a nervous hand over her tangled hair, frizzing from the water's mist. "I tried to bring Travis here. But he complained all the walk over. *There are too many bugs. The temp's way hot. No cell service.*" She sighed. "When we reached the falls, I didn't bother bringing him back here, because I knew he wouldn't cherish it like I do."

"Yet you brought me here."

She nodded as Chase moved close.

"Thank you." He slid a hand behind her neck, easing her closer with the most excruciating tenderness. "I cherish everything I see here."

"For my second secret." Her face was only inches from his. "I was disappointed you didn't kiss me in the basement." She was surprised at her boldness, but his penetrating gaze seemed to draw the words from her heart.

"Here's a secret to match yours." His head lowered, his breath warm against her cheek. "I wanted to kiss you the first time we met, when you were dancing on the stern."

She blinked and pulled her head back, his hand slipping to her shoulder. "But I was ridiculous."

"Ridiculously intriguing." He didn't stop his pursuit. His hand settled on the nape of her neck, his fingers catching in her hair. "I've never been more drawn to another person the way I am to you."

She flattened her hands on his chest, his heartbeat steady against her palm. "I can say the same about you."

"Let's tell each other another way." He lowered his mouth to hers, conveying his heart in the most thorough delivery.

Chapter 25

Hattie

"Clem?" I rushed into the pilothouse and nearly knocked into the gruff pilot. "Have you seen Duffy?"

He grunted, his jowls shaking with muted indignance. "Said he needed to run an emergency wire. Should be back any minute." He glanced at his pocket watch, and a scowl puckered between his bushy gray brows. "He better be, since we're launching soon."

Emergency wire? What was so important that the captain would abandon the *Idlewild* an hour before departure? Usually Duffy would send a deckhand or the young striker from the engine room to do his bidding, even the purser on occasion. Why go himself? Unless he didn't want anyone else knowing the contents of the message.

Had this to do with rumrunning? Was Duffy contacting that Mr. Jones fellow? My conscience poked my feeble will with an accusing jab. I couldn't protect Duffy any longer. But could I turn him in to the authorities? The suppressed secrets had piled in my chest, expounding, pressing so hard against my sternum, it hurt to draw breath.

I had to tell Jack.

But how could I deliver my message without anyone else hearing? An idea flashed, and I scrambled to gather a pencil and my songbook. I scratched the message, *Need to speak with you alone. Very important.*

My fingers snapped the book shut, and I set off in search of Jack. My legs carried me to all the decks only to find him on the texas roof near my calliope. The next few moments would determine my wisest decision or my biggest mistake.

He brightened when he saw me, and my heart lightened at his

welcome. Since our kiss a week ago, we'd hardly found any chance to be alone. Running excursions and shipments had filled our days, but that hadn't stopped him from slipping notes under my door in the morning once Miss Wendall had left to prepare meals.

Love notes.

Reading them were like gentle caresses to my heart. The sensible thing would be to get rid of them to avoid exposure, but I couldn't. So I had become creative as to where I hid the treasured words.

"There you are, Jack." My tone was more breathless than it should be.

"Afternoon, Hattie. Always a pleasure to see you." His words were formal, polite, but his eyes—my goodness—I could see affection welling in the crystalline blues.

"I need your opinion on a song."

His head tilted, but nothing else betrayed the confusion I knew he harbored. I'd never sought his thoughts on songs before. "Right here." I opened the calliope book to the spot I needed him to see. "Here's a pencil if you need to make corrections." I handed over both items.

He read my words, his mouth curling into a small smile at my endeavor of subterfuge. He scribbled something and handed it back to me, his fingers lingering longer than necessary.

My eyes scanned his return note.

Tonight. I'll handle everything.

The dread in my stomach unraveled. Soon, I'd share the weight of this burden with Jack, and he'd know what to do.

"Is my suggestion to your liking?"

"Of course." I hugged the songbook to my chest.

Jack took a step toward me and subtly caught my fingers in his. His voice dropped to a whisper, "One day, sweetheart—"

"Stand right there for only a second longer."

I turned toward the unfamiliar voice in time to hear the unmistakable sound of a lens shutter.

A man with a press label stuffed into his hatband lowered his camera. "Sorry for not giving a warning, but I wanted to capture you both as you were."

Jack released my hand and stood taller. "And you are?"

"Kent Winston from the *Steubenville Herald*. I'm covering publicity of the *Idlewild* during its stay here. My boss wants me to get some photos to go along with the article."

I put a hand on Jack's shoulder, raised on my tiptoes, and whispered in his ear. "Duffy never allows my picture taken. A matter of decorum, since I'm not an official part of the crew." I hated saying the words and seeing the flicker of anger in Jack's eyes, but if Duffy found out my photo was captured, he'd be furious.

"I'll deal with it," Jack reassured me. "It's probably best for my image not to be plastered as well. I don't recall ever meeting anyone from this area, but I should take precautions not to have my cover exposed."

Jack approached the gentleman and led him to the side. I couldn't understand what Jack was saying, but whatever it was the man readily nodded. Satisfied, I went to my stateroom to dress for the excursion.

Duffy returned only moments before launch. His mood was irritated at best, and so I did what I could not to aggravate him as he welcomed guests. He said all the right words, but I could see the splash of annoyance in his eyes. Whatever his trip up the hill was about, it hadn't been a pleasant one. Maybe he held regret over his actions. Maybe he'd told Mr. Jones he wouldn't go through with the illegal plans. I could only hope.

As the hours wore on, I busied myself in the main hall tending the needs of guests and helping the purser sell the confections Miss Wendall had baked early that morning. After we ended the launch, we had an hour to clean before the sunset excursion.

I figured Jack wouldn't seek me out, but disappointment still coursed through me as I lined up to count the boarding passengers for the evening's jaunt. The excursion ran smoothly, and we had a decent-sized crowd.

With the cleanup done, everyone, fatigued and sluggish, set off toward their staterooms. If tonight would repeat the last time Jack summoned me, he would approach my door about midnight. But the twelve o'clock hour came and went. My eyelids weighted. My stockings itched. With a sigh, I slipped my nightgown over my head.

Maybe Jack realized there was no way to easily sneak off the wharf, since we were moored in clear view of the town hotel. There weren't any trees to shield us. Nothing to keep our rendezvous hidden.

Careful not to jostle the double-framed bed, I climbed to the top bunk. A tight band stretched between my temples, the hammering ache keeping time with my thudding heart. I punched my pillow, fidgeted my sheet, straining to get comfortable without waking my cabinmate.

The pulsing intensified. No, wait. The tapping seemed external. Urgent. I rolled to my side and jolted at Jack's silhouette, unmistakable through the glass. He drummed the window again, the sound reverberating off the walls. I skittered off my bunk. Didn't he realize how loud he was being? Surely, he would wake Miss Wendall.

I scrambled to the door just as he was about to assault the window again. "Jack, what's the matter?"

"We have to hurry." His gaze darted left, then right. "I just left the watchman. He's on the portside of the hurricane roof. But we don't have time to dawdle. Everything's clear." He ringed my wrist with a delicate grip, tugging me outside. I quietly closed the door, and we rushed along the roof.

"In here." He hooked my waist and ushered me into his cabin.

His cabin! "Jack!" I said in a shouting whisper. "I can't be here."

He eased the door shut and faced me. "I'm sorry, my love, but this is the only place I can be assured of privacy."

My love. I tried to keep my head from floating like driftwood in the river, but his adoring tone made it impossible. A ragged snore startled me, and I spun on my heel. "Clem's right there." I sliced my finger through the air, pointing, the sight of the dozing steamboat pilot adding to my distress.

Jack smiled. "You and I both know the man could snooze through a typhoon."

That was true. Once a shanty had caught fire where we'd been wharfed, and Clem had slept through all the siren bells and men's shouting.

Jack's gaze dipped to my nightgown, and his smile slid from his face. In my haste, I'd forgotten my robe. I tugged the lacy collar tighter, but I wasn't sure how much that helped. Given Jack's averted gaze, not much.

"Here." He grabbed a blanket from the edge of his bed and draped my shoulders. "I wish I could've thought of a better place, but Ludwig was on the stern smoking a cigar and Face was rummaging the pantry. So much for curfew." Jack grumbled, even though we both were offenders as well.

My toes curled against the cold planked floor. My courage deserted me. It had taken reaching this precipice to realize I couldn't go through with it. I would never betray the man who cared for me when no one else wanted to. Who'd protected me for twenty-one years. No, I'd carry this secret to my grave. "Jack, I...I don't think..." My chin wobbled, my heart heavy with the weight of it all.

His thumb smoothed over my jaw, settling in the dip underneath my lip. "Don't think what, Hattie?"

"Never mind. I feel like a terrible person for even suspecting. He's been nothing but good to me." A tear leaked from the corner of my eye. Then another.

"You could never be a terrible person. Tell me, sweetheart. Tell me, so I can bear the burden with you."

At those words, I broke. Silent tears poured, and Jack gathered me into his arms. His hand smoothed over my back, his lips either whispering words of comfort or kissing the crown of my head.

I drew strength from the security of his embrace. He adjusted his grip but held on to me with a fervent protectiveness.

"Jack." I sniffled. "It's about—"

The door opened, and I pressed into Jack's chest, clinging. Duffy shuffled a step into the room, scowling fiercer than I'd ever seen. He must have been making a surprise round of the boat and spied us through the door window.

"It's not what you think, Duff." I released Jack, and the blanket fell from my shoulders, revealing my nightgown.

Duffy's eyes narrowed.

Drat.

Jack braved a commanding step toward his superior. "Sir, I take the blame for tonight's events. But I can assure you nothing untoward has occurred."

Duffy's glower had a dark glint to it. "Not yet."

I gasped. "Not at all." I shoved my hands on my hips. "You raised me with more morals than whatever outlandish thoughts you're having about us right now."

Duffy's jaw clenched. "Young lady, back to your cabin. We'll talk in the morning."

I opened my mouth to argue, but Jack set a hand on my back. "Captain, right now I want to make you aware that I intend to, with your blessing, pay court to Hattie. I'm in love with her."

My heart soared within me, but one look into Duffy's stern face, and all my elation plummeted.

Duffy's rigid shoulders curled forward on a heavy exhale. "I'm afraid that's impossible."

Jack's head reared back as if Duffy had punched him.

Panic seized me with a numbing grip. "Duffy, nothing happened here. I still have my virtue. And I'm in love with Jack. Can't you see that?"

Something crossed his face. Something terrifying. "You can't, Hattie." His leveled gaze was half sorrow, half adamance. "You are betrothed."

Chapter 26

Devyn

*D*evyn had just concluded a tour of the *Belle* for a newly engaged couple planning a late-summer wedding when her boss entered the banquet hall, a stylish younger woman in tow.

"Devyn." Steph approached, her wedge heels a clunky cadence against the wooden floor. With manicured fingers, she swept her red bangs from her forehead, and Devyn caught the slight twitch of her thin brow. "I'd like you to meet Jenna Henry. She's from *Once Upon a Wedding* magazine."

The judge!

The ball was less than three weeks away. Devyn had assumed the judges would visit on a day closer to the event, since they'd already be in town to attend. And even then, anonymously. Why make two trips? Clearly, to catch the finalists off guard.

Well played.

Adopting a warm expression, Devyn stretched out her hand. "Nice to meet you."

Ms. Henry's mocha-brown eyes flickered with recognition, then any traces of warmth melted cool. She shook Devyn's hand. "Likewise, Miss Asbury." Her bracelet poked Devyn's finger, but that wasn't what made Devyn stiffen against a wince.

No, the woman had called her Miss Asbury. Steph had only said her first name, and Devyn hadn't submitted her information on the contest entry. Only Steph's. So how would this woman know Devyn's surname? Unless she remembered Devyn from Space Station.

Maybe in Devyn's absence, Steph had leaked her full name to the judge. If that was the case, Devyn's heart rate had spiked for no reason.

"If you have time, could you show me around and answer a few questions?" Ms. Henry's perfectly glossed lips pulled into a conspiratorial smile.

Nope. She knew. "Of course."

"Very good." Steph shot Devyn an encouraging look and settled her gaze on the judge. "I'll let you two get to it. Pleasure to meet you, Ms. Henry."

Now her boss was abandoning her? You could bet Steph's eighties shoulder pads that Jenna Henry was practically bouncing in her Louboutin heels, ready to catapult questions at the rogue social media queen.

Steph descended the grand staircase and the twentysomething judge faced Devyn, her perceptive brow arching. "We've switched roles, Miss Asbury." Her tone was calculating. "Now *you* need something from *me*."

Looked like Devyn had been wrong. It appeared Ms. Henry had mistaken Devyn for somebody else altogether. But just to be certain. . . "I'm sorry, have we met before?"

Dark, long lashes framed probing eyes. "You really don't remember me?" She tugged the hem of her chic blazer with a sardonic smirk. "Last year I was assigned to contact you to see if our magazine could cover your nuptials. I worked late nights creating an entire promotional package." Her pointed gaze remained fixed on Devyn. "Then it was made clear that our *little* publication wasn't popular enough for your Royal Highnesses' wedding, and I was dismissed before I could even present my proposal."

"What? I had no idea." Devyn's jaw unhinged. "Who told you that? Never mind. I know who." Travis. Wasn't surprising. Might as well tell Ms. Henry to forfeit their entry, because there was no way this woman would look favorably on the *Belle*. Her heart twisted. Even now, Travis Leeman was ruining her dreams. And true to his mode of operation, Devyn was totally blindsided. Again.

Though unlike with her breakup, Devyn could get in the final word. And she'd better make it good. "I'm sorry about what happened." She paused, making sure she had the young woman's attention. "Travis was a complete jerk in how he treated you, but in a way, he did you a favor."

Ms. Henry made a disbelieving sound, but Devyn continued. "Think about it. You would've put in so much more work interviewing, writing every detail, reserving prominent space in the magazine, all for nothing. Because we broke up. You were spared a heartache. I wasn't so lucky."

The rigid lines framing her pinched mouth held firm for a few heartbeats then eased. "I'm sorry about your breakup."

Devyn welcomed the delicate olive branch with a friendly smile. "I need to remind myself of that too. Travis treated me badly, but he really did me a favor. We wouldn't have lasted." Realization dropped anchor in her heart. "Did you know that the *Belle*'s engine is older than the boat itself?"

Ms. Henry tilted her head at the turn in conversation, but Devyn could see it so clearly.

"The engine was built twenty years before the *Belle*, making the heart of the boat over one hundred and thirty years old. The *Belle*'s different than other landmarks because she navigates the waters. She's voyaged a million miles. Faced storms. Faced sinkings. Has seen more than other sites that are stationary. She's taken risks. But she's weathered it all, because she is made from strong stuff. She's something that lasts."

Ms. Henry folded her arms, her expression unreadable.

"What I'm trying to say is, if Travis hadn't broken things off, we obviously would've gotten married. And the wedding would have been stunning. My gown was to be custom-sewn by an elite designer. The venue was luxurious. The cake we chose was to be gilded with 24-karat gold flakes. Every detail gorgeous. No expense spared." Her gaze connected with the judge's. "But we wouldn't have lasted. Because the heart of our relationship wasn't strong enough."

"I know what you're trying to say, but celebrity weddings are popular with our audience. When we feature them, our readership grows." Her professional facade proved challenging to break through. "Plus everyone loves a beautiful wedding."

"But what about an enduring marriage?" Devyn posed the question even to herself. "I can't sell you on the *Belle*'s beauty, because she wasn't built for that purpose. She was built to endure. To outlast. During the first half of the 1900s, there were other steamboats, like the *J.S. Deluxe*, that were more decorated. Showy. They received accolade upon accolade for their extravagant furnishings. But. . ." She paused for emphasis. "They're not around now. They didn't make it half as long as the *Belle*. Carrying that point over, what's the use of an elaborate wedding if the marriage won't last?"

"And that's why you think the *Belle* deserves the timeless wedding award?"

"Her heart is strong, durable. And every couple who holds a wedding here is surrounded by that reminder. This boat has survived life's challenges with noble grace, and that's what makes her timeless."

Ms. Henry glanced at her tablet and then to Devyn. "How about you show me around for a bit?"

"Certainly." She showed Ms. Henry everything from the pilothouse to the engine room and everything in between. The judge only asked Devyn four questions during the tour, making Devyn doubt Ms. Henry's interest. They reached the bottom of the main staircase, and the wedding expert said her thanks along with an "I'll be in touch."

With the judge gone, Devyn retreated to her office, finally catching a deep breath.

"How'd it go?" Steph rushed into the room in a whirlwind of Vanilla Fields perfume and exuberance. "What'd she say?"

"She recognized me. Worse yet, Travis was a total jerk to her. I think she harbors a grudge against me." She pressed a hand to her pounding heart. "Steph, it would've been better if you'd shown her around."

"No, it wouldn't."

"Why?" Devyn plopped into her desk chair and sunk her face into her hands. "I no doubt just cost us the contest."

"Did you speak your heart?"

"Yeah. A little too much."

Steph placed a motherly hand on Devyn's shoulder. "You can't have too much heart. I'm proud of you. I wanted the judge to see the *Belle* through your eyes. And I'm not sorry for that decision. Neither should you be."

Devyn blinked. "I don't know what to say."

"I do." Steph beamed, her bright blue eye shadow sparkling beneath the fluorescent lights. "Go celebrate with that hunky boyfriend of yours."

"Celebrate? The judge hates me, and we still have the ball to pull off."

"You did a big thing today." She patted her shoulder. "If you aren't going out to celebrate, at least bring him over so I can look at him. It's been a while. Maybe I should invent another mystery for you two since you solved the one about the photo."

"We didn't solve it." No new information had surfaced about Hattie. Seriously, the woman had no trail on the internet, past newspapers, any record. Devyn wished she could learn her vanishing secret! As a dutiful daughter she had shared what they'd learned at the cabin with her parents, and both of them had been as surprised as she. "I think we've dug up all we can. The H and J hunt has hit a standstill." But while the search had gone to nothing, Devyn and Chase's relationship had been escalating.

It had been two weeks since their day at the waterfall. That day had turned out memorable in more ways than one. They'd spent more time than necessary picking the paw paws, because they'd gotten immersed in conversation, resulting in more than a few kisses.

Devyn had scored a sunburn, but it'd been worth it. Since then, they'd both been busy with work but still managed to see each other almost every other day.

She snapped out of her Chase daze to find Steph looking at her with a strange expression. How long had she been reliving those kisses? A couple seconds? Minutes? "Sorry, I totally zoned."

Steph held a hand up. "What you said struck me funny."

Devyn's nose wrinkled. What had she said? Oh the mystery. "Nothing so odd about it. The woman didn't leave a trail."

"No. The H and J part." She folded her arms, her fingers tapping methodically on her elbow. "You know how the *Belle* looked when the city of Louisville purchased her? You've seen those pictures."

"Yes. What about it?"

"My uncle was one of the workers. He helped remodel the staterooms before becoming one of the *Belle*'s officers. I completely forgot until you said H and J. Well, I didn't know about the J until just now. What does it stand for?"

Devyn swallowed. "Jack." Or Jonathan. "Steph, I found the other half of the picture. It was at my family's cabin."

Surprise splashed in her eyes.

"My great-grandfather and Hattie were both part of the *Idlewild* crew. And I think they had a romance."

"Oh, there was a romance. No question."

"Steph?" She leaned forward. "Why do you say that?"

"It was when you said H and J. The workers found love letters tucked into the wall of the stateroom. They were all addressed 'To H' and were signed 'Yours, J.'"

What? "How come I've never heard about this?"

"It wasn't really made known. I only found out because my uncle was part of the construction crew."

"The remodel was in the sixties. They're long gone by now."

Steph's gaze turned thoughtful. "There's a chance."

Hope billowed, but then deflated like a pin to a balloon. "You don't mean. . ."

"Sorry, sweets. If they're anywhere, they're in the Graveyard."

Chapter 27

"Is this the proverbial searching for a needle in the haystack?" Chase adjusted his worn ball cap and peered into the storage unit they'd just opened.

"I'd rather tackle a haystack than this." It had taken over an hour to go through the last unit, and the one she'd just stepped her Converse into was even more cluttered. Racks of clothes displayed everything from faded Santa Claus costumes to choir robes. Boxes were piled high everywhere. "I think it's a lost cause. Steph wasn't even certain the notes would be here."

Chase shrugged. "We can make a game of it."

Devyn's nose wrinkled at a set of decorative plastic pillars covered in cobwebs and layered with grime. "Like whoever sneezes most wins the sinus headache?"

Chase tugged her hand and led her farther into the unit. "I was thinking more on the line of—every time someone finds outdated Christmas décor, they get kissed."

Devyn snorted. "This place is packed with holiday stuff."

"See? This is going to be fun. Should we practice to make sure we understand the rules?" He hooked the belt loops of her jeans and pulled her close, dropping a quick kiss. Then as if realizing one wasn't enough, he claimed her lips again.

Devyn melded into him, and Chase took that as a go-ahead to up the intensity. His hands roamed the length of her back. His mouth wandered the contours of her lips, the slope of her neck, the edge of her jaw, with murmured endearments in between. Devyn imagined the rack of plush Easter bunnies to her left shielding their plastic eyes with their floppy ears.

She finally broke away, feeling heady. "We're not getting anything done."

"I disagree." His grin unleashed, and he held out the hairband he'd divested her of.

Her shock of laughter bounced off the low ceiling. She had no idea when he'd tugged her topknot free, but her hair spilling over her shoulders evidenced his cunning handsiness. "What am I going to do with you?" She snatched the elastic band from his fingers as he lifted a shoulder in a bogus display of innocence. She worked her locks into a messy ponytail, all while under Chase's hot gaze.

Thankfully he rallied some self-control and pulled his eyes from hers to drift over the unit. "So the city uses all this space?"

She nodded. "They built this storage complex. We call it the Grave-yard because once things are thrown in here, they're pretty much left for dead." Devyn had only visited this place twice. The first time was to locate retired wedding decorations Steph had sworn were boxed with the artificial flowers. She'd been wrong. The other was to store leftover plastic eggs used for the *Belle*'s Easter event. Both times Devyn had felt overwhelmed by the clutter. Today was no different.

He picked up a glittery top hat with gaudy lime-green tassels stapled around the brim. "I have questions."

She smiled. "That was probably a prop for a float or talent show. We share this space with the chamber of commerce."

He returned the hat to its place beside a heap of multi-colored streamers. "So which units do you have access to?"

"This one and the last, obviously, and the next two down the row."

Chase rubbed his jaw with a slow nod. "That's gonna be a lot of kiss-ing. Not that I mind."

She hip-checked him. "Focus, wildcat. We're looking for a box from the sixties."

They searched the front and middle section. Devyn almost turned her ankle tripping over a rusted gallon of paint. Chase was a good sport when a pile of mini American flags toppled onto his head in a patriotic avalanche.

"Is this something?" Chase pointed to a gray plastic tub labeled *Alan Bates*.

She pumped a fist. "Score! Alan Bates led the remodeling crew for the

Belle." She joined Chase, a thread of hopeful energy stitching through her.

They sorted through wrinkled brochures and invoices for labor done on the *Belle*. Chase held up a flyer advertising the *Belle*'s steamboat race with the *Delta Queen* in 1963.

He scanned the crumpled paper. "They raced each other?"

Devyn nodded. "It was a huge event. The city had bought the *Belle* and were in the process of fixing her up. They were so confident in the progress of the repairs that they challenged the *Delta* before they were even certain the *Belle* would run."

"Bold move."

"They worked right up until the start of the race. But were unsure if she'd go the distance."

"Let me guess." He absently toyed with the end of her ponytail. "Not only did the *Belle* run, but she smoked the *Delta*."

"Nope. The *Belle* got roasted. She fell behind the *Delta* by three miles in the twelve-mile race. The *Delta* even played "Goodbye, Little Girl, Goodbye" on their calliope as it passed."

His fingers stilled on her hair. "They didn't."

She smiled at his surprise. "They did. Though if you think about it, it's not just being the first to cross the finish line that makes you the winner. There's also having the courage to enter the race even when the odds are against you. The *Belle* was all but totaled when the city bought her, but in a short time, she braved the waters again. Her resiliency is champion material." And for the second time in one day, Devyn got emotional over a steamboat.

Chase looked at her.

"I know." She fidgeted. "I can be too much."

"Never." He tossed the flyer aside and slid his hands around her waist. "If I stare, it's only because of the way you talk about things others over-look." The edges of his mouth lifted. "That, and how adorable you look with tinsel in your hair." He disentangled the shiny offender from her locks. Holding it up for her inspection, he waggled his brows. "Look at you, wearing Christmas decorations. I didn't realize how much you loved our game." He reached for her with a playful growl.

She shirked away with a laugh. "Back to the search, Jones." With a saucy grin, she sank her hands deeper into the tub. He gave an exaggerated sigh and accommodated her, grabbing a pile of papers to sort through.

More brochures, receipts, and a few pictures of the construction work. But no notes.

A box, burdened with vinyl tablecloths, peeked from the bottom shelf, the label *Lost and Found* stirring her interest. Devyn removed the table coverings and shimmied the box forward. They found vintage sunglasses that Devyn adored—very Audrey Hepburnish from the beginning scene of *Charade*. There were some leather purses cracked with age. Magazines that would sell for a fortune online, if they weren't warbled and the pages not stuck together. It didn't seem like the letters would be shoved into a random box like this, but she wouldn't be satisfied until they ruled out every avenue.

A canvas pouch, that must've been leaning against the box before Devyn disrupted it, had fallen over and was on its side. She unzipped it and found a dozen or so small slips of paper bound by a paper clip. Her eyes landed on the *J* at the bottom of the page topping the stack and her breath stuck in her throat.

"You found it." Chase pressed a celebratory kiss to the side of her head. "Your great-grandfather's letters."

The notes were small enough to sit in the hollow of her hand. With care, she slid off the paper clip. The first note was faded and torn. She held it up to the natural light flooding in from the door.

> *H,*
> *I enjoyed our chat on the stern last evening.*
> *But for the first time in my life I pitied the sunset.*
> *It could never be as beautiful as you.*
> *Yours, J*

"Nice." Chase nodded his approval. "Your great-grandpa had game."

"It's weird though." She thumbed through them, suppressing a grimace. "Reading his romancy words to someone other than my great-grandmother."

His fingers covered hers as she handed him the notes, his gaze unusually serious. "Just because he loved Hattie doesn't mean he didn't love your great-grandma too."

How many times had she told herself that very thing?

He released her and lightly chucked her under the chin. "Besides, maybe we'll finally discover what separated him from Hattie."

With that in mind, they skimmed through more notes, the letters being along the same lines as the first.

"Whoa." Chase nudged her. "This one's different."

"Hmm?" She set down her stack. "How?"

"It's not addressed *H* and *Yours J* like the others. But it's written in Jack's handwriting." He read aloud. "*Are you okay? Knowing you're a Fair-view doesn't change who you really are. You are God's child. You are the woman who captured my heart. I'm praying for you. But the decision belongs to you, my love.*"

And just like that, a new name entered the search.

Fairview.

Chapter 28

Hattie

*M*y joints locked, frozen. I stood numb in Duffy's cabin, the devastating word plunging like an icy dagger into my chest.

Betrothed.

We'd moved from Jack's stateroom to Duffy's. His quarters had always been a place of comfort for me, but tonight, it was drafty and dark, the night pressing in with a chilling force. The kerosene lamp flickered, shifting the shadows on the walls. "What's going on, Duff?"

He sank onto a chair and dragged a hand across his weathered face. "This isn't easy, Hattie." His voice, usually so decided and gruff, was brittle. "Your real name is Harriet Fairview."

A shiver rocked my body, and Jack's hand infused delicate pressure to my spine, almost upholding me. My gaze probed Duffy's, searching, hoping, for hints of deception. But his dull eyes held so much clarity it made my own blink in rapid succession. It had to be a trick of the night, or illusions from my exhausted state, but it seemed even the carved lines in his aged face lost their rigidness, as if he'd strained for years bearing a devastating secret. "You've known my identity all along, my entire life, but never told me?" Betrayal wrestled with anger, crashing into my heart, breaking it into jagged shards.

"I'm sorry." He slouched. "Your mother was scared. She had—"

"My mother?" Duffy knew her? "You. . .lied to me." For twenty-one years, I'd been led to believe a nameless woman abandoned me on the Louisville wharf. And all this time, the man I'd trusted most had deceived me.

"I know."

"No, you don't know." My voice rasped. I was barely aware of Jack's arm wrapping my waist, anchoring me to his side. "Everything I know about myself is a myth. I lived a lie. How. . .how could you do this to me?"

"Because your life was in danger." His scruffy throat worked. "Still is."

Jack flinched. "Sir?"

Duffy didn't pull his weary gaze from mine. "You're the heiress of Fairview Steel and Rolling Mills in Pittsburgh."

I scoffed. He might as well have said I was heir to the British throne. How ridiculous. Duffy sounded like he'd lost his—I inhaled sharply. Jack strengthened his grip as if expecting me to swoon. But for the first time in twenty minutes, I drew the right conclusion. Duffy's behavior. His increased backwardness. Understanding and compassion flooded me. I left the security of Jack's arms and took a gentle step forward. "Duffy, I think it's time to see a doctor. Tomorrow before the noon excur—"

"You think I'm going mad?" His eyes saddened, his mouth tugging down at the edges.

I'd hurt him. Challenged one of the only strengths he'd had left—his intelligence. "Not mad, Duff. Maybe a little confused. Perhaps you dreamt all this. Or maybe the stress of the *Idlewild* being sold. . ."

Duffy stood and shuffled to his locked box. He shakily grabbed the keychain from his pocket, fumbled searching for the correct key, and struggled inserting it into the lock. His arthritis flared to alarming levels, choking the air in my chest. If I dashed over to help, it wouldn't *help* at all. Because coddling Duffy equaled bruising his pride. Finally, he opened the wooden lid. He scrambled through the box, the rustling of papers muting my spurts of breath. What was he looking for? Had he been to the doctor without my knowledge and was now hunting for the report? With a jerk of his head, he motioned me forward.

I rushed to his side.

"I can't lift it," he muttered, and I followed his pained gaze to a yellowed paper sticking out from the stack.

Commonwealth of Pennsylvania Certified Record of Birth.

My eyes widened at the bold lettering. I pinched the paper free from the smothering articles stuffed in the box, my hand shaking as fiercely as Duffy's. I sensed more than felt Jack's commanding presence behind me.

But I couldn't tear my eyes from the certificate.

My birth record.

The date listed was the exact day and year Duffy had told me. My birthday. Faded ink in a masculine scrawl drew me. Harold Fairview. My father. My finger traced his signature, my heart tying to a man I never knew but whose blood coursed through my veins. My vision blurred at the edges, but even that couldn't stop me from reading my mother's name. Ruth Young Fairview. Fiery tears scorched a blazing path over my flushed cheeks. My mother had given this to Duffy. She'd touched this very paper even as my father had.

"It's true?" Jack whispered. "Hattie's an heiress?"

Out of my peripheral, I saw Duffy dip his chin, assenting to Jack's words. "Sit, Hattie. There's more to discuss."

I couldn't peel my gaze from my birth record. I didn't want to let it go. But with all these emotions came the heavy realization that Duffy was telling the truth. I was a Fairview. In line to own a company. Even I was aware of the steel empire and the kingdom of factories based out of Pittsburgh. And somewhere in this story was a terrible twist in which I was betrothed. I set the paper down as if it turned to fire. Because of that certificate I was bound to a total stranger, whose name I'd yet to hear, an impending union my heart screamed to deny.

Duffy lowered onto a stool. "As you see, your papa is Harold Fairview. He and I were good friends. Like brothers. His father handed over the company to him when he was in his early twenties. Harold was a brilliant man."

A brilliant man with a misfit daughter. I'd been right all along. They had known I'd never measure up. They hadn't bothered to give me the chance to prove my worth.

Jack gently squeezed my waist. "Sit, Hattie. You're shaking."

"I don't want to sit." I wanted to run. I wanted far away from this conversation. Yet my legs wouldn't budge, my soles rooted to the floor. My own being was torn, half begging to retreat and never know, half yearning for answers to lifelong questions.

"Please?" Jack grabbed a chair. The same one I'd sat on when opening my birthday presents. The same day I'd kissed Jack. It seemed a lifetime ago. Another person ago—one that had been Hattie Louis. A woman belonging to no one except the waters she loved. Now, I was Harriet Fairview? An heiress belonging to a man I'd never met? The hairs on my arms raised, the tendons behind my knees weakened.

I sat, but remained at the edge of the chair, gripping the handrails, my thumb digging into a decorative brass rivet. "What about my mother? Was it a joint agreement to be rid of me?"

"No, my dear girl." The sadness returned to Duffy's eyes, along with something else. Muffled insistence. "You were wanted. You were loved."

My lashes flitted shut, damming the tears surging against my lids. Loved. Wanted. How I'd craved those words all my life. Duffy had the power to tell me the truth about my parents, yet he hadn't. The only papa I knew withheld a secret, rather several secrets. The tears escaped in a wild fury. Jack pressed a handkerchief into my trembling palm, and his finger stroked a soothing path on my wrist before pulling away.

Duffy leaned forward, a struggle evident in the lowering of his gray brows. "Harold had an. . .accident that took his life not long after you were born."

"What?"

Duffy shook his head. "Ruth panicked and found me when I was wharfed in Louisville waiting for the river to lower. She was desperate. She asked me to keep you safe until your twenty-first birthday."

I felt Jack's hands flex then tighten on my chair's back.

Duffy's mouth pressed tight as though wrestling his words. With a roughened exhale, he raised his eyes to mine. "Ruth believed Harold was murdered."

I gasped. "By who?"

"Your uncle."

"My uncle?" Another relation I never knew existed. One rumored to be a killer? What next? My quivering insides couldn't bear to know.

"He's the younger son and reckless. Harold owned the steel company and Bradford resented it. Your mother believed he killed your father because he wanted the fortune and factories. But Bradford didn't know about you."

My sharp breaths stabbed my chest. "How could he not know?"

"Ruth had trouble staying in the family way. She'd had several miscarriages." Duffy's tone lowered to a gruff rumble, and I leaned forward to catch his words. "She took to staying at the country estate when with child. They decided to keep your presence a secret until they knew for certain she could carry you through birth."

My stomach knotted. What hardships my parents had endured.

"You were only hours old when news came that your uncle had returned to the states. He lived overseas for years." Duffy's gaze hardened. "Your father traveled to the city to meet him, but never made it home. A carriage accident."

"That's too much of a coincidence." Jack echoed my very thought. "I'm guessing Hattie's father didn't mention her arrival to his brother."

Duffy shook his head. "Ruth wanted a week alone with her new daughter before telling the world."

"And where is my mother now?"

Duffy averted my stare, his gaze fusing to the floor. "She's dead."

Jack's protective hand gentled on my shoulder.

I would never get the chance to meet either of them. Could anything be crueler? To learn of my birth parents only to be informed in the next breath that they were both out of my reach. How many ways could they be ripped from me? "What happened?"

"It's uncertain. She fell down a staircase, but the housekeeper reported hearing a fight before her tumble."

I shuddered. How much more of this could I take? I shot to my feet.

"Hattie." Duffy's weak protest stilled my retreat. "He knows about you. I don't know how he found out but he did. He knows you're aboard the *Idlewild*."

Jack tensed. "Are you saying he'll come after her?"

"He already has. Remember the incident on the Louisville wharf?"

My fingers flew to my mouth. The two men. The assault. Everything fell into place with a sickening click. "He told me who I was."

"What?" Jack rounded the chair and knelt before me, his concerned eyes searching my face. "Who did?"

"The man with the gun. He said, 'You're a Fairview if I ever seen one.' I thought...I thought he was mocking me about my looks, but he must've meant my resemblance. He knew who I was. That's why he tried to steal me away." My gaze darted to Duffy. "Was that my uncle?"

"No. One of his henchmen. The plan looked as if it was for him to sneak aboard in the secret cargo and get rid of you." Duffy's voice trembled, fear strangling every word. "If he'd succeeded...I don't know how I'd live with myself." His eyes glossed. "You're my world, Hattie girl."

I was angry with Duffy. He'd lied to me. He'd wronged me. But my heart couldn't handle the anguished sheen in his eyes. The stern steamboat captain was more fragile than I'd ever seen. "I'm okay, Duff." I leaned over and hugged him. "It'll be all right."

"He won't stop." His whisper was urgent. "He knows what the will says. It all became yours the day you turned twenty-one."

I eased away. "But I don't want it." What on earth would I know about running a steel factory? "Can't I just refuse it all?"

"It's not that simple."

Jack paled. "The coded message the Coast Guard intercepted. The one that brought me here." His haunted gaze swung to me. "There was never alcohol aboard, was there? The diamond in the message referred to Hattie."

"Shakes Donovan didn't send it. Bradford Fairview did." Duffy shifted on the stool. "I knew the moment you showed me. The last portion of the missive sealed it—to unload before Pittsburgh."

My heart thudded dully, then with each passing, fearful thought, picked up momentum, rolling into my throat.

"I let you come aboard, Marshall, under false pretenses, and I'm sorry. I figured you would help keep my girl safe. And you have." He turned to me, and I barely registered he'd called Jack by his given name. "Once we dock in Pittsburgh next week, I'm taking you to Mr. Jones. He's your father's lawyer. He knows all the particulars of the will and the...arrangement."

My gut twisted. "You mean the stranger I'm promised to?" Did arranged marriages still happen? This was the 1920s, for heaven's sake. Women were voting, competing in the working world, running for legislature. Surely we could choose our own husbands.

Duffy's sigh was heavy enough to cave through all the decks. "The will states you must marry Mr. Arthur Thomas. He was Harold's right-hand man. He'll run the company and take care of you."

The man had to be at least twice my age. "Mr. Thomas knew of this agreement? While I was still a nursing babe, he agreed to marry me?"

"It's a clause in the will should something happen to your father." He cleared his throat and glued his gaze to the crummy floor again. His jaw worked a full three seconds before his words seemed to budge. "The marriage will be a formal one. He's a bachelor set in his ways and has his own. . .methods of relationships."

Jack launched to his feet. I'd seen enough tempests to recognize the power behind them. And Jack's eyes held thunder, lightning, and all the fury of a hundred stormy nights. "You mean take on mistresses? This man will pledge his life to Hattie while being unfaithful to her?"

My head swirled. I was disgusted at the idea of a stranger's touch, but what kind of life would that be? A union without love. "I won't marry him." My pleading gaze bore into Duffy's. "My heart belongs to Jack. It always will."

"This is all for your protection from your uncle. The best way to keep you safe. Accepting your inheritance will ensure the protection from him that I can't afford to give you. There's too much to explain right now. But the bottom line is you must marry Thomas. This has always been the plan. Your destiny. You're a Fairview."

He'd spoken the name as if it were a gavel's strike. It wasn't a plan, it was judgment. I paced the small area. "What about this." My feet halted in front of Duffy, my fingers lifting the helm pendent around my neck. "When you gave this to me, you said I held the power to navigate the course of my life. Was that a lie too?" Surely he'd remember that fatherly advice he'd given only three years back. Surely he'd fight for me.

Instead of taking up my case, his set jaw told me he wouldn't rally to my side. "I knew you'd reject this, Hattie. That's why I didn't tell you earlier. But I made a promise to your parents to watch over you until the appointed time. Which is now. I was afraid that if you knew, you'd run away."

He spoke as if it were too late to flee. A notion I intended to challenge.

Chapter 29

"This plan will work." I'd spent four sleepless nights, seven uneaten meals, and eight chewed fingernails on this strategy. Now to convince Jack. "I'm going to the papers with my story. Better yet, radio!" I snapped my fingers for a greater punch, but my thumb and index finger were slimy from my current task of peeling potatoes.

"It seems risky." Jack set down the paring knife he'd been slicing carrots with and wiped his hands on a towel. Two weeks ago, he would have been too busy with first mate duties to help me in the galley, but since learning of the threat on my life, things had changed. Jack had not only been the founder of my protection squad, but the appointed president and sole member. The man hardly left my side.

I continued with my practiced delivery of my upcoming adventure. "I'll publicly denounce my inheritance and make it known I want nothing to do with Fairview Steel." Though the famous KDKA station was based in Pittsburgh, their broadcasts reached across the nation. If Duffy wouldn't come to my defense, perhaps I could persuade a sliver of the northern hemisphere.

"Let's think on it more, Hattie. I'm not convinced this is the best route to take."

"I'll be sure to not-so-subtly hint to the world that if I wind up as fish food in the Ohio River, then it was by the hand of my rotten uncle."

Jack pinched the bridge of his nose, his thick lashes squeezing shut. "Don't talk like that. He won't touch you. I'm not letting you out of my sight." His determination was evident in his voice. But his red-rimmed eyes, and the shadows that hung beneath, told the story of his exhaustion. Duffy had withdrawn, practically abandoning all his captainly duties, leaving Jack to run the entire boat while keeping a diligent eye on me.

Early this morning I'd caught Jack sleeping on a deck chair outside my cabin door. He guarded me as if my life depended on him completely. There was no way he would agree to my idea. It required me to go alone. "I have to try. I need to let them all know I'm not interested in the Fairview kind of world."

Jack's steady gaze faltered. "Are you sure this is what you want?"

"What?" I emptied the excess potato skins down the Dollar Hole, tapping the aluminum plate hard against the tube, sending the peels down to the river. "You can't believe I'd enjoy the pampered life."

He scratched the back of his ear, knocking his mate's cap askew. "Some women do."

Oh. His former fiancée. The one who'd discarded him down the relationship chute, like I'd just dumped the peels, regarding him like garbage because he'd lost his fortune. "Jack, listen to me, and listen good. You told me in your last note the choice was mine and mine alone. And I choose us." How I'd recited his words over and over.

The uncertainty in his eyes looked out of place among the definite angles and sure plains of his face. "I can't give you all that you're giving up."

"No." I rounded the small island and caught his fingers in mine. "You can give me much more."

He opened his mouth to object, but I placed my other hand on his heart, stilling his protest.

"You're worth more to me than a million family fortunes."

"You say that now, but—"

"Nothing can convince me to accept those terms. I won't be forced to marry that man, and I refuse the heiress role."

The lines at the edges of his eyes relaxed. "I'll never stop you from pursuing your heart."

"Well, that's good." I turned over his hand and lifted it. "Because it's resting quite snugly right here." I kissed his calloused palm.

Gaze fervent on mine, he leaned closer, curving his raised hand to rest against my face. His thumb stroked my cheekbone. His mouth hovered near mine, but not close enough to satisfy the excruciating pang of want. His hands slid into my hair as his lips met mine.

We could be happened upon any second, but at the moment nothing mattered except Jack and his touch.

He was the first to pull away, and I was pleased his breathing was just as ragged as mine.

Jack cut a glance to both galley entrances then settled on me. His hand found mine and he drew me close. "You know there's nothing I want more than to be with you always." He pressed a lingering kiss to my forehead.

I eased back in his arms to look fully into his handsome face. "Then I must follow through with my plan."

"Tell me when, and we'll make our escape."

This really was unfair. His broad stance was so noble, his tone resolutely protective. Jack Asbury would battle all monsters for me, but this was a fight I needed to wage alone.

"Hattie?"

"You need to stay and run the *Idlewild*." I stepped back, only for my heel to hit the wall of cupboards.

"No." His shoulders tensed. "You aren't leaving without me."

"Duffy's been neglectful." I never thought I'd utter those words. It almost felt like I was betraying the riverman code by speaking against such a faithful captain. But there was more to it. I feared Duffy was slipping away, his health failing. What if something tragic happened to him while I was gone? At least Jack would be aboard and know what to do. "There's an excursion tonight and two scheduled for tomor—"

"Blast the excursions. Blast this boat." He moved toward me, palming the wall, bracketing me within his arms. "Your life's been threatened. You're my first priority. Not the *Idlewild*."

His nearness held power to sway me.

"Duffy needs you." My argument was feeble.

His chin lowered, his lips murmuring against my temple. "I need to be with you."

He was too close. Too enticing. Too Jack.

My will was like a brittle pinecone in a strong current. I had no choice but to duck away and place distance between us. Otherwise all my planning would be swept away in the force of his beautiful declarations.

"Hattie?" His voice broke on my name.

"There's no direct streetcar route from Beaver Valley to Pittsburgh. We must get there by bus." I sighed. "It leaves tomorrow morning at eight."

He pulled me to him and gave me a thoroughly appreciative kiss before bounding out the door to see to his next duty.

I pressed my fingers to my racing heart. I hadn't lied. There was a bus leaving tomorrow. But there was also one leaving tonight.

⁂

I'd played the calliope thirty minutes before departure, summoning the folk of Beaver, Pennsylvania, to a sunset cruise. I'd stood beside Jack and counted the boarding passengers. The efficient first mate then headed up to the wing bridge to command the deckhands, leaving me to the *watchful* eye of the purser. But the older man proved too easy to distract. When an elderly couple argued about the price of the trip, I took that as a divine cue and grabbed the bag and Duffy's old cloak I'd hidden behind a stack of preservers. With rushed steps, I sneaked off the boarding stage.

I draped the dark fabric over myself and lifted the hood. Thank goodness the sky was blanketed gray. Any passerby would think I was preparing for rain. I hustled as fast as I could, not stopping for breath until the *Idlewild* was out of sight. Guilt pinched my ribs. Jack would soon know I wasn't aboard, but he wouldn't be able to do a thing about it for at least three hours while the boat was coursing the river.

The cab I'd arranged for earlier waited for me at the corner I'd requested. By ten tonight, I would be in Pittsburgh, arriving a full day and a half before the *Idlewild*. If my uncle was tracking the boat, he'd no doubt have his henchmen waiting for me there at the dock. It felt good to outsmart him.

"Are you Miss Irene Simmons?" The young driver wearing a faded cap and bright smile waved me over.

It took me a second to remember the alias I'd given this morning on the phone at the drugstore. At the time, I'd been so flustered about slipping out unnoticed from the boat that my preoccupied brain had me rattling off the first name that came to mind. "I am. Thank you for being prompt." I waited as he opened the back door, and I slid inside the black Ford.

The driver positioned behind the wheel. "Where to, miss?"

"The bus terminal, please." I clutched my bag in my lap, my nerves jostling with each quickened heartbeat. The terminal was only a few miles away. I could have easily walked, but I was already pressed for time after waiting for the *Idlewild* to leave shore.

With dark clouds moving in, daylight faded even faster on this charming small town. All of the businesses were locked up for the evening, except for the corner drugstore. The same place I'd visited this morning to call a taxi and splurge on a chocolate soda.

Soon the bus terminal came into view and my pulse kicked faster. But. . .the taxi wasn't slowing. "Here's my stop." My voice cracked along with the remains of my composure. "Sir, you missed the terminal."

"No worries, miss. I will get you to the proper destination." His final two words caused my fingers to bite into the seat cushion.

I swallowed, trying to get my throat to obey. "Who are you?"

"The name's Charles Jones."

Jones! This was the man Duffy had been corresponding with? The lawyer who represented my family? He seemed far too young. Too unpolished. And I found considerable fault with how he ran his practice, considering he'd just abducted me. How had he—

"Sorry about the strange means of introduction." He braked, allowing a young couple to cross the street. He glanced at me over his shoulder. His hat cast a shadow over his eyes, but I could tell from his smooth jawline that he was indeed young. Maybe even younger than me. "I'm surprised you don't recognize me."

I blinked. "How could I? I've never seen you before."

"Ah, you're wrong. I followed you to the drugstore this morning and stood in the booth beside yours. That's how I knew you were running away. I took it upon myself to cancel the cab you booked and decided to escort you myself. With your captain's approval, of course."

What? Of all the crazy things. Duffy knew about this? "You followed me?" My head spun faster than the quaint town scenes outside my window.

"I've been scouting the *Idlewild* at the ports since Steubenville. Captain sent me an urgent wire a week or so back. He was concerned the closer we got to Pittsburgh, the greater the chance Fairview's men might try to kidnap you."

"So you kidnapped me first. How kind of you." My tone dripped with sarcasm. It all fell into place. That was the emergency message Duffy had sent the day of the excursion when I couldn't locate him. He could have at least said something. Then again, the man had a habit of withholding precious information from me.

"When I saw you bounding off the boat this morning, I knew right away it was you." He held up a half-torn picture, angling it my direction.

It was a photo. . .of me.

I squinted at the image of me dressed in the same frock I'd worn the day I asked Jack to meet me. My right hand held my calliope book. Comprehension struck. "That's the picture the newspaperman took. How'd you get it?"

"The captain." He lowered the picture and stuffed it in his pocket.

Duffy. My fingers bunched the fabric of my cloak. I should have known. He'd no doubt spoken to the journalist. The steamboat captain had muttered here and there about being quoted in the local paper, but conveniently refrained from mentioning he'd acquired the picture.

"He wanted to be sure I knew who I was protecting. Pretty important."

No. What was important was me getting to the terminal before my bus departed. "I have my own plan, thank you very much. And it doesn't include you."

"Best for you if it does." He turned, checking the traffic, giving me a better glimpse of his profile. His lips were pressed together, making a dimple dent his smooth cheek. "You see, Bradford Fairview wants you dead, and he's gone to great lengths to see to it."

I pushed past the nausea invading my stomach. "I'm disclaiming my birthright. I don't want it."

Mr. Jones's snort of laughter sent a wave of agitation through me. "A man like him, so consumed with money and greed? Nah, he won't believe you."

"Then I'll put it in writing. Have witnesses. Make it as legal as the will itself. Then I won't have to marry a man I don't know."

He scratched the back of his neck, bringing my attention to his dark hair curling beneath his cap. "I'm not sure if it's something you can denounce."

I sniffed. "I'm sure I could."

"Tell me, you ever plan on having babies?"

I blinked at his intrusiveness. What a time to be asking something so personal. "Someday," was all I could bring myself to mutter.

He shook his head. "Then it won't work."

I crossed my arms. "You're not making sense."

"The will is specific about the generational succession. If you turn over the company, it would return right back to your children. The company is to stay in the family line. *Your* family line."

My lips trembled. "You don't mean—"

"That he'd kill your children? I absolutely mean that. The man's a devil."

All the fight I'd so stubbornly clung to fled in a defeated whoosh of breath. "Then how is he ever to be stopped?"

"Mr. Thomas."

The man I was to marry. "What role does he have in all this?"

"A powerful one."

A chill trickled down the length of my body, and I pressed my back against the cushion.

"Even a murdering crook like your uncle won't mess with Thomas. You've got an impenetrable ally with him. Thomas has powerful friends and just enough dirt on your uncle to keep him in his place. When you marry him, that protection extends to you."

This was what Duffy had meant when he said there was more to explain. I slid my eyes shut. The only way to stay alive was to unite myself with Mr. Thomas. The oppressive sorrow I'd been snubbing the past week smiled smugly and settled in for an extended stay. My heart mourned for the life I craved but that was fading away and for the sad existence I was forced to accept. Darkness invaded the skies even as it had my soul. I had to find another way. I prayed with everything in me.

"The wedding's set for tomorrow. It's my job to get you there."

My hand slapped over my mouth. I was going to retch. I sat in queasy agony for several minutes before braving to speak. "Where are you taking me now? And exactly who are you in all this rigamarole? I've never known a lawyer to be so unorthodox."

His laughter filled the car's cabin. "I'm not your lawyer, lady. My father is. We're on our way to see him now." He braked at a stop sign and looked over his shoulder again. "No doubt you'll find the great Garrison Jones a bit pompous, but it's in your best interest to listen to him."

Something crashed into us from behind. I lurched forward, colliding into the back of the front bench. The crunch of metal on metal scraped my ears.

Mr. Jones cussed and jumped out of the car. "What are you doing? You can't run a stop sign if someone's right in front of you, genius."

I peered out the window. This stretch of road had no streetlamps. All I managed to see were moving shadows. The dark profiles launched at each other, and I gasped at the unmistakable sound of fists against flesh.

What could I do? Should I leave this man to fend for himself and make my getaway? I couldn't rightly interject myself into their fight. But I could run for help.

I reached for the door, but it swung open before my fingers grasped the handle. A giant of a man crouched in the opening.

"Miss Fairview, nice to see ya 'gain." He leaned forward, and I caught a glimpse of the beastly man from the Louisville wharf. The one who'd gotten into fisticuffs with Jack. "This time you're comin' with me."

⁂

I'd screamed, clawed, and kicked, but my captors had withdrew pistols. Instead of aiming at me, one of the two men leveled their weapons on an unconscious Mr. Jones, who had already been bloodied up something awful. They'd wisely targeted my compassion, and all my courage died as the night choked the last drops of daylight from the ominous sky.

They'd bound my wrists and ankles with coarse ropes and dragged me to the back seat of their vehicle. The jostling ride had only triggered the pounding in my skull and now my stomach was two panicked breaths from emptying itself all over the rattling floorboards. I hadn't the luxury of anxiety. Not when I needed to determine the best means of escape. My sense of time had been cruelly skewed. Had we been driving for thirty minutes? An hour?

The automobile veered off the county road. In the weak headlamp's glow, I could identify shadowed outlines of trees, their branches like skeletal fingers clawing the night sky. We entered the pit of a forest. A place where one could easily hide a villainous act. And bury it. Dread coiled around my chest and squeezed, constricting my breaths to agitated spurts. The brute who'd split Jack's lip on the Louisville wharf was the driver. The other fellow, the one I'd clobbered with the crowbar, sat in an unsettling state beside the driver, his beady glare bouncing between me and the pistol he clutched.

The car lurched to a stop. Before I had time to work the exit lever with my elbow, the back door burst open. I pushed off the seat with my feet, scrambling to the other side of the bench, the ropes burning tender flesh.

Gun Man poked his head inside the car cabin. The dim moonlight twisted shadows across his face, but I clearly glimpsed his venomous snarl. "Out ya go, missy. And no funny tricks this time."

I pressed my shoulder blades against the other side of the car, thankful at least the goons had bound my hands in front rather than behind my back. But my temporary partition gave way as the door yanked wide. I fell backwards, smacking my head on the handle.

The driver laughed, hovering over me like a sinister gargoyle. "It's easier to get her out from this side."

"Yeah." Gun Man's fingers lazily walked up my leg. "But not half as fun."

I resisted the urge to thrust my knee into his throat and squirmed to a seated position. "What are you going to do?" The two ruffians sandwiched me, and I toggled my narrowed gaze between them.

Neither answered. No. I shouldn't expect a response. No matter how desperately I needed to know their intentions, this wasn't a silent film where the villains revealed their evil plot with climactic music and title cards. But maybe I could take some hints from the silver screen. "I—I... please don't hurt me." I was never one for theatrics, but tonight I'd be Clara Bow, Greta Garbo, and Lillian Gish all squeezed into a dramatic heap. "Please. Please, I'll do anything."

Gun Man's lips peeled back in a vicious smile. "How 'bout we test that theory." His hand slid up my leg.

At his pursuit, I screamed like a banshee, then collapsed against the seat, forcing tension from my limbs.

"She conked out." The vulgar man sounded disappointed.

"Probably for the best. Now she can't put up a fight."

I prayed they wouldn't take my pulse. No amount of pretending could keep my blood from pumping fast.

Coarse fingers bit into the sensitive spot beneath my arms and pulled my limp body from the car. They dragged me over the rough forest floor. Twigs stabbed the backs of my legs, a rock scraped my ankle, shredding my stockings into ribbons. My jaw rattled with each jostle, causing my teeth to slash my tongue. Pain ravaged, but I couldn't release the pressing cry. Darkness pushed in, but I envisioned the ice blue of Jack's eyes. Those luring hues that gazed at me with aching affection. Would I ever see those eyes again?

One of the men tripped and cussed.

Were they planning on ending my life out in these woods? Or were they taking me to him? To my uncle?

Dewy grass slimed the hem of my dress, the backs of my legs.

"You got the lockpicks, Briggins?" the man clutching my right arm groused.

The jingling sound of metal met my ears. "Got 'em. But I ain't happy about being on Hatcher property. We can get ourselves in lots of trouble messin' with the likes of that man."

Hatcher? As in Kenneth Hatcher, Duffy's friend that owned lumber mills? If only I could find a way to get to him. But his land extended over a hundred acres. I doubted the goons would be anywhere close to the Hatcher mansion.

"Alls I know is we can't do anythin' near Fairview's place. It'll look suspicious." His tone dripped like poison from a serpent's fangs. "Boss says make it look like an accident. Like all the others. So no puttin' any bullets in her."

All the others? Did he mean my parents? And now he spoke so casually about my own death! Fear and fury battled for prominence. I cracked my eyelids, slightly craning my neck. The fleeting moonlight allowed me a glimpse of a wooden shack. Desperation clawed. I had to do something.

They yanked me up two splintery steps. Briggins disappeared around the side of the shack, leaving me with the giant thug. He grabbed me beneath the shoulders, dragged me inside, then stomped out the door and locked it. His footsteps faded, and I struggled to sit up.

My prison reeked of wet earth and mildew. Blackness smothered me, and I rapidly blinked my weary eyes into adjustment. There was a window, but it had been boarded shut. Maybe I could pry it free. But first I needed to cut my bindings.

"Hurry up!" one of the cronies yelled to the other. "Douse it good."

Douse? The tang of kerosene singed my nose, igniting my panic. Within seconds, bright yellow flames glowed beneath the door, licking the wood with raging appetite.

Chapter 30

Devyn

*D*evyn swirled her french fry in her milkshake and popped it in her mouth.

"I'm going to ignore your doing that." Chase feigned repulsion, but the crinkles framing those gorgeous grays totally gave him away.

"You said finding those notes is a cause for celebration. Nothing says party like french fries dipped in chocolate ice cream." For good measure, she did it again. "You didn't cheat on our agreement, did you?" Brinston's Hot Dog Shoppe was a local favorite. Unfortunately their service wasn't as hot as their jalapeno crunch petals. So while Devyn waited in line through several bad nineties songs, she'd trusted Chase not to be googling the name Fairview. They'd made a deal—no internet searches unless they were together.

He cracked a smile more delicious than her calorie fest. "Wouldn't dream of it."

She withdrew her tablet and tapped the screen, lighting the display. "Besides the promise of a mild case of heartburn, this place also offers lightning speed Wi-Fi." She waved him closer. "Ready to find out who Hattie really is?"

He scooted his chair next to hers. The warmth from his thigh melted into hers. "Did I ever tell you how much I like this adventure of ours? All this togetherness." He gave her a quick kiss.

Her phone buzzed on the table. She didn't recognize the number, but then again, she'd given her contact info to all those steamboat museums. "This is Devyn Asbury."

"Devyn, what's up? It's Peirson."

She sat straighter. "Hey there. I was going to call you tomorrow and let you know all the details about—"

"Sorry, Dev." His normally smooth voice was rugged with apology. "I can't sing for your event."

She fumbled her phone, nearly giving it a death by chocolate milkshake. "What? Why?"

Chase's brow crumpled with concern, and she forced a smile as plastic as the vine winding around the light fixture overhead. It would be all right. She could convince Peirson Brooks. She had to.

"My agent put in my name to sing the national anthem at the World Series. I thought it was a no-go since we hadn't heard anything, but we just got the call." He tried—oh, he tried—to tame the excitement in his voice, but Devyn could read it just as clear as the FAILURE sign flashing in her mind.

"That's a great opportunity, Peirs." And with a far better advancement for his career than singing on the *Belle*.

"I'm sorry. I hate to cancel."

She bit her lip, sampling salt from her fries and the foretaste of future tears. "It's all right. I'll come up with something else."

"I'm in town again in December for the holidays with the fam. I'll give you a call. Maybe I can do something for your boat then."

The *Belle* would be docked for the winter, but he could always perform on the *Mary Miller*—the smaller steamboat ran all year long. Steph would love that. But this wouldn't help her situation now. "Thanks, Peirson." She ended the call and the milkshake turned to molten lava in her stomach.

"What's wrong?" Chase wrapped a protective arm around her, pulling her close.

She rested her head on his shoulder. "That was Peirson Brooks. He just canceled. He's gonna sing the anthem for the World Series. I get it. I do. Why sing for a hundred people when you can sing for millions?"

His exhale ruffled her hair, and he kissed the top of her head. "How can we fix this?"

"I don't know. The entertainment was going to be the highlight of the evening. How am I going to get a jaw-dropping entertainer in less than five days?" Good thing Devyn hadn't listed Peirson on the invitations.

She'd wanted it to be a surprise. To wow the judges. Now they'd be shocked by an empty stage. "I've exhausted all my connections."

Well, almost all of them. Travis had ties to celebrities, artists, probably even some royals. But asking him to pull strings for her would only be a tighter cord around her neck. She would not be indebted to him again.

"Wish I could help you." The rumble of Chase's soft voice pulled her back to the moment.

"Let's get back to our girl." Her high-pitched tone made her wince, but she pushed through. "Do you want to run the internet search or should I?"

"We don't have to. There's no rush on this."

Devyn enjoyed his comforting embrace for a few calming seconds, then faced him. "Please? I need to have at least one thing go right today."

"We found the letters." He caught one of her wayward locks between his fingers, swept his thumb over it in a reverent caress, then tucked it behind her ear. "That was a win for us."

"C'mon, wildcat. I need this." She reawakened her tablet and typed *Fairview 1920s* into the search bar.

They leaned forward to review the results. The top hit referenced Fairview Steel. She tapped it and the site popped up. "It's a huge steel factory in Pittsburgh."

Chase's brows pulled together, his gaze thoughtful. "Pittsburgh was a leader in the steel industry. And also where my great-grandpap was born. His family had a very successful law firm there."

"Think that's a coincidence?"

"Probably not. We know my family is tied somehow to Hattie."

She tapped one of the links, bringing up a page with several pictures of massive buildings. "Wow, looks like this place would take up half the city." The paragraph underneath provided a quick summary of the plant. Established in 1860 by Douglas Fairview, the empire went to his oldest son Harold. Devyn raised a brow at the photo of a man with perfectly parted hair and a waxy moustache. "It's nothing but a long-winded Wikipedia page."

"Wait." Chase scanned the screen. "Look here. Scroll down."

She did as he asked and read aloud. "'When Harold Fairview had a tragic accident, the steel kingdom went to his brother, Bradford Fairview. The younger of the siblings had control of the company, but another heir surfaced in 1927. Harold and Ruth Fairview had a daughter named Harriet.'"

"Isn't Hattie a nickname for Harriet?" Chase's hand clasped hers.

"Could be. And the date lines up with your picture." Then realization sank in. "Was Hattie a steel factory heiress? Was that why she couldn't marry my great-grandfather?" Had Hattie's family disagreed with the match like something from an Austen novel? "But then, we can't be sure this is the same woman."

"Oh yes, we can." Chase zoomed in. "Read this. 'The younger brother didn't know about Harriet's existence until she was an adult, because she'd been raised by a riverboat captain, living aboard the *Idlewild*.'"

"It's her! And no wonder this site didn't come up on our searches. They spelled *Idlewild* with two 'll's at the end."

Devyn exhaled a sigh as Chase kept scrolling. They'd found her. Harriet "Hattie" Fairview. "Now we can run a search on Harriet Fairview and get all the goods on her."

Chase shifted his gaze from the screen to her. "We may not want to."

"Why not? What's a better ending than becoming an heiress, marrying someone like American royalty, and living happily ever after?"

"But she didn't." Chase stared at her, eyes troubled. "Devyn. . .it says she died that same year."

Chapter 31

Jack

*J*ack bounded the stairs leading to the texas roof, his joints jarring on each step. His muscles screamed for relief, but he refused. He couldn't rest until he found Hattie. Daylight teetered on the edge of the horizon, but the serene view was in direct contrast to his riotous soul. He knocked on her cabin door. No answer. He opened it. Miss Wendall was away visiting family, but it was Hattie's bunk that stole his stare.

Empty.

She hadn't returned. It wasn't like he'd expected her to, but he had to make certain. He shut the door and checked his pocket watch. He had a little over an hour before the bus would leave for Pittsburgh.

And he was going to be on it.

Last night, when Hattie didn't appear on the excursion, he knew immediately she'd fled. Without him. Blast it all if he hadn't been hurt by her deception.

The moment the *Idlewild* reached shore, he'd dashed off in search of her. His first stop was the terminal. A bus had departed for the steel city last evening. Not only was Hattie's name absent from the passenger list, but the attendant said there hadn't been any females on board.

Where on earth had she gone? He'd scoured the streets for hours until dawn, achieving nothing but a heart full of worry and a body fraught with exhaustion.

He strode toward the captain's cabin and pounded on the door, uncaring if he blistered a knuckle or disturbed his superior.

Duffy grunted and Jack all but tore off the brass knob entering the cabin. Duffy was seated at the small table, Bible opened in front of him.

"I can't find her, sir." His voice cracked. A pathetic delivery, but he could do no better. His girl was missing.

Duffy said nothing at first, just leaned back in his chair, studying him. "I've been waiting for you to return." His casual address riled Jack's temper.

"Didn't you hear me? Hattie's gone."

"I know." He motioned for Jack to sit, but Jack could barely stand still as it was. Realizing Jack wasn't to be placated, Duffy sighed. "She left with Charles Jones. He took her to Pittsburgh. Jack, I'm sorry, but she's getting married today."

No.

He yanked his hat from his head, crushing it in his grip. "She can't be." Not after her heartfelt declaration only yesterday. How green her eyes had been when she'd sworn so faithfully that he held her heart. Her kiss had all the evidence of a woman in love.

But was love enough?

He knew all too well the lure wealth and grandeur possessed. He'd suffered at its powerful hand. Now it appeared the thief of prominence had stolen from him yet again. But this time, he may not recover.

He met Duffy's eyes. "Are you certain, sir?"

He gave a solemn nod.

Fire seethed his skin. "Then I'll have to go and win her back." He wasn't about to lose her. Not without a fight for her affection. "If you'll excuse me." He slapped his hat back on his head. "I have a bus to catch."

"Don't do it." Duffy's feeble protest stopped him midstride. "You can't protect her."

Jack faced him, and he worked to keep his breaths even. "What aren't you telling me?"

Duffy's hand shook as he closed his Bible. "Her intended is the only one who can—"

The door burst open. A young man stumbled in. His left eye was swollen shut. His lips bruised and puffy. Poor chap had been in a rumble and appeared to be on the losing end. "It's all gone wrong." The man whimpered. "Very wrong."

"Charles." Duffy flinched. "What's happened? Where's Hattie?"

The young man lowered his head, revealing an angry knot on his scalp. But nothing looked more painful than the anguish in his eyes. "They took her."

"Who took her?" Jack stepped toward Jones. "Where is she now?"

Jones recoiled as if Jack would strike him. "I'm sorry. They found us."

Duffy's jowls trembled. "What do you mean?"

"Fairview's men. They knocked me out cold and took her."

The words pierced Jack like a thousand harpoons. "Where'd they go?" He would find them. And if they'd harmed a single hair on her head, he'd tear them—

"It happened on Hatcher land. The old grump ran me off his property, but not before I found this." Jones dug in his pocket and retrieved what looked like a tarnished necklace.

Jack snatched it from Jones's trembling hand. It was Hattie's. The helm pendent was half-melted. The links charred and molten together. He looked to Jones, horror slicing through him.

"They burned the cabin to the ground with Hattie inside."

Jack's heart collapsed. He thumped his chest, hard, refusing to forsake hope. "You're wrong. She's alive. I can feel it."

The young man's busted lip quivered. "She's gone."

Duffy's chin lowered in defeat and sorrow. "My girl," he said on a sob. "My girl."

Jack couldn't believe it. Hattie was a fighter. She wouldn't let them kill her. But even she had her limits. The thought of her in pain, burning, rent his soul. No. No! "This is her uncle's doing. I'm going to destroy him. Make him suffer like he did her."

"Won't bring her back, son." Duffy's voice trembled. "Nothing can bring her back." He stood and shuffled away, shoulders heaving.

Jones gave a slow shake of his head and left.

Jack's soul cleft in two. Hattie. His Hattie. With a guttural cry, he kicked the stool and stormed from the stateroom.

He didn't know where he was going, but he needed off this boat. Away from it all. But his heart yanked in another direction. He tore into Hattie's room. The sweet smell of rosewater and talc taunted him. He grabbed her songbook from the small desk. Clutching it to his chest, he wept.

Chapter 32

$\mathcal{D}$evyn had never gotten emotional over bluegrass music before, but today she could cry along with a tinny banjo's strum commemorating another failed endeavor. The Mountain Road Boys had just rejected her request—more like pleading—to perform this Saturday. Even after she'd offered season passes for the *Belle*, a year's worth of free food at MJs Pizza (Mitch would've understood. Emergencies called for sibling backup!) as well as her lifetime gratitude. Still, nope.

She rolled her head back against her chair and groaned.

"I take it the Mountain Road Boys aren't coming?" Steph entered Devyn's office, clipboard in hand.

"They're booked all weekend." The ball was three days away. Devyn had lowered her sights from A-list music artists to local-and-loved bands. No one was available. Yes, it was short notice, but somebody had to be free to perform. "I'm getting desperate. My mom's uncle can play a mean rendition of "Moon River" on his accordion."

Steph winced. "Sweetie, that's too desperate."

"You're right. Plus he has a weird habit of scaring children by popping out his glass eye."

Steph's pencil-lined lips pursed in thought. "You're thinking all on the lines of music. What about something else?"

"Like a standup comic? All I have to do is stand up there, and it's a guaranteed laugh." She sighed. "I'm bombing this opportunity."

"This isn't your fault."

"No, but I should've had backup plans on all fronts." The non-existent entertainment wasn't the only glitch. The forecast predicted bad weather this weekend. Not just any regular thunderstorm, but a walloping gale. Rain would be bad enough, causing the guests to be huddled inside, watching gloomy skies rather than an amazing sunset. But with the expected high winds and limited visibility, the boat would be forced to remain docked, taking away the entire charm and uniqueness of the *Belle*.

Her phone buzzed. She read the incoming text and moaned. "Now my brother's saying the breaker in his basement blew. It's been out for days without him knowing. The paw paws in his spare fridge are spoiled." Her breathing tightened, darts of pain shooting across her chest. "I think I'm going to have a panic attack." She pinched her eyes shut, buried her face into her folded arms on her desk, and prayed.

"Oh good." Steph exhaled, but Devyn refused to lift her lashes. "Your cure's here. Handsome, go play doctor and fix our girl right up."

She hadn't the strength to look up at Chase or else the tears she'd been bottling would burst free, like shaking a two-liter then popping the lid. Booted steps crossed her office, but she would have known the moment Chase drew near without the sound of his rhythmic footfalls. No, his amazing cologne enveloped her in a soothing cocoon. And she couldn't help but sniff through her only unclogged nostril.

Two solid hands slid over her shoulders, massaging. "What's the matter?"

"Everything," she mumbled into her sleeve.

His talented fingers worked the knots on the base of her neck. "Care to talk about it?"

She allowed him to knead her shoulders for a few more comforting seconds before glancing up. The pinch of concern in his eyes made her own well with tears. "I need outta here. I feel an all-out sobfest coming." Thankfully Steph had already left them alone.

Chase tugged her up and into his arms, cushioning her head against his chest. "Let's go back to your place. We'll talk, order pizza, and watch one of your old movies." The man really was the sweetest.

She sniffled. "Sadly, not even carbs and Cary Grant can fix my problems."

"That bad, huh?"

Through her choking tears, she explained all the snags in their event. Chase simply held her and ran a soothing hand along her back.

"On top of that, I can't stop thinking about Hattie." She wiped her soggy cheeks with the edge of her sleeve. "It's stupid, I know. But I feel like I'm in mourning."

"It's not stupid." He released her to grab her cardigan from the chair back and handed it to her. "We were fully invested in this girl, and her end was tragic."

Very tragic. Now that they knew her real name, they'd been able to discover everything about her death on the internet—her obituary, pictures of her humongous headstone in a Pittsburgh cemetery. They'd searched several newspapers, but they'd all run the same story, stating Hattie had intended to meet up with her beau—Devyn assumed he was her great-grandfather—with plans to elope. The pair had planned to meet at the cabin in a secluded spot, but Hattie had dozed off and knocked over a kerosene lamp.

Harriet Fairview had been burned alive.

But if Hattie and Devyn's great-grandfather both had worked on the *Idlewild*, why would they have had to meet up somewhere? Wouldn't they have already *been* together?

Several of the old articles had quotes from Garrison Jones, Chase's great-great-grandfather, who'd been the Fairview family lawyer. They hadn't complete clarity on his great-grandpap Charles Jones's role in all of it, or why he'd been so anguished over Hattie. But they assumed Charles had known Hattie through her connection with his lawyer father, and her death had impacted him.

Devyn's breath shuddered. "Here I am whining about a ball, when Hattie had an awful demise. She died at twenty-one, robbed of an entire lifetime with the man she loved." Though if Hattie had lived, Devyn wouldn't exist now. Nothing like a loaded dose of survivor's guilt to add to her neurotic meltdown.

"Let's not think about that right now." He smoothed the hair back from her cheek. "Ready to go?" He threaded his fingers through hers, and they walked out of the lifesaving station offices to Chase's Jeep. The sky blanketed dark gray, promising rain.

He held open the passenger door, then rounded the front, only to pause and tug his cell from his jeans' pocket. He peered into the windshield, holding up his index finger, letting her know he had to field the call.

She waved him off. Might as well call Mitch back and try to get something figured out for dessert. But her phone buzzed, displaying a number she didn't recognize. No doubt it was another potential entertainer turning her down. Or the florist saying all the flowers had been destroyed by zombie beetles. At this point, nothing would surprise her. "Hello, Devyn Asbury speaking."

"Afternoon, Miss Asbury, this is Phil Beaumont from the Ohio Steamboat Museum. I found some information that might be useful in your search."

Their search had hit a deadly end, but she hadn't the strength to say that. Poor Hattie.

"We located some inventory logs and purser books for the *Idlewild* during the timeframe you're interested in."

She straightened. The logs would include a payroll and have the crew names listed. "Was there a Marshall Asbury on the crew? Or maybe Johnathan Asbury?"

A few sprinkles alighted the windshield. "No Asbury, but there's a Jack Marshall here. Says he's the first mate."

Marshall? Why would her great-grandfather use his first name as his last? There must be more to the story. "Was there a Hattie Fairview?"

"There wasn't any lady by that name. But the cook's name was. . .let's see. . ." She heard pages flipping. "Miss Agnes Wendall."

Maybe Hattie hadn't been on the payroll. Maybe the steamboat captain who'd been her guardian had taken care of all she needed. Which reminded her. "What about the captain's name?"

"Ah, that would be Finnegan 'Duffy' Woodruff."

"Let me grab something to write with." Her gaze scrambled. Chase's notebook rested on the dash. Surely, he wouldn't mind her taking a piece of paper. Especially since she already knew his secret. She snagged the notepad and flipped to find a blank page. Her brow furrowed. These weren't food logs, med dosages, or appointment info. These were phrases, words.

Sunset shone in her eyes and it set my soul aflame. Dated the day of their first date. When they'd been on the evening cruise.

He wrote poetry? About her?

She flushed with warmth but then another thought drained her cold.

Her fingers skimmed to the front of the notepad. All poems with dates. One group of words made her heart clench. It was the poem Travis used in the breakup video. Dated two years ago.

Before that ridiculous book of poetry had even been printed.

⚜

"Sorry about that." Chase settled behind the wheel. "Feeling any better?"

She couldn't pull her distraught gaze from his eyes, his granite—no, *slate*-colored—eyes. Rain droplets had caught in his hair, curling the tips. But she was the one soaked in unbelief, abject shock.

"What's wrong?" The easy smile slid from his face. "Still thinking about Hattie? The ball? We'll get it—"

"I know." Her voice warbled, and she hated the sound.

"Know what?" He reached to caress her face, but she shrank from his touch. "What happened?"

"You're Slate."

His gaze fell to the notebook in her lap, and a muscle leapt in his jaw. "You knew that already. We talked about it."

What? "No, we haven't." Her snappish tone was accented by a rumble of thunder. "I would've remembered that conversation. I have no recollection of you saying, 'Hey Devyn, you know that worst moment of your life? I was part of it.'"

He jolted as if she'd slapped him. "I had no idea your jerk of a fiancé was going to use my poem. That's not my fault."

"But you're at fault for lying to me this whole time." She picked up the notebook and shook it. "How could you? I trusted you. Fell in lov—" No, she was *not* going there.

"Wait. Devyn, back up." He dropped his keys in the cupholder as if saying he wasn't going anywhere until they'd worked this out. "The day at your family's cabin, when we were by the falls, I tried to tell you. But you said you knew all about it. That we didn't need to discuss anything because it was a personal part of my life."

"No. No, no, no." This wasn't happening. Her fingers skimmed her pounding temple. "I thought you were sick."

"What?" His forehead rippled. "What gave you that idea?"

"Your phone conversation a while back, I kept hearing the words *insurance*, and *agent*, and *overdue*. Then I saw you jotting words on the *Belle* before dinner. I thought you were logging what you ate. My mom did that when she was on lots of meds." She shifted her stare toward her window, watching rivulets of rain twist down the glass. "I totally assumed the wrong thing."

Chase sat for a long minute. "I was probably talking to Melanie. My agent. She's pressuring me to accept Travis's offer. I told her my biggest insurance right now is staying anonymous." His laugh held no humor. "But that won't last unless I give my publishers some more material. I've been struggling, and I'm overdue on my deadline."

All those words she'd thought had to do with sickness had been aimed at him being a writer. Slate. "Why didn't you mention it even before?" Agitation renewed, she nailed him with a glare. "You had plenty of opportunities to tell me before that mix-up at the creek."

"Because, Devyn." His tone was deep and heated. "The very first time we met you basically strangled my book and called it trash."

Ugh. She did.

"Then. . ." He palmed the back of his neck, his eyes sliding shut for a few sharp breaths. "Then we got close. I wanted to tell you several times, but I didn't want to lose you. To lose what we have."

What did they have? Clearly communication issues. But the bold-faced truth rose from the swell of chaos—she had fallen in love with Slate.

"Say something." His imploring gaze made her look away. "Anything."

She bit the inside of her cheek. "I don't know." This day had been disaster upon disaster. The ball planning was in shambles. Her relationship with Chase now teetering like a Jenga tower—one more unwise turn, and it could topple completely. "You're not who I thought you were."

He blew out a shaft of air. "You know who I am."

"Do I?"

His gaze latched hers. "Devyn, you know me. More than anyone else outside my family. I don't want to lose what we have here."

At this moment she wasn't certain what she felt. It wasn't his fault about the misunderstanding at the cabin. She wasn't too unreasonable or proud to accept the blame for her part in that. But still, the truth was a shock to her core. More like an explosion. And now her emotions were fragmented debris scattered all around her.

"You also know how important it is to remain anonymous."

Oh, she knew. Travis had been prepared to toss a lot of money at Slate for a reveal on Space Station.

Chase was waiting, but she couldn't offer a response. Her thoughts were jumbled, too mixed up to understand, let alone voice. But her choice in remaining silent seemed to make Chase more anxious, his searching gaze never straying from her face.

"I know you're upset with me. Angry, even." He scraped both hands through his hair and then collapsed his head against the seat back. "Just please, don't do anything rash."

Her jaw unhinged. "Like?"

"Like break up with me or. . ."

"Or what?"

"Ruin me."

Her breath iced over in her lungs. "You can't be serious." Was that what he thought of her? "Chase, I know exactly how it feels to be *ruined* in the public eye. I would never do that to anyone. Anyone! Let alone the man I—" She'd said enough. Her shaky fingers managed to open the door.

Chase looked stricken. "Devyn, please stay. I didn't mean it to—"

She exited the Jeep and hurried down the Riverwalk toward her apartment building, the rain mixing with her tears.

Chapter 33

*T*he storms had rolled in earlier than forecasted. Two days after Devyn and Chase's explosive argument the sky had cracked open and unleashed its wrath on Louisville. Electricity had flickered on and off. Some areas of the city had flooded.

But Devyn had work to do.

She'd tried—but failed miserably—to keep her thoughts focused on the ball and off Chase. He'd called a dozen times. Texted more than that. And like the responsible adult she was, she hadn't responded. Finding out her man was Slate had been a crazy mountain of emotions to scale, but realizing he was afraid she'd purposefully expose him? That was like an avalanche tumbling down said mountain and burying her in hurt. And she'd yet to climb out.

Relationships were built on trust, and if he didn't trust her to keep his secret, then what was the use? This morning she'd located a general non-disclosure agreement at work, filled out what she could, and signed it. Soon UPS would supply him with legal proof that she had no intention of destroying him.

All afternoon and into early evening, Devyn and Steph had been decorating the ball room, transforming it into a river dreamland. But even that couldn't keep Devyn from checking her phone. The few stragglers she'd been waiting on about the entertainment hadn't gotten back to her, but she was mostly curious if Chase would reach out again. His last text had been five hours ago.

Maybe she should—

"Hey, Devyn?" Steph called over her shoulder while standing on a stepladder, screwdriver in her hand. "Leave the entertainment to me." She resumed unscrewing the faded No Smoking sign as if what she said wasn't a huge deal.

Devyn shook her head. Maybe she'd misheard. She hadn't been too awesome in the communication department lately. "What's that, Steph?"

"Leave the entertainment to me. I'll handle it." She tugged the sign from the wall.

"That's really kind of you, but—"

"It's my responsibility now." Steph stepped down from the ladder and approached Devyn, a sympathetic smile in place. "Look at you. You've been micromanaging this entire event."

"Isn't that what you told me to do? To take care of everything?"

"Yes." She sighed. "And I'm sorry for it." She pulled out a chair and sat then motioned for Devyn to sit too. "You've been running yourself ragged."

"I really want the *Belle* to win."

"Do you?" The twist in her tone paired with the knowing lift of her brow. "Or do you have something to prove to yourself?"

Devyn glued her stare on her chipped thumbnail rather than let Steph glimpse the truth no doubt flooding her eyes. "I just want something to go right." Was that too much to ask? "But even this spun out of control. Thank God, it's manageable again." The weather now seemed cooperative, promising clear skies for the event. The décor had come together and the parts they'd already arranged looked stunning. Mitch had called earlier with news of salvaging enough fruit to make pawpaw crème brûlé for dessert. Which would be a tastier dish than the pudding. And yet Devyn still felt like a failure. Was it the missing entertainment factor? Or more likely her rocky relationship with Chase? Her pillow was probably still soaked from her unending tears. "I'll rest after the ball."

"That's where you're wrong, honey." Steph pushed off the table and stood. "I'm sending you home. Now."

"What?" She glanced at her phone. "It's only six. There's still a lot of decorating to finish." Hanging the twinkle lights. Arranging the display tables.

"All of which I'll do. Hubby's on his way. He'll help me with the rest."

"But—"

Steph's head tilted, her face adopting that parental don't-challenge-me look. "You're only content when things are under your control."

Devyn blinked. "That's a bit harsh."

"Not meaning it to be cruel, hon. Just honest. What happened when things didn't go according to plan with this ball? You immediately fell into panic mode."

"Because this event's a huge deal."

"It is, but not worth losing your mind over. Or your health. When things are out of your control, you struggle."

Devyn's chin sagged in quiet defeat. Steph was right. Devyn had accused Chase for not trusting her, when she'd been the one with trust issues. She'd thought she relied on God, but suddenly realized she relied on herself more.

"Go home, sweet thing." Steph squished her in a hug. "You did a great job. Rest, and I'll see you tomorrow at five."

Devyn nodded, too exhausted to put up a fight. She hadn't made two steps off the *Belle* when her phone buzzed.

Mitch.

She couldn't handle any more bad news right now. If there was a problem with the—

Enough.

That was what Steph was talking about. Devyn needed to open her clenched fists and release her control to God. Let go and let God. If Mitch had terrible news, then she'd view this as an opportunity to trust Him more.

"What's up, Bro?" She skirted an enormous puddle. The skies were blessedly clear, but the sidewalks were a hazard to her satin flats.

"You sound better."

"Huh?"

"When we talked earlier, you seemed close to a meltdown."

"I was. But I'm better."

"Things are going your way then?"

She faltered midstep. "Why'd you say that?"

"Just figured you got a handle on everything, since you sound happier now."

Then and there Devyn decided her happiness would not hinge on circumstances. She could be filled with joy despite the changes in life.

"Nope. I'm happy because I'm out of control. I'm giving everything to God. Though I think I may need some accountability. Bad habits being hard to break and all."

"You know I'm always here for you, Devs."

"Thank you." She inhaled a deep, calming breath. "Now, what's up?"

The following beats of silence made her wonder if they'd disconnected. But then her brother's sigh pushed through the speaker. "Those storms that came through here were bad, but they're worse in Carrollton. Lots of strong winds. Let's pray our cabin survives."

⁂

"I still can't believe you tagged along." Mitch gave her a sideways look as they drove up the wooded lane to the cabin the following morning. "Your party's tonight. I didn't expect you to come."

"I couldn't leave all this to you. Besides, I wanted to see the place for myself." Or did she? She glanced out her window, taking in the damage. So many trees were down.

"I hope the roof's okay." His grimace reminded Devyn of their dad. "That would be a beast to repair. Plus any damage to the interior."

Deep breaths. *God, I trust You.* She'd spent a lot of last night in prayer for the cabin, for her life, for Chase.

She had a small window before she had to get back and ready herself for the ball. Which she'd attend dateless. She'd called Chase earlier and left an apologetic voice mail for how she'd handled their fight and his subsequent attempts to reach her. With each passing moment he didn't return her call, worry slipped in that she'd waited too long. Or what if he saw her sending the NDA as a petty act to hurt him? Okay, she'd acted rashly. She'd wanted to send him a clear message that she wasn't bent on destroying his carefully kept secret. But had she instead sabotaged her chances with him?

Tears burned. She faced the window, not allowing her brother to see her distress.

The cabin came into view and Devyn squeezed Mitch's beefy arm. "It's okay." She exhaled relief. "It's safe."

They exited Mitch's truck and took in the sight of an uprooted pine beside the cabin. Close call. A smaller sapling had fallen into the barn, breaking a window. But the cabin itself stood tall.

Mitch hefted a branch from their path. "That storm was no joke, but I'm glad the old place held its ground." His gaze drifted about the property, and he gave a satisfied nod. "I need to check farther out. See if there's any other damage." He started toward the barn.

"I'll ride with you." She caught up to him.

"Better not. There'll be a lot of brush and debris. You don't need scrapes and cuts before having to get all purtied up."

"Did you just say *purtied*?" Her brother always had a way to make her smile, most often when he was being dorky. "We're in this together, Bro." He was forfeiting his Saturday night to cook a gazillion dessert dishes; it was only fair to help him any way she could this morning.

"Always." He slung an arm around her shoulder. "All right. Let's go."

He hitched the cart to the back of his four-wheeler and loaded it with tools in case they needed to clear the trail. They spent the next hour surveying the storm's monstrous touch. There wasn't too much harm on the north part of the property, but there was a lot of fallen trees and limbs on the south region by the water.

They abandoned their quads and walked the path toward the creek. Devyn's mood sank lower with each step. The memories of picking paw paws with Chase, of their unforgettable first kiss, surged to the lonely realms of her heart. And now everything between them was broken like the gnarled branches she was tripping over. She lifted her gaze and caught yet another wreckage. "Look, Mitch, the sign."

A paw paw tree had crashed into the SECRET CREEK sign, splitting one of the posts. Now only upheld by one wooden pillar, the sign drooped in sorry surrender.

She could identify with its fragile, humble state. "Think we can fix it?"

He scratched his stubbled jaw. "Yeah. We can dig out the ground and pour new cement for another post. My schedule's full over the next few weeks, but I think I can get to it before the ground freezes."

She eyed the carved letters on the weathered board. "Let's take it back with us. The way it's wobbling makes me nervous. I'm scared it'll fall into the creek and we'll never see it again." She grabbed a shovel from the cart and tore into the soil surrounding the broken post while Mitch focused on detaching the sign from the solid one.

Judging by the amount of cement, Great-Grandfather had obviously wanted this sign to remain until the next century. She was about to give up, but her shovel struck something tinny and hollow. Using a smaller spade, she dug until a square outline appeared. Her fingers brushed away the dirt, and she gasped. "Mitch, I found a box!"

"Cool. Think it's someone's bones?"

"You're such a weirdo." She crinkled her nose. "Besides, the box is too small for even a femur. But it must be something important. Why else would it be buried here?" Hattie leapt to mind. What if it was something about her and Great-Grandfather's past?

Mitch helped pull the rusted box from its earthen home and handed it to her.

Her gaze took in the sage-green metal pocked with rust. The tarnished latch, when unhinged, could reveal something amazing. Or terrible.

"Aren't you going to check it out?"

She pressed her lips together. "I don't feel right without Chase." Though what if it had nothing to do with their search? Her thumb swept over the rough corner. The metal container had been buried directly beneath the word *Secret*. It had to be significant. But significant didn't always mean something good. And from what Devyn knew of Hattie's plight, it probably wasn't. What if it was a memory box of sorts? Used as closure for Great-Grandfather?

"I'll take it home and call Chase again." That was the right decision. Their relationship had started with this mystery. Maybe it was fitting that it ended with it too.

Chapter 34

$\mathscr{D}$evyn made her way through the *Belle's* ballroom, her breath sticking to one of her vertebrates. She'd worn this designer dress once, years ago, when she'd been under pressure to be a thinner version of herself. But the blue bodice crushing her ribs had nothing on the crowd pressing in from all sides.

There were more people here than invitations sent. How had that happened? What if they ran out of food? She cringed at the tacky image of herself throwing dozens of fishing lines over the deck to make up the bass deficit.

The orchestra played river-related music, welcoming couples onto the dance floor. Twinkling lights glinted off the decorative tin ceiling, giving the illusion of a starry sky. Women in formal gowns mingled with men in tuxes, and beyond the indistinct chatter there was a certain energy, a hum of expectation.

But no Chase Jones.

On the way home from the cabin, she'd texted and left voice mails like a creepy stalker, practically begging him to attend tonight. Mitch was here offering his support in between blowtorching desserts. Mom kept spamming her phone with well wishes and requests for pictures. But nothing from the man she'd given her heart to.

Her focus snagged on several camera crews. Were they *Once Upon a Wedding's* people? Or had Steph called the local news?

Her boss strolled by, chatting freely with an older gentleman, and Devyn caught the woman by her gold lamé elbow. With her slinky, sparkly gown, blue eye shadow, and teased bouffant hair, Steph looked as if she'd be accepting an Emmy for her role in an eighties soap opera.

The second her superior finished her conversation, Devyn pounced faster than one could say Aqua Net. "What's going on?"

"Everything's a fabulous success, if that's what you mean." She flapped an exuberant wave to someone on their left, and then aimed her Revlon smile at Devyn. "Love your gown. That blue looks stunning on you."

"Thank you. I tried to match the theme." Though she doubted anyone would draw that conclusion. "I see lots of press, Steph. Is that your doing?" Or had Travis leaked where Devyn worked? Worse, was *he* here?

"I went overboard. Pun intended."

"How?"

She shrugged, her hoop earrings bouncing on her shoulder pads. "I invited every source of coverage I could think of."

Devyn pressed a hand to her abdomen. Breathe. Well, half-breathe. Dumb dress.

For the umpteenth time today, she reminded herself to give up the worry. "Okay. Well. God's got this." She'd even refrained from nagging about the entertainment. Steph had said she'd take care of it, and that was enough. Devyn was out of control. And maybe a bit out of her mind too.

The *Belle* was arrayed in all her finest. Every deck bulb was lit and shining into the sunset. It was as if she'd been waiting for this moment. To shine. Her steam whistle rent the air like a sassy introduction, letting the guests know it was time to leave the dock.

Devyn would face the evening without Chase. Emptiness pricked her heart. What was all this effort worth if she hadn't him to share it with? He'd been an integral part of bringing this event about, from the theme to the décor, and keeping her sane through it all.

The next hour flew by in a fantastical whirlwind. She'd made small talk with some beneficiaries. Avoided Jenna Henry, judger of the contest, loather of Devyn Asbury. Thankfully Steph had run interference where the tall brunette was concerned.

It was almost time for the entertainment to take the stage. Apprehension crashed into Devyn. What had she been thinking? Should the woman who claimed to have a lip-shaped sofa in her living room really be the one handling such a taste-delicate matter? Then again, Devyn had almost contracted her polka-playing, one-eyed uncle.

People thronged the stage, packing in like a bunch of junior high girls at a boy band concert. She froze. If Steph booked the Jonas Brothers, Devyn would scour the internet and buy her every lip-shaped accent pillow imaginable. Dozens of cameras and phones were lifted high, aiming at the empty stage. Shouldn't the band have at least set up? There were no instruments. Only the lone microphone Devyn had arranged for the emcee. The orchestra, situated off to the side, had stopped playing. A hush fell over the room, making her heart jam in her throat.

Veteran Louisville sportscaster Jim Rogers, tonight's emcee, strolled center stage. "Ladies and gentlemen." His low voice floated through the PA speakers. "On behalf of the *Belle of Louisville*, we welcome you to tonight's ball."

A round of applause and cheers followed.

"This evening's theme is Dream River. We hope you enjoy the savory cuisine. All the dishes nod to the Ohio River as well as the décor." He made a sweeping gesture to the surrounding floral arrangements. "Now, how about a special predinner treat? The officers and crew of the *Belle* are proud to introduce to you, tonight's entertainment."

Oh here goes. Devyn bit her lip, no doubt smearing her makeup.

Jim glanced off stage and nodded. "Let's give a hearty welcome to Louisville's own celebrity poet, Slate."

Hollers and gasps charged the cramped space. Devyn blinked. What was going on? She pushed through the mob, stepping on someone's foot, knocking elbows with another patron. Her mumbled apologies would have to suffice because she couldn't pause for anything more. She needed to get to that stage.

"At his own request, Slate chose the *Belle of Louisville* to reveal his well-anticipated identity."

"What?" Devyn's shrieked word jarred the room, earning her multiple looks and glances. How was this possible? She snaked her way to the front, ready to storm the platform.

Chase stepped out, and she almost face-planted into a vase of wildflowers.

His athletic frame looked right at home in a tuxedo. His gray gaze sought hers and clung. So much filled his expression. Whistles and applause, so grating a second ago, dimmed in the glow of the moment. He flashed her his winning smile, then with sure steps, moved beside Jim and exchanged handshakes.

The emcee moved past Devyn, leaving Chase alone with an awaiting crowd.

"Good evening." He poised behind the microphone as if he were born to stand there. His confident demeanor arrested every soul in the room. "My name is Chase Graham Jones, and I have a confession to make." He glanced Devyn's way for a pulse-pounding second then returned to his audience. "My debut, *The Fault of My Heart*, may have been noted here or there." Several chuckled at the downplay of his success. "But after its release I struggled to pen a single verse. Believe me, I've tried. I wouldn't claim it as writer's block, but more of a soul block." He paused, then deliberately set his gaze on Devyn. "One gloomy afternoon, I stepped aboard the *Belle*, and everything changed."

That day he'd caught her dancing with no one. Heat crept up her neck, and he smiled at her blush.

"That day set me on a course I never expected. All that I thought dead came to life. The dream revived. My heart was no longer my own." He stepped toward her and stretched out his hand, inviting her.

Her heart gave a loud thump, and her ankles threatened to cave. Someone lightly pushed her back. She glanced over her shoulder. Steph.

With a stabling breath, Devyn joined him on the wood-planked platform.

He leaned toward her. His head dipped closer, and she feared he'd drop a kiss on her right in front of everyone. Instead, he angled to the side, his lips brushing the ridge of her ear. "You look beautiful." His warm breath tickled the wisps of hair on her neck. "I love that you're wearing wildcat blue."

She almost snorted.

With flecks of mischief shining in his eyes, he winked. Chase took her hand and returned to the microphone.

"In honor of the amazing woman beside me and the *Belle of Louisville* that brought us together, I give you the first verse I've written in two years. Dream River."

There was a collective gasp. Additional phones raised in the air. Chase had not only revealed his identity, but was also presenting new work? It was too much. All too much.

He gave her hand a gentle squeeze and angled toward her.

"Adventure tasted like moonlight and a thousand stolen moments. The water beckons, its silvery voice a tide of longing, sweeping us together. Dream River is what they call it, but to me, it's our awakening. In those shimmering depths your laughter hints of music, your touch a silky whisper, your kiss a mystery needing a lifetime to explore."

"The waters won't always glitter. The current will cut through storms. But I want this journey with you. Let us drift on this river of dreams. For infinite tomorrows became ours when your heart slipped into mine."

His gaze never left hers. One of her most devastating moments had begun with one of Chase's poems, and he'd sweetly redeemed it. His own words, from his own voice, in a public setting to restore her heart. To free the chains of the past.

The audience clapped, and Devyn launched into his arms, their lips meeting tenderly until the chemistry between them ignited. Forget the contest. Forget the beneficiaries. This night was theirs.

From some far-off place, the emcee spoke. The orchestra strummed a jazzy version of "Moon River." The world began its rotation again.

Devyn lowered from her toes. "I'm sorry," she whispered.

"I'm sorry too." His thumbs caressed her sides.

"You just told the world who you are."

"I did." He led her off stage.

"Why?"

His grin was as full as her heart. "Because someone once told me that love is bold."

"Well, that was bold. You wowed everyone."

"I did it for you." His gaze roamed her face. "I'm thinking that's my new goal in life. To make you happy."

"I like that goal." She laid her hand over his heart. "Thank you for that poem. You know that's going to be broadcast everywhere on social media."

He shrugged. "It doesn't matter. I have a whole folder of new works. All inspired by you and God."

She couldn't wait to read them. "I thought you were angry with me. I've been trying to get ahold of you all day."

He groaned. "And it was torture not answering your calls." The soberness in his eyes confirmed his words. "But Steph made me promise not to talk to you until tonight. She said you'd try to talk me out of the reveal."

"I would have."

"And she also knew I'm crazy about you and would do anything you asked."

Her meddling boss caught her attention, and with a megawatt smile, pointed to the deck, mouthing. "Go!" Then she puckered her lips in a kissy face.

This time Devyn did snort. "My boss is suggesting we make out on the deck."

Chase breathed a laugh. "I've always liked her."

"But first." She grabbed his hand. "I found something this morning buried by the waterfall." She filled him in on how she discovered the box. "I brought it with me, hoping you would show up tonight, and that we could open it together."

His smile dimmed. "Are you sure? It might contain something upsetting." He stroked her cheek with his knuckle. "Tonight you're to celebrate. Your eyes are too pretty to fill with tears."

"I'm sure." She pressed her hand over his. "If the box holds something about Great-Grandfather and Hattie, what better place to open it than right here where their relationship probably began?"

The concern tightening the edges of his eyes relaxed. "In honor of love that was gained and lost."

"You almost sound like a poet." She quipped a sassy smile, and he reached for her. Getting caught up in his arms was such a beautiful pastime.

He kissed the tender spot behind her ear. Then her neck. "Go get your box, love. We'll go through it together. And then we'll obey your boss and make out on the deck."

Her grin widened. "Deal." She rushed to the galley where her brother was expertly torching the crème brûlés. He flashed a thumbs-up and went back to work. Within seconds, the box was in Devyn's hands, and she joined Chase on the stern, overlooking the paddle wheel.

With everyone settled for dinner, they were the only ones out there.

Chase glanced at the box and then her. "Ready?"

"I am." She unlatched the lid and lifted it. Her gaze fell on a note, zeroing in on the first line. "Oh." The container wobbled in her hand.

Chase steadied her. "What is it?"

"Something I never expected."

Chapter 35

*J*ack scrubbed a hand over his face and winced at the sunlight spearing through the cabin door's window. He must have fallen asleep. Surprising, considering he'd hardly rested since learning about Hattie. He'd only existed in a dismal haze.

His bags stacked beside his bed. His bus ticket for Kentucky tucked in his coat pocket. He couldn't leave this boat fast enough. Everywhere he turned, he'd expected Hattie to appear. Visions of her, so full of life, so beautiful, invaded his every waking and non-waking moment.

For sanity's sake, he needed to escape the torture.

A knock at his door triggered his scowl. He was in no mood to deal with people. Thankfully the *Idlewild* would remain docked all this week. The excursions had been canceled, the crew released from duties until the following Monday. By then, he'd be gone.

Someone rapped again.

He grunted a haphazard, "Come in."

Duffy shuffled inside, his face as ghostly white as his captain's hat. Since that awful morning, the aged riverman seemed to lose all will to go on. He'd kept to his room, rejecting food and company. In those late-night hours, Duffy's broken sobs had bled through the hollow walls.

Jack had no more tears to cry. Only scorching anger and emptiness.

"Have you changed your mind about coming?" Duffy's hunched posture emphasized his loose-fitting uniform. "To pay your respects."

"No." Jack refused to attend Hattie's funeral. Her body wouldn't even be there. Fire had destroyed her remains. His stomach twisted hard, the nausea resurfacing. He missed her. Ached for her. Misery consumed him, making him wish it had been him in that blaze rather than his beloved. For it was no different than what he experienced now. He'd no life in his bones. No solid beat of his heart. All because of Bradford Fairview. "If I go, I'll hurt him. Or worse." Authorities had closed the case. They'd refused to consider foul play—even with Charles Jones's account of the thugs. Bradford Fairview no doubt paid a small fortune to keep things quiet, to publish his version of Hattie's death. "Do you know what they're saying happened?"

Duffy nodded. "Bunch of rot."

Radio. Newspapers. All the places Hattie had once wanted for allies had turned against her, claiming she'd fled to the cabin to meet a beau. His hands clenched. They'd further stated she must have tired of waiting and drifted asleep only to knock over a kerosene lamp, setting the place on fire.

Lies. Jones's descriptions of Hattie's abductors matched the men at the Louisville wharf. No doubt hired by Hattie's uncle, but Jack had no proof. "What can we do, sir?" Agitation simmered beneath his skin. "We can't let Fairview get away with this."

Duffy's shoulder's lowered. "I don't know. I don't know anything at the moment."

Jack ground his jaw. Couldn't this have been avoided? If Duffy had only told Hattie sooner, they could have thought through it all. They would have had time to invent a sound plan to keep her from harm. She could still be here. In his arms.

"I better get going." The man who could navigate any boat through stormy waters had no grit left in his eyes.

The memorial service Fairview arranged for his niece was predicted to be a fancy fanfare. All the while the man himself was utterly responsible for Hattie's death. It was maddening.

Duffy turned toward the door, then stilled. "Here's this." He shakily pulled something from his trouser pocket and held it out.

It was a torn photograph. But only of Jack. He recognized it immediately—the picture taken by the newspaperman the day he and Hattie had talked on the texas roof. "Where's the other half? I'd rather have the side of her."

"Charles Jones got it. I gave it to him so he'd know who'd he be protecting." He shuddered, and Jack felt a slice of pity. Hattie had been

Duffy's daughter, maybe not in blood but in everything else. "I was going to ask for it back, but the young'un disappeared. He took what happened personally."

He should. The kid had failed to keep the woman Jack loved alive. He glanced at the photo with a tight grimace. What would he do with a picture of himself? Why would Duffy even give this to him? But upon closer inspection, he saw it.

Hattie's hand was in his. His fingers wrapped around hers.

Jack made a fist then unclenched, trying to summon the feeling of her warm palm against his. But no, everything was cold. Numb. "I'll keep an eye on the boat while you're at the funeral."

Duffy left without another word. With the rest of the crew gone, Jack would be alone aboard the *Idlewild* for his last remaining hours as first mate.

He set up patrol on the far side of the bow, sitting in the drizzling rain, letting the sound of water slapping against the hull fill his vacant thoughts.

By heaven, he'd loved her. Still loved her. He didn't want his admiration for her to wane. Didn't he owe that to—

Something moved to his right. He launched to his feet. Someone was on the boat. A flash of black. But then, nothing. Had he imagined it? He bounded up the deck stairs two at a time, his gaze darting. Light footsteps came from behind. He pivoted toward the sound. There. The dark figure slid into a cabin.

Hattie's.

Smart move, Fairview. The man would know that everyone who loved his niece would be at the funeral. What better time to send his crony to search Hattie's cabin for evidence that could be used against him, or to find something to further besmirch her character.

Fury sluiced his veins. If he couldn't protect Hattie in life, then he would in death. He stormed the deck and threw open the door. With a growl, he lunged, tackling the trespasser, sending them both to the floor.

"My goodness, Jack." That voice. That familiar, haunting voice.

The hood was drawn, veiling the intruder's face, but Jack had to see.

Had to be sure it wasn't his morbid imagination. He pushed back the damp cloak, revealing an angelic face.

How? He needed sleep. *Was* he asleep? Because the woman pinned beneath him looked identical to the woman he loved. The woman who'd died.

"Jack." She cupped his face, her fingers icy, her eyes intent. "It's me."

"Hattie." He could only whisper. If he spoke too loud, she might disappear.

She pressed her cold lips to his. "I know this is a shock. But it has to be this way."

He blinked. She was here. "You're alive." And before she could respond, he lowered and kissed her. He'd never been so desperate, and his touch was nothing if that. His hands buried in her hair, slid over her slim shoulders, down her arms. He pressed his body closer to hers, making sure she was real.

Hattie responded in kind, fully convincing him she was indeed flesh and blood. "My word, if that doesn't bring a lady back from the dead." She spoke against his lips.

Jack should probably get off her, but he was mesmerized. Her eyes took on a dark greenish tint against her cloak, her golden hair fell in loose curls around her feminine jaw. Dirt smeared her face, but it only made her more beautiful. The markings of her survival.

"Now we're even." Her mouth lifted into a teasing smile, and he kissed it. "I mistook you as a stowaway, and now you've thought me one." Her gentle laughter was the most captivating sound in the world. "Though I have to say, your tackle had a bit more umph."

Her words snapped his alarm. He rolled away, his gaze sweeping her form. "Did I hurt you?"

"Not in the least." She moved to a seated position.

He moved beside her, keeping close. "What happened? We thought . . .that is. . .you're supposed to be—"

"Charred to ash." The good humor slipped from her expression. "About that. Well. It's a bit of a long story."

"Tell me." He savored the melodic sound of her voice. A voice he thought he'd never hear again. The look of love she shot him compelled his arm to slide around her. She was here. Thank God, she was here!

"The brutes tied me up." She pushed a lock of hair from her cheek. "You keep looking at me like that. It's hard to concentrate."

"I can't help it." He leaned over and kissed her again.

"Fine by me." She smoothed his brow, her eyes filling with concern. No doubt she saw how rugged and fatigued he was. "I'm sorry." Her other hand scraped against his stubbled cheek.

"No apologies, my love. I only want to hear how it is you came back to me."

"Like I said." She removed her touch. "The men bound me and threw me in a cabin. Then torched it."

He stiffened.

"But remember, a lady always keeps her weapon at the ready." She hiked up her skirt, revealing the garter and knife. "It came in handy. I was able to slice through the ropes and escape."

"But the cabin was on fire. We thought you were trapped inside. Young Jones found your necklace." He withdrew the scorched links from his pocket.

Her eyes widened. "I must've lost it when I was crawling beneath the stove."

"The stove?"

She nodded, her smile adorably smug. "Those idiots couldn't have picked a better place. You see, I knew of the Hatcher family from Duffy. He told me stories about their role in the Underground Railroad. Those seeking freedom hid in the cabins, and if there was any trouble, they fled through tunnels."

"That's how you escaped?"

"There was a trap door under the woodstove. It was dark and thrilling!"

That was his girl. His adventure-loving girl. And for the life of him, he couldn't stop kissing her.

She blushed at his attention. "I'm glad you missed me."

"Missed you? It was more than that. I never knew such pain. I thought the woman I loved was dead."

Her smile sobered. "You love me?"

"With everything I am." He'd tell her every day of his life if she gave him the honor. "I love you, Hattie Harriet Fairview Louis." He said all her names like she had his on the night of their first kiss.

She leaned into him and he crushed her close, not wanting to let go.

"Jack." She nestled into his chest. "What I'm about to say might shock you."

"More than you being alive? I think I can handle anything."

She leaned back, her gaze steady, resolve in her features. "I want to remain dead."

Chapter 36

Hattie

*J*ack's brows lowered to a straight slash across his forehead. "I don't understand."

How could I explain? "It has to be this way. Harriet Fairview has to remain dead to the world." And with that, Hattie too. I couldn't return to the way things had been.

"My uncle needs to believe I'm dead."

Jack's mouth opened, but I cut him off. "I know it seems drastic, but after hiding in a tunnel for a day and half, and the miles I've walked under the cover of darkness to get here, I've had plenty of time to think it over."

Jack launched to his feet and helped me to mine. "You can't let Fairview get away with this. Confront him. Make him pay for what he did to you and your parents."

Revenge swept on the shores of my soul, but I wouldn't wade in the bitter waters. "It won't work. It wasn't Uncle who tried to kill me."

"It was men he hired."

"But I can't prove it."

Jack's shoulders lowered slightly but his jaw set like stone.

"Don't you see?" I grabbed his hand and pressed it to my cheek. "Even if I denounce my inheritance, it still falls to my children. My uncle won't stop. It's safer for me to be dead in his eyes. In everyone's eyes."

"That's letting him win."

"If he knows I'm alive it puts us all in danger. This is the escape I prayed for. Jack, I don't want the heiress life." I reached for his other hand, clasping them both. "I don't want to marry a stranger. I don't want to live in fear of my uncle. I want to be free."

"But then you'll have to give up your life here as well." Sadness crept into his gaze. "You won't be able to return to the *Idlewild*."

And that hurt the most. My boat. My life here. Everything I'd ever known. But God had taken me this far. "I know."

"Hattie." Jack slid his hands from mine and lowered to one knee. "Marry me."

My balance went askew, and I placed my hand on his shoulder to steady myself. "Are you serious?"

"I just got you back. I can't give you up again." His face was ruggedly gorgeous, his eyes so brimming with affection I could hardly breathe. "Please say yes. We can return to my land in Kentucky, build a cabin near your creek." He stared at my left hand. "I don't have a ring, but I promise to buy you one that will—"

"Oh, Jack!" I lunged into his arms, nearly sending us to the wood floor for the second time today.

"Is that a *yes*?" He laughed into my hair.

The door to my stateroom yawned open, and Jack scrambled in front of me.

Duffy poked his head inside. "Jack, what are you doing in Hat—" His gaze landed on me, and he startled. "My girl?" His voice filled with wonder, then broke upon a withering sob. "My girl!"

He shuffled forward as if in a daze. I'd witnessed the disbelief in Jack's eyes, but it was ten times more severe in Duffy's.

"It's okay, Duff. I'm well." I rushed to him and hugged his neck. His arms clasped around me in a trembling embrace.

I informed Duffy of all that had happened. He scratched his gray temple, his gaze never leaving mine as if I'd disappear into thin air. I finished with how I'd accepted Jack's proposal, and Duffy squeezed my elbow.

"I'll marry you two."

As a steamboat captain he was licensed to officiate weddings. Something of course I'd known, but still, it was all happening delightfully fast.

"What about a license, sir?" Jack stood and grasped my hand in his.

"Leave that to me." The twinkle was back in Duffy's eyes. "I've a friend who works in the courts who owes me a favor."

I was to be married to Jack Asbury. "But I can't go by my name anymore."

"The papers all know you by Harriet Fairview, and you can't return to Hattie Louis either. Thanks to Face." Duffy grunted. "He leaked to the press about you living aboard here. Told them your name, everything. He said it was to honor your memory, but I say it was to put himself in the spotlight." His head shook in disapproval, his gaze sharpening on my face. "You look pale. I'll fetch some food." He slipped out the door.

I turned my attention to Jack. "I must be renamed." Changing identities was becoming an irksome habit of mine.

Jack's lips twitched. "I have a suggestion."

"Don't you dare say Admiral."

He laughed. "Maybe not the full, but how about the heart of the word? Mira." His gaze turned tender. "Mrs. Mira Asbury has a beautiful ring to it."

With that enamoring look in his eyes, he could call me Bernadine Buggywampus and I'd dumbly answer. But he was right, Mira was a lovely name. "I like it."

His head lowered, lips brushing my temple. "I'll only call you Admiral when we're alone." His husky undertone spurred my blush. Soon we'd be very alone and closer than I'd ever been to anyone.

Duffy returned, setting food and drink on the dresser. "Time to have us a wedding." He smiled, but there were hints of sadness in his face. He knew the result of this. That after today, we'd never see each other again.

I couldn't dwell on it, or my heart would chip into pieces. This plan was for Duffy's safety too. The sooner I left this boat and Pittsburgh, the sooner all our lives would be free from danger. At present, I needed to focus on getting married. My gaze landed on the ivory gown Duffy had given me for my birthday. "Would you gentleman give me a moment." I went toward the small closet and pulled the dress from the hanger. "I want to at least look like a bride on my wedding day."

Jack flashed an affectionate smile, and Duffy nodded. They left, and I washed my face, fixed my hair with the fancy grooming set, pulling wispy sides up in the jeweled combs. Today Harriet Fairview was mourned at some memorial service in Pittsburgh and Hattie Louis would remain in the deep breadths of the *Idlewild*. From this day forward, I'd be Mira, the devoted wife of Jack Asbury. Together we would build our life on God and our love for each other.

In the main hall of the *Idlewild*, while the rest of the world was oblivious, I pledged my life to Jack. The adoration welling in his gaze overwhelmed me. Duffy had even choked on a few words. He announced our union, and it was I who couldn't hold back the tears of gratitude, especially when Jack kissed me. I'd been given a second chance at life. A life that wasn't attached to a family with cruel intentions. I now belonged to a man who'd cherish, protect, and grow old with me.

I gathered what few belongings I had, and Jack took them so I could say farewell to Duffy.

His age-spotted hand cupped my cheek as a tear slid down his.

I hugged him fiercely, taking in the scent of his cigar and the choppy beating of his old heart.

He patted my back. "Never forget how much I love you, child."

My soul swelled at the words that I'd longed to hear from him. And now I was to leave and never return. I couldn't say farewell. I just clung to him. "I love you too, Papa." I turned away, afraid my heart would snap into splinters.

I had one more goodbye to deliver.

I pressed my cheek against the white-washed wall of the *Idlewild*. "So long, dear friend." I could almost feel her pulse. "Thank you for the adventures." This ole gal had embraced me, carried me on beautiful journeys, and sheltered me when I feared stepping out onto the shores.

I peered beyond the rails, beyond all I'd ever known. My courage, so robust only moments ago, shriveled and twisted, the familiar dread clutching with renewed strength. Could I do this? Spend the rest of my days in an unfamiliar world? Face the strong winds of life without the shelter of this place? My home?

Jack's warm hand pressed my lower back. "What's wrong?"

My palms still flattened against the *Idlewild*'s wall, I lowered my lashes. "I don't know if I have enough in me to face the wind." My voice was as willowy as the reeds lining the river.

Jack hands bracketed my shoulders, and he turned me to face him, realization settling in the softening of his brow. He must have recalled our conversation on the texas roof after he'd commanded Clem to steer into the gusty weather rather than back into it.

"That's where you're different from her." The pad of his thumb gently swept over my cheek. "The *Idlewild* fails when low on power, but your supply of strength comes from a greater Source. God's in you." He pressed a kiss against my forehead then laughed.

I pulled back, mildly hurt at his ill-timed humor.

"Hattie, you tackle stowaways, raise your chin at gunpoint, bash attackers' kneecaps, race through forbidden tunnels." Admiration built in his beautiful eyes and his tone hushed to a reverent whisper. "You cheated death." His lips feathered against mine. "No, my love, fear has no victory over you. It's the other way around." His mouth captured mine, sealing his words in my heart.

The kiss was brief for we hadn't time to linger, but it would forever remain one of my most treasured moments. Jack helped me back into my cloak. With one final wave at Duffy, we stepped off the *Idlewild* and into our new life together.

Chapter 37

Devyn

$\mathcal{U}$sing a gardening spade, Chase patted down the last scoop of concrete around the 6 x 6 pine beam. The man cut a fine figure in a tux, but seeing him in work jeans, a worn T-shirt, and his toned arms dusted with Quikrete mix, it was a whole different kind of attractive.

Warm spells were scarce this late in October, so they'd taken advantage of the sunny afternoon to repost the creek's sign. The trees shed their colorful leaves with each kiss of wind upon their branches. Fall had always been Devyn's favorite season, but this year it was more meaningful, for she saw the beauty in letting go.

Chase stood to full height and examined his efforts. Satisfied, he set his sights on Devyn, the sunlight playing in his artfully mussed hair. "You really know how to throw a wild celebration party." The curve of his full lips belied the slow shake of his head.

"We have each other and a host of insects." She swatted at a cluster of gnats swirling above her. "What says party more than that?" Since today was the first day they'd had off together, they'd decided to celebrate the liberating fact that the Dream River Ball was over.

He shrugged. "Your great-grandmother faked her own death. I think you can come up with something a bit more exciting than this." He gave a slow wink and tugged the gloves from his hands. "Genius is in your blood."

She warmed at the hints of pride in his voice. It still amazed her how it had all unfolded—that Hattie and Mira were the same person. "I happen to remember this being your idea." After Chase had revealed his identity, he'd been swarmed with press, invites from talk shows, and casseroles from hopeful women. The man had practically begged her for a trip to the cabin, away from the demands of his growing fan base.

"I wasn't aware you'd put me to work." He tossed the gloves into the four-wheeler's cart. "Though I think you've been enjoying watching me swing a hammer." He wagged his brows and she laughed at his ridiculousness. Even if it was the truth.

She snapped off a twig and tossed it at him, and he deflected it with ease. "You know full well we came here to work. For the record, I love my present." She glanced at the new sign resting on the seat of the quad. Chase had surprised her this morning with a slab of cherry-stained wood complete with chunky framing, decorative routered detail, and the engraved words HATTIE'S CREEK. "This place will be restored to its original name." Though they couldn't hang the sign until the concrete hardened, Devyn was thankful to have things exactly how her great-grandparents had first intended.

The box she'd unearthed contained letters from both her great-grandparents, sharing their full love story. Apparently Bradford Fairview had believed the steel plant should remain in his greedy hands and had been prepared to kill for it. While she'd been able escape his murderous plan, she hadn't wanted to risk anyone knowing she was alive. The letters even mentioned Chase's grandfather, Charles Jones, who'd been charged with protecting her. Mira had expressed remorse about letting him believe she'd died that fateful night, but she couldn't contact him without blowing her cover. There were no witness protection programs back in the twenties, so they'd done what they could to remain safe—she'd taken on a new identity.

A line her great-grandmother had written feathered Devyn's thoughts. *"I had to say goodbye to all I knew. Up to then, my entire life was spent between the banks of rivers. The first step was the hardest, but the most important. I ventured past, and in losing sight of the shores, I caught a glimpse of truth. Of what love is. Love is bold. It takes a good deal of courage and a trusting heart."*

There was that stirring again. "Chase?" She waited for him to look up from putting away the tools in the five-gallon bucket they'd brought. "I think I'm going to go for it." After the ball, Devyn had awoken at two a.m. with a snippet of an idea. One that blended both her loves—coding and history. She wanted to create a website that linked ancestry, newspaper, and historical document sites. Even a bit of social media tossed in by allowing subscribers to connect with relatives they discovered through the site. And make it all user-friendly. That way those who were tracing their family tree would have one stop for all their genealogy needs. Of course, she'd need permission from the other sources, but they'd benefit from the cooperative effort as well.

His grin stretched wide. "Really?" He jogged toward her, catching her in a swirling hug. "That's my girl." From the moment she told Chase, he'd been encouraging her to follow her heart, but she had to overcome the fear of stepping out. He set her back on her feet with a kiss to her forehead. "What about your job with the *Belle*?"

"Maybe Steph will let me work part-time." She really did enjoy her role as wedding coordinator, but maybe, just like her great-grandparents, she was only meant to be with the *Belle* for a season. "If not, then at least I'll be leaving on an amazing high."

His brows rose. "Did you hear from *Once Upon a Wedding*? I thought the winner won't be revealed until next month."

She swept her thumb over his jaw, rubbing away a smudge. "You're right. No news until the end of November, but win or lose, I already count the event a success." The ball hadn't even ended and the steamboat was already making a jaunty virtual voyage across the social media seas. Videos of Chase's reveal had gone viral. Of course, Devyn's identity hadn't gone unnoticed, but for once she didn't care if she was trending on Google. Her security came from God, not what the world said about her. She glanced at the sign. No more secrets. No more hiding. "Thank you."

Chase followed her gaze. "For what? Fixing the post?" He tsked her. "I'm more than a pretty face, you know. I can work with my hands."

She laughed and moved to lightly push him, but he caught her hands and pulled her to his chest. "Yes, I appreciate both your pretty face and you fixing the sign. But I was referring to what you did at the ball."

Smiling, he rested his forehead against hers. "I believe you thanked me for that already. At least fifty times."

But he'd taken a risk. For her. "You never said why you remained anonymous."

He shrugged. "Not a huge mystery behind it. I wasn't sure if I wanted to make a career out of it. Wasn't certain I was good enough. And so when my agent suggested I use a pen name, I figured it couldn't hurt."

"From a marketing standpoint it was brilliant. The intrigue alone about the man behind all those romancy words did nothing but further your career." Her fingertips feathered back a lock of his hair that had fallen across his forehead. "You did an amazing job keeping it all a secret, only to tell everyone at a humble steamboat party."

"I'd do it again in a heartbeat." He slipped his arms around her hips. "In case you haven't noticed, I'm in love with you, Devyn Asbury. I realize I have to share you with all those old dudes from those archaic movies. That you'll always roast me in Skeeball. And while I have a personal goal to mature your taste buds, I'm already resigned to accept defeat in that as well."

She grinned, his words of love bolstering her heart. "Well, since your secret's out, I now have to share you with half the female population."

"Never." His head dipped close. "It's only you."

"And you're the only one for me, Chase Jones."

They stood on her great-grandparents' property. A place built on love. And here she had the man she loved within kissing reach. She stood on her toes, closing the distance, and brushed her lips against his.

Devyn was still in the process of learning to trust beyond her own means. Trust God and those like the man with his hands buried in her hair with her heart, but she was making amazing progress.

God had a way of leading His children. It may not be the course Devyn had imagined, but as long as she stayed in the current of His love, she knew she could rely on Him in both the still and the troubled waters. He was faithful to steer her through it all.

Chapter 38

Mira Asbury
June 14, 1987

I gazed at one of the loveliest sights my aged eyes could take in. My dear old friend. My steamboat. Today our grandson Stephen Asbury would marry his college sweetheart aboard the same vessel Jack and I had been united on.

But no one knew.

The lifelong secret wiggled against my ribs, making it tough to breathe. Though at the ripe age of eighty-one, deep breaths were hard to come by. Jack squeezed my hand, gently urging me to follow the moving line onto the boarding stage.

Here I stood, silver-haired, wrinkle piled upon wrinkle, but the boat that had carried me on the waters over six decades ago had a regal bloom. Even the dual smokestacks had a fancy crown-looking topper. Quite the transformation from its humble beginnings as a packet boat.

The main deck, once open and airy, was now a smooth wall of windows and wood. The words *The Belle of Louisville* had been painted in vivid red and gold, the fancy lettering stretching from the stern to mid-deck. The cargo hold where Jack had emerged that life-changing night was no longer. But I could envision our first meeting as if it had happened yesterday.

My gaze lifted to the pilothouse. All framed in with glass. A smile graced my lips. Wouldn't Clem have loved to see that. No more chapped skin from the biting breeze.

I shuffled forward. Excitement charged the air with tangible hints of romance. The sun slung low on the horizon, wispy clouds dappling the pink and purple sky. Such a perfect ambiance for a summer wedding.

I turned and found Jack watching me. That pleasing smile of his prompted my own. Being his bride for over sixty years still seemed too short.

His eyes gleamed, and I wondered if he was reliving memories too. "Are you ready for this, Mira?"

Was I? When I'd heard rumors that the city of Louisville had purchased a damaged steamboat and was raising funds to restore it, my heart had known it was the *Idlewild* even before I'd read about it in the paper.

And today, I'd walk her decks again. Though with a slightly slower pace than before.

I smiled at my husband. "Lead on."

He leaned close and lowered his tone. "Atta girl, Admiral." His rascally wink earned him a swat on his suit-sleeved arm.

I moved across the boarding stage, supporting myself on the rails, and stepped onto the bow like I'd done hundreds of times, but it felt different. Like revisiting one's childhood home after it had changed ownership again and again. The swell of nostalgia was palpable, but I couldn't help but feel like a visitor.

"Aunt Mira. Uncle Jack." The sweet voice of our great-niece, Kathleen, reached my ears. "I've been waiting for you."

"Got stuck on the interstate," Jack grumbled. "That construction is going to last clear into the millennium."

"Well c'mon, you two." Kathleen squeezed between us and linked her arms through ours. "The ceremony will be starting in just a few. I've heard rumors Stephen's bride-to-be spent a whole grand on her dress."

Jack let out a whistle. "That's enough to get us box seats for the Cardinals all season."

We greeted the captain, a nice man in his fifties, and my mind traveled to another steamboat captain. The one who'd raised me. Our wedding day had been the last time I'd seen Captain Finnegan Woodruff. After he married us, the *Idlewild* was sold to a company in New Orleans. Duffy had hung up his officer's hat, and two months later had gone on to meet the Captain of our salvation.

I blinked back the sting of tears. Being here, on these familiar decks, brought a new pull on old memories. Or perhaps it was the tug of heaven on my heart.

I'd lived a beautiful life. One that had almost been cut short by a conniving uncle.

The steel empire Bradford Fairview had kept under his thumb crumbled only seven years later during the Great Depression. Fairview Steel was bought by a neighboring company. Uncle had tried to rally again, attempting to purchase rolling mills, but the venture failed. He died of tuberculosis the following year, penniless.

We approached the grand staircase, and my breath bounced in my lungs. The curve of the wall, the same twenty steps leading to the main room. Or ballroom, nowadays. It was all too much. I pressed a hand to my heart.

Kathleen leaned close to me. "I was chatting with one of the crewmen. You know what he told me?"

Jack humored her. "That there's a brig in the engine room for stowaways?"

I subtly pinched him, and his shoulders shook with silent laughter.

"Stowaways." Kathleen's tinkling laugh rose above the chatter of the other passengers. "You're such a character, Uncle Jack." She sent him a fond smile as we climbed the stairs. "No, he said he was part of the renovation crew and he found love letters behind one of the cabin walls."

I paused, squeezing the handrail.

"You okay, Aunt?" She gripped my elbow. "Only a few more steps and then we'll get you to your table."

Jack cast me a sidelong glance. He knew very well my pause had nothing to do with feebleness. *My love notes.* The day of our wedding, I was able to scrape a few from the wall, but the rest had slid out of reach. We'd been in a hurry to leave Pittsburgh, to get miles between me and my uncle, so I'd left them behind.

While I would never recover those letters, with Jack's encouragement, I wrote my own, detailing the secrets behind the three names I'd been bestowed. Jack had penned one too. He had the sentimental idea of burying the notes near my creek. Though I doubted anyone would ever find them.

I flattened my hand on the doorframe of the main room, the hum of her life thrumming into my palm. The *Idlewild* and I shared a rare connection. This steamboat had taken on three separate identities, just like me. First the *Idlewild*, then after World War II, she'd become the *Avalon*, and now *The Belle of Louisville*.

I patted the wood paneling. Yes, old girl. But just because we'd gone by different names didn't mean our souls had changed. Our hearts were very much the same. As for me, there was only one name that stuck with me throughout the years—*Beloved*. Cherished by Marshall Jack Asbury. Loved by God.

And that was the identity I would forever cling to.

Author's Notes

This section is one of my favorite parts to write! My inner geek gets unleashed, and I get to gush about all the things that were true in this fictional story. First off, it was my intention—and dearest hope!—that the *Belle* is portrayed as a character in this story. The steamboat was indeed built in 1914 by James Rees and Sons Company, in Pittsburgh, Pennsylvania for the West Memphis Packet Company. The workers constructed the boat with repurposed engines from the mid-1880s, which are still working to this day!

She's been employed as a packet boat, hauling freight; as a ferry boat, carrying passengers to theme parks; and an excursion boat, tramping from town to town and delighting crowds with pleasure jaunts along the river. The *Idlewild* even aided the World War II effort by pushing oil barges along the river, as well as serving as a floating nightclub for USO troops stationed at military bases.

After the war, the boat had a new owner and was renamed the *Avalon*. She tramped along American waterways for the next fifteen years.

In 1962, the mileage and decades had caught up to her, and she'd fallen in disrepair. The city of Louisville purchased her at an auction for $34,000, and she gained a new home and her third name—*The Belle of Louisville*.

Marine architect Alan L. Bates was hired to oversee the restoration. You may recall this name from the story. This man was responsible for the entire reconstruction of the *Belle* and later became first mate and captain. Capt. Bates's writings about the *Belle* were useful to me while writing this story. From his books, I was able to understand how she worked, along with her strengths and weaknesses. (Such as, the boat had a difficult time facing the wind when low on fuel.) Those resources also carried detailed information about the steamboat race between the *Delta* and the *Belle*. I was amazed that the city of Louisville challenged the *Delta* even before they were certain the *Belle* would be able to run! So I had to include that fun tidbit in the story.

It's said that this hundred-year-old steamboat holds the all-time record for most miles traveled, years in operation, and places visited.

Another interesting truth to this story is about the vessel where Devyn's office was located. It's known as "Lifesaving Station #10" and is registered as a National History Landmark too. For more information on *The Belle of Louisville* and the neighboring Lifesaving Station, visit belleoflouisville.org.

One last sliver of truth included in this story is the mention of Elizebeth Friedman. She worked for the Coast Guard during the 1920s and '30s. She was known as America's first female cryptanalyst. Without the aid of computers, Elizebeth armed herself with a pad and pencil and took down rumrunners and drug rings. Using mathematics, she broke over 12,000 codes intercepted by the Coast Guard, single-handedly exposing many notable cases.

I always find women like Elizebeth Friedman inspiring. During the twenties, women gained the right to vote, but they still weren't accepted as equals in the workforce. Ms. Friedman not only proved a woman could pull her weight in a male-dominated profession, but she excelled, stamping history with her name as one of the most legendary codebreakers of all time.

Acknowledgements

This story came together with the help of many amazing people! First, a giant thank-you to my agent, Julie Gwinn, for championing this story! I'm so grateful to work with you and to call you friend. To Becky Germany and the Barbour team, for taking a chance on me. I have never written a dual timeline story before, and I was encouraged by your faith in me. Ellen Tarver, thank you for your amazing insight and help with taking this story to the next level. My sincerest apologies for not knowing the names of steamboats are supposed to be italicized. Thank you for graciously correcting all 5 million of them.

CAPT Dan Laliberte, USCG-ret, you have no idea how much you helped me. Thank you for answering all my incessant questions about the Coast Guard during the prohibition era. It was you who helped me decide on making Jack a prohibition agent, which worked out wonderfully.

Rebekah Millet, you are one of my favorite humans, and the best critique partner, friend, and soul sister anyone could ever ask for. Thanks for all your help with this story. Janyre Tromp and Janine Rosche, you ladies have bolstered my heart and strengthened my story ideas. I'm so grateful for your friendship. I'm extremely appreciative to Natalie Walters. Without you I would've struggled to even write this book. Thank you, friend. For everything. Pepper Basham, I get to be in a series with you! Thank you, friend, for always being there and encouraging me. A giant thanks to my early readers Abbi Hart and Ashley Johnson. Also to my incredible launch team, I can't even express how much your enthusiasm and awesomeness have blessed me.

This story would not have been possible without the constant support from my family. To my husband, you were the first one who believed in this writing dream. Even before I did. Thank you. You listen with interest to my story ideas, take the kids places so I can have quiet time to write,

Rachel Scott McDaniel is an award-winning Christian romance writer. Her stories inspire with faith and heart, yet intrigue with mystery and suspense. Her first novel was nominated for the ACFW Carol Award for best debut. She's also the winner of the ACFW Genesis Award and the RWA Touched By Love award. Rachel can be found online at www.RachelScottMcDaniel.com and on all social media platforms. Her work is represented by Julie Gwinn of the Seymour Agency. She enjoys life in Ohio with her husband and two kids.

and feed my inspiration for my heroes. Also, I really appreciate it when you help me reenact certain scenes so I can get them just right. To my kiddos, Drew and Meg, thank you for being the best kiddos. You teach me so much, and I'm grateful to be your mama.

To Jesus, You're the reason I write, the breath of my stories, and the author of my life. Thank You for being my everything.